PENGUIN BOOKS

Bertie the Blitz Dog

Libby Parker grew up in the countryside in Somerset surrounded by animals of all varieties. She has been, and always will be, an animal lover, so when she began to write she knew that they would play a central role in her fiction. Libby still lives in Somerset with her husband, two children, three dogs, two cats, two alpacas and the rest of the menagerie. *Bertie the Blitz Dog* is her first novel and she is working on her second.

Bertie the Blitz Dog

LIBBY PARKER

PENGUIN BOOKS

PENGUIN BOOKS

UK | USA | Canada | Ireland | Australia
India | New Zealand | South Africa

Penguin Books is part of the Penguin Random House group of companies
whose addresses can be found at global.penguinrandomhouse.com

First published by Michael Joseph 2017
Published in Penguin Books 2017

002

Copyright © Libby Parker, 2017

The moral right of the author has been asserted

Set in 12.5/14.75pt Garamond MT Std
Typeset in India by Thomson Digital Pvt Ltd, Noida, Delhi
Printed in Great Britain by Clays Ltd, St Ives plc

A CIP catalogue record for this book is available from the British Library

ISBN: 978–1–405–92822–9

www.greenpenguin.co.uk

MIX
Paper from
responsible sources
FSC® C018179

Penguin Random House is committed to a
sustainable future for our business, our readers
and our planet. This book is made from Forest
Stewardship Council® certified paper.

We'd been hearing about it for months but nothing had happened yet. No gas. No dreaded bombing. Then one day we saw them. Out of nowhere, wheeling across the sky. The siren went off as usual. We hid in the shelter and huddled together like we always did. But this time it was different. First the deafening crack crack crack of guns. Then a distant thud thud thud as the bombs began to drop, one after another, like heavy rain. I could feel the vibrations right under my skin as they exploded; they seemed to go right through my nerves. I looked up for a moment and sniffed the air. There was a bitter burning I had never smelt before. The planes passed right over and flew away again, off into the distance. There was a moment's quiet. I breathed out in relief and dared to hope it was all over. Then the roaring came back again, louder than before, as they wheeled their way back towards us, getting ever closer, and then the whole earth seemed to split in two.

CHAPTER ONE

It was a hot late-August day; one of those days when you can't move, you just have to lie still by an open door and hope nature will cool you down. Every now and again, I plodded into the kitchen to drink some cooling water, then returned to the back doorstep to lie stretched out in the shade and wait for evening. But that afternoon, instead of a relaxing lie in the shade, I got the shock of my life. Walking down the garden path was . . . I don't know what . . . a creature, the like of which I'd never seen before. It was tall, like a human, but with a crazy, strange face, a large nose and eyes. I sat up with a start and arched my back, laying my front paws flat to the ground. I barked as loudly as I could. I was doing my best to scare the alien creature away. Then, horror of horrors, the creature lifted its face right off. All of a sudden, there was Annie, my owner, smiling, petting me and telling me it was all right.

'Don't be silly, Bertie,' she said. Then, realizing I'd had quite a shock, she continued, 'I'm sorry. Did I frighten you?'

I was just relieved that my Annie was there and not that alien creature I had seen before.

'It's a gas mask,' she explained. 'We've all got them now, though I don't think they've got any for dogs just yet. It's to protect us. If the worst happens.'

I didn't know what 'the worst' was, or what gas was and why we needed a mask for it.

3

I looked up at Annie for some kind of reassurance, and she knelt down and calmed me. I felt silly for being so frightened, and soon nuzzled into her lap, but I couldn't help thinking these gas masks and their scary faces meant something was coming and that, perhaps, it really was something to be frightened of.

I'd lived in Annie's house ever since she had adopted me as a pup. I was just a few weeks old then and don't remember much about it at all. I remember being in a dark space for hours. I remember a man with green boots kicking me and then being tied up in something. Then blackness for what felt like days. Then a kind, smiling face appeared.

Annie told me I had been left in a bin in a canvas bag. But by who, I can never be sure. I must have blocked out who my first human owners were. I was just lucky Annie happened to be walking past that day and heard me crying out.

'You were such a skinny bundle,' she said. 'All eyes and tail and fur.'

After that, I moved into her house and we soon became inseparable.

As soon as I was big enough to go out on a lead, we started to go for walks together, but at first I wasn't very well behaved. I hadn't ever been taught how humans do things. I wasn't house-trained, and I didn't know anything about walking nicely at her side, so she spent a long time teaching me the rules, using tasty treats to get me to behave. I had to learn not to bark at every person I saw, run about like a wild thing every time she let me off the lead, chew up everything in the house or scratch up the carpets. Once I had learnt to come back when she called me and didn't run around chasing my own tail every time we went out, we started going for some really nice long walks, and Annie would take me to see all the sights of the city.

We would walk past the big clock tower and its chiming bell, Big Ben, then all the way along the river to the Tower of London and over its bridge. We loved to cross the river there, and then from the other side, we would watch as Tower Bridge lifted up and huge ships passed underneath. There was also St Paul's Cathedral with its huge dome, which must have been one of the biggest things I had ever seen. Annie loved the cathedral and spent hours just sitting there looking at it.

She wanted to show me everything, and while she could, she did. But for the few months before she came home with that gas mask on, we hadn't gone out as much as we used to.

'My old lungs aren't what they were, Bertie,' she said, trying to make light of it as she came in with her bag of shopping. She went into the kitchen to make tea. 'You should have seen me as a girl. I couldn't keep still. Ran for miles! Not any more, though,' she said sadly.

Annie stopped to catch her breath and held on to the edge of the door frame. I wagged my tail and followed her into the kitchen. Something smelt tasty in her shopping bag, and I was getting hungry, although I had long ago learnt to wait until she served the food to me and not to grab it straight out of the bag like I used to as a puppy.

'Don't you worry. I've got a nice couple of chops for you,' she said with a smile.

She knew me well. I wasn't exactly spoilt. Well, OK, I was a bit.

As she reached down to scratch my head, I looked up at her and felt again that everything was all right.

The sun went down and the air chilled off to a comfortable temperature. I joined Annie in the sitting room. I had eaten my chops, and she was eating her dinner at the little table on her lap. As she ate, she chatted, partly to me and partly to herself, about the things she had wanted to do in her life. The plans she had made; her and Albert and the child.

'He was a clever one. Good at the sciences. Could have been a doctor, that boy,' she said.

The radio, the wireless as we called it then, was on in the background, and a man began to talk about a thing called war. Everyone feared it was coming.

'All I know is that man Hitler needs stopping,' said Annie, putting her knife and fork down on the plate. Her face settled into a frown. 'I don't know. I feel so helpless now. As if we have no control over what happens. It's out of our hands. I just hope . . .' She looked across the room. On the mantelpiece was a grainy photograph of a man in an army uniform, holding a violin. 'Not again, that's all,' she said and began to eat her dinner again slowly.

When she had finished eating, Annie shuffled over and picked up the photograph, as she had done many times before. The man in the picture had a sad look in his eyes.

'When we were married, you know, I was quite a catch myself, if you can believe it! And Albert. Those eyes. Then little Bertie was born . . .' She stopped and looked into the distance as though she was looking at a ghost just outside the window. 'I couldn't believe his feet. Such tiny feet . . .'

I knew Annie's story well. When war broke out in 1914, her husband, Albert, had left his job on the buses and joined the army. Most men of his age did the same thing, she told me. I wasn't sure what the army was, exactly, but I knew it meant leaving and going away somewhere, and the people back at home were usually frightened of what would happen to those who had gone.

It wasn't long before she was waving her husband off at the train station with her son by her side. He was sixteen at the time.

'Albert didn't really want to fight a war. He didn't have a fighting bone in his body,' she said, 'but that was what you did then, wasn't it? Put on a brave face. Then the telegram came. Killed in Action. Shot by a sniper. They buried him right there at the front line and we never saw him again.' She looked down at the photo.

'Of course, little Bertie wanted to go after that. Duty, he called it. The arguments we had. It was easy enough for him to lie about his age, you see. They wanted them to join. Willing to turn a blind eye. "You're only seventeen. A child," I said. "You're all I've got," I said. He was tall for his age, you see.'

'You know it's right,' he had replied to her before he left. But she didn't know.

'You've got the same eyes,' Annie had said to him as they stood on the train platform just as they had the year before. She wiped a tear from her eye. 'The same as your father's.'

After that, there was nothing she could do except wait. And just a year after he left for the war, little Bertie was killed. His body was never found.

'Such a waste,' she whispered as she put the photograph back on the mantelpiece and started the long walk back to the kitchen.

There was more talk of the thing called war. I knew the effect it had on Annie so I knew it wasn't a good thing. And with all this talk came panic, rumour and speculation.

'If the Germans do attack us, or gas us,' said Mrs Barlow from three doors down, 'all those animals will run wild, you know. Dogs. Well, they're wolves really, aren't they? They'll be running wild, in packs.'

'It would be kinder just to get rid of them now, before it gets that bad,' said Mr Fitzpatrick, another neighbour who was passing by at the time. 'Easier to put them down. Make it safer for everyone.'

I was sitting on the doorstep, trying not to listen. I didn't really know what they meant by 'put them down', but I didn't like the sound of it.

'Don't worry, Bertie, I would never do that to you,' said Annie, poking her head around the door. I wandered back into the house and put all thoughts of animals being 'got rid of' out of my mind.

The next morning, Annie didn't come down to feed me at her usual time. I waited until the big clock in the living room chimed ten times. She was usually down by the time it chimed seven times. I ran upstairs and pushed the bedroom door open with my nose.

'I'm sorry, Bertie,' she said weakly. She was lying in the bed. Her face looked a kind of yellow-grey colour.

I ran over and licked her hand.

'I don't know what's got into me! I just can't get up. It's not like me at all.'

She had a sudden fit of coughing and was straining to breathe. Every time she managed to pull herself to the edge of the bed and sit up a bit, she just fell back down again, coughing and wheezing. I barked anxiously. I'd never seen her like that before, so pale and weak. She was usually so strong and in charge of everything.

I ran downstairs and kept barking, hoping someone would hear me and do something. I felt helpless. Eventually, after quite some time, Mrs Evans from next door appeared in the kitchen. She had been taking me for some of our walks lately, to help Annie out.

'I'm more of a cat person, to be honest, Bertie,' she would say, 'but I'll make an exception for you.'

'Halloooo,' she called out as I barked so much my throat began to hurt. 'The door was open. I heard a noise. Is everything all right? What's all this hullabaloo? Is it you, Bertie, you horror?'

I ran over and looked up at her and barked some more. Then I turned and ran back upstairs. Mrs Evans followed me into the bedroom.

'Hello, Jean,' Annie croaked. 'Did old Bertie fetch you? Clever thing. Listen. I'm so sorry to ask again. There's a crown on the dresser. Can you fetch something for Bertie? A nice bit of beef. I know, I know. I spoil him. I can't help it. He's all I've got.'

Mrs Evans smiled. 'Don't you worry. We'll pop over to Mr Poultney's. And while we're at it, I'm going to make sure Dr Tippett comes over first thing, whatever you say!'

I didn't really want to go, but we left Annie there and walked to the shops. On the way, Mrs Evans told me about her daughter who was in a place called Wales. She had just had a baby. It was her first grandchild and Mrs Evans was eager to go back and see them both as soon as possible.

'What with this war likely now on top of it all,' she said. 'I can't stay here any more. You know, they're going to send the children away, for safety, if the war comes. It'll be us next. Mark my words.'

Send the children away? It was all very confusing. Why were they thinking of getting rid of things, and sending people away? By the time we got back with the food, Annie was asleep. Mrs Evans put a glass of milk on the bedside table and a bit of bread and butter on a plate, just in case Annie got hungry. Then she fed me a nice bit of beef and said goodnight.

I sat in the kitchen on my own. The room felt cold and lonely. There were strange noises I didn't normally hear because Annie was usually there with me, comforting me until bedtime. I crept back upstairs quietly to check she was all right. She must have managed to get out of bed while we were gone because the photograph of Albert and the violin were now lying next to her.

I couldn't bear to go back to the cold kitchen and decided to sleep there in the bedroom. I never usually did. It was Annie's rule. I had my own blanket downstairs by the stove. But that night I didn't want to leave her alone and I didn't want to be alone. So I jumped up and lay at her feet.

'Night night, Bertie,' she mumbled, her hand resting on the photo. 'See you in the morning.'

When I woke up, Annie was strangely still. I listened for the familiar rhythm of her breath. She was silent. I jumped up and started licking her face. She didn't move. I nuzzled her and barked, but whatever I did, she just would not respond. I had no idea what was going on. She wouldn't wake up. She was so cold. I started to panic. A man in a grey suit walked in.

'Mrs Peel,' he said softly. Then he called out a bit louder. 'I let myself in. I hope it's OK. The back door was open.'

But Annie did not move. Her eyes were closed as though she was asleep, but she had a strange expression on her face, kind of contorted, anxious. The man, who I assumed must be Dr Tippett, lifted her arm and felt her wrist. His face began to look serious. There must be something you can do, I thought. There must be something in that bag of yours to wake her up.

'Sorry, old chap,' he said and patted me on the head. 'I'm afraid she's gone.'

I couldn't understand it. Gone. What did it mean? 'She hasn't gone anywhere. She's right there!' I barked. But it was no use; I couldn't get through to him. I could always get through to Annie, but now she wasn't moving. I barked and jumped up at the doctor. 'You must be able to do something.' I was desperate. But from the expression on his face, I could tell there was nothing he could do. When I finally realized what was happening, my head started spinning. I had never lost anyone before. She was all I knew. I felt sick. It was as though something or someone had ripped out my insides. Annie was dead.

CHAPTER TWO

Mrs Evans sorted out the funeral. She put on her busy face and got hold of Reverend Jeffreys, from the local church, to arrange things quickly. Mr Poultney, the butcher, came along, and Mrs Barlow and her three children from next door, and Mr Fitzpatrick, our neighbour; they were all at the church. But I didn't want to see any of them. I felt angry inside that they were all still there and Annie was nowhere. Mrs Evans took me along, but I waited in the porch by the church door as the Reverend murmured some words I couldn't make out, and everyone sang a song about 'Christian Soldiers'.

After that, they all shuffled out to a nearby place they called the 'cemetery' and the Reverend said more words while some men lowered a big box into a hole. Then they filled in the hole with earth until the box could no longer be seen. I suppose this is what humans do, I thought, when someone dies. Cover them up. I hid behind a nearby gravestone, trying not to think about Annie down there in that box. I tried to remember the nice times – our walks along the Thames and snuggling up together by the fire. Her laugh. Her kind voice. Her face.

When it was all over and the people started drifting away, I heard Mrs Evans calling out for me. My ears pricked up. I wondered whether I should go back with her. But I couldn't bear the thought of returning to the house and Annie not being there. So I stayed where I was, hiding behind a large grey stone.

'I don't know where Bertie is,' she said to Mrs Barlow. 'I'm worried about the poor thing, out here alone.'

'Well, we can't stay here all night,' said Mrs Barlow who was on her way out. 'He'll probably just find his own way back. Dogs can do that, you know. They have a sixth sense. Don't you want a lift back in my Peter's motor car?'

I was very close to running out to greet them. But something inside wouldn't let me. Mrs Evans called out a few more times, but Mrs Barlow was getting anxious to get home, so in the end she had no choice but to leave.

When they had all gone I came out from behind the grave and sat next to where Annie had been lowered into the ground. I sat there for I don't know how long, until it got cold, then dark. I heard something in a nearby tree, hooting. A bird. I might have stayed there for ever, who knows, if I hadn't seen a large green van approaching. It slowed down then stopped, and the lights went out. A man got out and flashed a torch around in the early morning half-light.

'Someone reported a stray around here earlier,' he said, 'sniffing around gravestones.'

Another man got out. I could hear a dog barking from inside the van. It sounded desperate to get out and was crying for help.

'I'm not saying I enjoy it, Reg,' said the other man, as he slammed the door shut. 'But what can you do? Someone's got to. If we don't do it now they'll only starve, or worse. Not because they're bad, but . . . The wife and I decided it would be best for the little puss. Scratch, the black one, the kitten. Little Janey doesn't know yet. Thinks the little thing's on a holiday . . .'

I didn't know who they were but I knew one thing: I was not going to get picked up by them and put in that van. No way. I looked at the stone they had placed next to Annie's grave. Mrs Evans had read out the words to me when they ordered it, and I would never forget them.

In Loving Memory of Anne Mary Peel
  Who Fell Asleep 27th August, 1939
  Aged 62
  Devoted wife to Albert David Peel and mother to Bertram
  Who lost their lives in The Great War

Her body might be down there, I thought, but Annie was gone.

'Over here, Reg, prints.' A light flashed. I turned and ran.

I don't know how long I ran for. I had no idea where I was going. I was in a kind of blind panic, frightened I would get caught by the men with the van, and desperately missing Annie. I ran along the streets for hours, darting this way and that, dodging between the crowds and getting shouted at for being in people's way. By the time I stopped, I was on a main road with a line of buses and cars honking their horns. A horse that was leading a milk cart veered off to one side when it saw me. The horse neighed and I barked, and the milkman hauled it back over on to the road. When I reached the other side of the road, I suddenly felt overwhelmed with thirst and exhaustion. I had no choice. I would have to find some-where to sleep out here. I looked down at the river below. There was a space underneath the bridge and it looked as though I could climb down to it.

I made my way to the water, and when I got there, I drank in great gulps from the river. It didn't taste great. In fact, it made me feel a bit sick, but it was better than nothing. After that, I lay down on the stone steps and breathed in and out heavily. A bell chimed over and over again. It seemed to go on for so long I couldn't tell whether it was actually ringing or whether it was eventually just in my head. For the first time I could remember since I had been abandoned as a puppy, I was completely alone. A pair of pigeons sitting on a ledge above me settled down, ruffling their feathers and tuck-ing their heads into their wings. My head hit the cold stone and I slept.

I was dreaming. I was running through London, looking for Annie. Faces, large with gas masks, flashed in front of me, hunting me down. I found her. She was sitting, asleep in a chair. Her face was cold and grey. Her eyes opened. All of a sudden, it wasn't her any more. It was the man at the cemetery with the van. He jumped up and chased me. I ran. There was a loud blaring sound. I opened my eyes and jumped up, barking. Where's Annie? But I soon realized I wasn't at home in my bed. I was by a river. There were boats passing by, honking their horns. I remembered, felt the pain all over again. Annie was gone.

A stream of people were hurrying across the bridge towards a big building on the other side. I sniffed the air. There was a bakery somewhere near. My stomach growled. I seriously needed something to eat. I crossed over the bridge and passed a newspaper seller. 'Hitler invades Poland,' he was shouting over and over again as he handed out newspapers.

People were talking to each other as they read it.

'What will he do, do you think?'

'What does he want with Poland, anyway?'

There was a sense of nervous anticipation. I didn't know who Hitler was, although I had heard Annie mention him once or twice, and I didn't know what Poland was, or why that man was invading it, but I didn't like the sound of it one bit.

I ran about for a while, unsure where I was or where I was going. Eventually, I found myself inside a large building by the side of a main road. There was a crowd of children milling about, all done up in little hats and coats and carrying suitcases. Some of the cases were nearly bigger than they were, and the children all had boxes hanging around their necks, like the one Annie had shown me for her gas mask. They also had numbers pinned on their backs and labels around their necks. How strange, I thought. I wondered if they were the children Mrs Evans had told me about, the ones they were sending away. I thought for a moment that I might see Mrs Evans on the platform. Then, as if by magic, there she was! I ran over and barked, so relieved to see a friend. But when I got to her and the woman turned around, she had a different face. It wasn't Mrs Evans at all.

She shouted at me. 'Get away, you beast.' She put her arms around a small child she had with her, who started to cry. I ran away, confused.

A huge thing came into the building and screeched and shuddered to a stop. I was terrified of the shiny, smelly metal creature, and didn't realize that it was a train. All the children were bundled on board. Some had to be pushed on because they didn't want to leave. Some looked excited, others just afraid. After a while, the train pulled away in a cloud of smoke. Children's faces were hanging out of the windows. As many as could get to it were calling out and waving. Some of them were crying, and some of the adults still standing on the platform were crying too and blowing kisses. I thought about trying to jump on a train to escape from London and all the scary things and people there. But before I could, a man in a funny hat ran over, waving his arms.

'Get out of here, you scoundrel,' he said. 'You're not allowed here. Go away. Shoo!'

I wasn't used to being chased and shouted at. I was used to kindness and safety and a smiling face and gentle voice. The world suddenly didn't seem like a very nice place.

CHAPTER THREE

I ran away, out of the station, on and up the road past shops and cafes and restaurants. Smells of every kind wafted out from doorways, and from the flats above the shops I could smell food being prepared for people's dinner. I was dizzy with hunger. I found an old newspaper on the roadside with a few bits of potato in it. I ate them, but the hunger still gnawed in my stomach. I smelt something nice and meaty coming from an alleyway. Around the back of one of the nearby buildings, I could hear a radio from an upstairs flat. A cat stalked past me, scowling and hissing. It was clearly his area. I barked a greeting, and he leapt up on to a wall and eyed me warily.

'What do you want?' he asked after a while, when he realized I wasn't going to chase him.

I jumped. I didn't meet many cats. I usually avoided them around our way. Or they ran away from me as soon as they saw me. Generally, I thought they were best kept well clear of.

'Nothing,' I stammered. 'I mean. I'm lost. Just looking for something to eat, that's all.'

'Well, you won't get much around here,' he said airily. 'And what is here is mine, anyway.'

I ignored him as best I could and decided it was safe enough to poke around, anyway, and see what I could find. There must be something, I thought. I was far too hungry to let a cat put me off. I found two bins, one with its large metal lid half open. There was an old pigeon walking about, pecking up scraps around it. I put my paws up on the edge and tried to reach my nose in, but in my haste I managed to knock the lid fully off. Then the whole bin fell over and clattered to the ground. The sound echoed around and around the small courtyard.

'You've done it now,' said the cat, jumping off the wall and sniffing at one of the bins. I ran behind and hid. When no one came out, I crept back again and stuck my nose inside. I was overjoyed to find there were a few scraps of left-over meat and some bones. I gobbled up the meat and grabbed one of the bones and started to chew it. Most of the juice seemed to have been boiled away already. It was certainly a far cry from the dinners I was used to, the best cuts of meat from Mr Poultney's, and Annie's special gravy. I was starting to realize just how good my life with Annie had been, now that it was gone. But at that moment I was starving, and it was certainly better than nothing.

A voice came from inside the building. I jumped back behind the bin.

'Julia. I'm just out for a fag. Keep an eye on the soup.'

A man with grey hair and a moustache came into the courtyard. He took out a cigarette, put it in his mouth, struck a match, then leant back, inhaled deeply and started humming. I thought he looked friendly, but I had met so many scary people these past two days, I was starting to get nervous of strangers. I looked up at the wall. The cat was now stalking up and down, looking at me with its hackles up, probably because I had invaded his bin. He let out a 'meow' and jumped down and rubbed against the man's leg.

'Chico,' said the man, and he stroked the cat's head. 'You catch any big fat rats for me today?'

Chico purred as if to say, 'Yes, plenty.'

The man stubbed his cigarette out on the wall and noticed that one of the bins had been knocked over. 'Naughty puss,' he said as he bent down to pick it up. Chico shot me an angry look. Then the man caught sight of me cowering at the back. 'Hello. Where did you come from?' he asked, bending down to look at me.

I flinched. I hadn't realized until then that I was shivering with fear. Chico hissed again and arched his back. I tried to bark, but only a weak kind of squawk came out. Eventually, Chico started to look bored by the whole thing and went off in search of more rats.

'You hungry, fella?' said the man. 'Got a name?' He looked at my collar, the one Annie had given me for Christmas one year. She'd had my name inscribed on a copper token.

'Bertie,' he said, and scooped me up and took me inside. We went through a narrow, badly lit hallway and the man peered around into a kitchen where a woman was stirring food in a big pot.

'You want to take over, Lou?' said the woman. 'I must get the pastry ready . . .' She suddenly noticed me. 'What's that you've got there?' She put the spoon down and walked over for a better look.

'Found this fella outside by the bins,' said Lou. 'Must have been abandoned. Clean, though. Not much of a stray. Bertie, his name is.'

'Hello, Bertie,' said the woman, smiling. 'Let's get you fed and warm. Just two soups and bread for Gerald in the cafe.' She left her husband to take over in the kitchen while she took me upstairs to their small flat above.

I couldn't believe my luck to have found such nice people. Julia – that was her name – boiled up a kettle of water and put me in a metal bath tub full of hot water. She washed off the dirt that had collected on me over the last day and night. I wasn't usually very fond of baths, but this one felt nice, and it was a relief to feel clean again. Then she filled a big bowl with scraps she had in the kitchen, some bits of fish and even a slice of ham. It felt like a proper feast, and I could hardly move, I ate so much. After that, she made me a small bed from some blankets and tucked me up and went downstairs. For the first time since Annie had gone, I managed to relax, and I drifted into a deep sleep.

By the time I woke up, Lou was back and the radio was on. He was sewing up an old sock, and Julia was writing a letter.

'Doesn't sound good, does it?' said Julia after a while, putting her pen down. 'He'll never pull out now, will he? Don't you think?'

'But the old man, Chamberlain, doesn't want another war,' said Lou. 'And, believe me, neither do I. But is there any choice? That's the thing. We can't just let him get away with it.'

'Gets my nerves on edge,' said Julia with a shiver.

The next day was Saturday, and I discovered that the couple ran a busy cafe downstairs from their flat. They served many of the shops and businesses in the area. I was pleased to be allowed to sit down there, and I was coddled and petted by all the customers who came in.

A group of lads arrived, all talking loudly and laughing with one another. They were wearing green clothes, all the same. They said they had been putting sandbags outside the buildings along the road. I wondered why they needed bags of sand all around the city. But a lot of strange things had been happening lately. They came in for cups of tea all round. One of them had a small rubber ball, and he threw it for me. I chased it back and forth across the cafe until Lou told them not to encourage me while the other customers were in. After that, they got me to catch sneaky bits of sandwich while Lou wasn't looking. Then the owners of shops along the street came in for their 'usuals': bacon sarnies and Julia's special apple pie, which everyone said was the best in London.

All throughout the day, the radio was on, and every now and again everyone would stop what they were doing and listen to a man talking in serious tones. I could sense people were nervous, on edge, as Julia had said, although they carried on laughing and joking as though it was business as usual. But, suddenly, it was no longer business as usual. By the time Lou and Julia closed up the cafe, people were saying that Hitler had not 'pulled out of Poland' as he was meant to, and they all thought this war everyone talked of was finally coming for real.

I have to admit, I didn't really know what war meant then. I knew what Annie had told me about the last one. I knew it made people sad. But, really, it was still just a word, an adventure even, for some people. The lads who were laying the sandbags seemed almost excited by everything that was going on. They were all dressed up in their green clothes and seemed ready for anything.

The next day was Sunday, so the cafe was closed. Lou and Julia took me to church for what they called 'mass'. It was different to Annie's church. It smelt different and the front was very ornate. I waited outside while they went in. It was nice to be outside in the sunshine. From inside the church, I could hear a very calming voice from the man at the front, who was wearing a kind of dress. Then there was some chanting and singing and a strong, pungent smell from a large metal thing he was shaking everywhere. Then everyone came out and shook his hand, and some took hold of his hand and looked serious as he spoke soft words to them.

We got back to the flat just in time to hear a man talking on the wireless again. It was the man Lou called 'old man Chamberlain'. Julia and Lou sat down at the table and I could hear the same voice echoing out from other flats along the street. I didn't know what it meant then, but I remember the words he said:

This morning the British Ambassador in Berlin handed the German Government a final note stating that, unless we heard from them by 11 o'clock that they were prepared at once to withdraw their troops from Poland, a state of war would exist between us. I have to tell you now that no such undertaking has been received, and that consequently this country is at war with Germany.

The words echoed in my head. 'At war with Germany'. That was what they had all said would happen. But I still didn't know what it meant. He carried on talking about the days of stress and strain that may be ahead, and how everyone should take their part as volunteers, and most importantly, carry on with their jobs. I wondered what my job was. It used to be taking care of Annie. But I had no idea what it was any more.

'Now may God bless you all. May He defend the right. It is the evil things that we shall be fighting against – brute force, bad faith, injustice, oppression and persecution – and against them I am certain that the right will prevail.'

When he finished, some music played. I looked over at Julia and saw tears were in her eyes. Humans did that, cried. Sometimes when they were happy. Sometimes when they were sad. This was the sad kind. Lou didn't say a word. He stood up, quietly kissed his wife on the head and began to prepare lunch.

I had discovered, to my relief, that Chico was more of an outdoor cat. But, unusually for him, he wandered up the stairs and into the kitchen that day, and started to meow as though he knew something wasn't right.

'What's going on?' Chico asked me. 'Julia seems sad.'

'I don't know,' I said, and instead of going back out like he normally would, he came and sat near me and seemed reluctant to leave.

Another official-sounding voice came on the wireless. This time it was telling people what to do, and what not to do, now the war had started.

'No whistles or horns,' it said, in case people thought they were 'air-raid sirens'. 'Observe the blackout. Carry your gas masks.'

The instructions droned on. I understood none of them, although I did explain to Chico about gas masks. I was about to get bored by the whole thing and wander into the kitchen to see what there was to eat when, all of a sudden, a horrible sound started up, a loud wailing noise, a ghostly moaning, rising up and down. It nearly burst my ears. I howled. Then Chico joined in the howling.

'What is it?' he yelled out. 'I knew something was going to happen. I just knew it.'

Julia jumped up and Lou dropped a spoon on the floor. I dived under the table.

'Already?' said Julia, nervously grabbing Lou's arm. Lou had started rummaging through a pile of papers on the side.

'I'm sure it's here,' he said.

'What?'

'That damn leaflet.'

'Damn the leaflet,' said Julia. 'We should go.'

I was still cowering under a table. I think they had almost forgotten I was there until Julia saw my tail sticking out.

'What shall we do?' she said, signalling towards me. 'We can't leave him here.'

'I don't know. I don't think they're allowed in,' said Lou.

'Well, we can't leave Chico. Get the basket. We'll have to take them both.'

Not allowed in where? I wondered. And why wouldn't that awful noise stop? It was hurting my ears. Julia was trying to get hold of Chico and put him in a basket, which caused a lot of meowing and a bit of scratching. He was clearly very confused and frightened and didn't know what was going on. I surprised myself that I managed not to panic very much. Perhaps being out on the street had started to toughen me up just a little bit. But I was sorry for Chico, who was in such a state. Julia eventually managed to get him into the basket, but even when he was in there, he was whining and wailing. I tried to calm him down, telling him it would be OK, although I had no idea, of course, whether it would be.

Lou grabbed his hat – he never went outside without it – along with his gas mask and his cigarette case. Julia picked up her bag and coat, and we were all about to leave.

'Wait, we're meant to turn off the gas, aren't we?' she said. 'In case of a fire. What else was it? Fill the bath?'

'I think so. I don't know. We haven't got time. Do the gas,' said Lou. 'I'll go down and check the cafe. I'll meet you outside.'

Julia ran a bit of a bath and did all the other things she could remember she had been told to do by the man on the radio, then she turned the lights off, and with me at her heel and Chico in the basket, we walked out on to the landing. As we made our way down the stairs a young couple from the upstairs flat came running past us. The man was in a panic.

'I knew this would happen,' he said, jumping down three steps at a time.

'Don't be daft,' said the woman, trying to catch up. 'It's just a false alarm, probably.'

'This is it,' he continued. 'It's all over.'

'Always the end of the world with you, isn't it?' said the woman. 'Anyone would think you want it to be over.'

Out on the street, no one seemed to know whether the noise meant someone was going to attack the city. Everyone was confused and didn't know what to do or what was going to happen next. Some people were running into buildings for shelter, while others were running out of the same buildings looking for shelter somewhere else.

'All done in there?' Julia asked Lou as he locked up the cafe.

'All done.'

'Where are we supposed to go?' Julia asked, looking up and down the street for some information.

'What about Gerald's?' said Lou. 'You know he said we could use his basement.'

'But it's so small. And it smells. We could be down there for hours. And he never stops . . .'

'Well, it's better than being blown to bits up here,' said Lou, suddenly angry. 'Come on, let's go this way.' We started to run down the street.

Blown to bits, I thought. That does not sound nice at all.

A policeman in a tin hat was riding a bicycle up and down, directing people along the road and telling everyone to take cover.

'This way. Remain calm. No running,' he said. But he sounded more nervous than anyone else as he pedalled away.

'Is it really real, then?' asked Julia.

A woman with a crying baby in her arms stopped to answer. 'I've no idea,' she said. 'I'm not risking it, though. Not with this one.' She looked down at the baby, which she had tied on to her front with a scarf.

'It must be. Look,' said Lou, pointing up to the sky. Dozens of giant silver objects were rising up above London.

'Barrage balloons,' said a man in a posh suit who was walking past hurriedly. 'That'll stop them flying too low.'

'Aeroplanes?' asked Julia. 'I didn't see any.'

'You won't be able to take *that* in, by the way,' said the man suddenly, pointing at me. 'No pets allowed in the shelter.'

Julia held on to the cat basket tightly. 'We'll sneak him in,' she whispered to Lou. They both looked at me and then at each other with a worried expression on their faces.

There was a loud bang and someone screamed.

'Was that a gun?' asked Lou.

'I feel sick,' said Julia

'Motor car,' said the woman with the baby.

There were quite a few cars on the street by then, and people were getting off buses, which had come to a stop. Some people began abandoning their cars and running towards the train station, which caused more confusion and honking of horns.

'Look at them, like they own the place,' said Julia, stopping to look at people in their cars.

'Well, they won't last long if they stay in there when the bombs come,' said Lou.

I didn't know what bombs were, but I was beginning to get the sense they weren't very welcome.

It turned out what they called the 'official shelter' was next to the main railway station where I had seen all those children getting on to trains a few days earlier. But when we got there, a long queue of people trying to get in had built up outside and there was a lot of jostling and shouting going on. Another man in a tin hat was trying but failing to organize people into groups. One very tall man was pushing his way forward, saying he had to get down there right now and that he didn't want to die.

'It's chaos,' said Julia. 'We won't make it.'

'Gerald's, then,' said Lou, and we ran the other way, down another street. We turned on to a side alley and came out on to another busy road next to the river. I could hear Chico howling in his basket. Then, suddenly, I couldn't hear him any more. I had lost them.

A crowd of people ran past me, heading towards the shelter. A man trod on my foot and I yelped. A little boy who had been crying bent down to stroke me and started to laugh and pull at my ears. His mother pulled his arm and they kept running. By the time the crowd had cleared, Julia and Lou were gone, and I had no idea where 'Gerald's' was.

I could try and find them, I thought, but hadn't that man said I wasn't allowed in the shelter? I could make my way back to the cafe and wait for them there. I had a pretty good sense of smell and could probably find the way. I was sure I would recognize their street if I saw it. But then I might get 'blown to bits' or who knows what. Or I could keep going and find somewhere to hide on my own until this horrible war, and all the confusion it seemed to be bringing with it, was over.

With the sound of those awful sirens still ringing in my ears and a biting hunger growing in my stomach, I kept on up the street towards I didn't know where. I was alone, again. And it felt like the end of the world was just beginning.

CHAPTER FOUR

I must have gone into some kind of shock because I can't remember exactly what happened next. Eventually, I found myself at the bottom of a flight of stone steps. My body was pressed up against a metal grill beyond which was a small tunnel. The air was filled with a strong and nasty sour smell. A pair of rats scuttled in and out of the tunnel. They hardly seemed to notice me, or care about the confusion going on above. The first sound had stopped blaring out some time ago, but another sound started up, this time one long ghostly siren. After a while, it gradually faded to nothing. Then it was quiet again. All I could hear was the scratch, scratch of the rats. Every now and then they stopped to wash their noses, before disappearing off into the darkness of the tunnel.

When I got my strength back, I climbed to the top of the steps and the street above. People were emerging from the various places in which they had been hiding. They looked dazed but relieved as they came blinking into the midday sun. One man, who had been crouching inside a red telephone box with his head in his hands, stood up and opened the door cautiously.

'Is that it, then?' he asked. His voice was shaking.

I wondered whether maybe the war was over, maybe that had been it, the thing they had all been talking about.

Perhaps that *was* the war, and life would get back to normal now.

'False alarm, do you suppose?' asked a woman who had just come up some steps from where she had taken cover in a basement. A newspaper seller was returning from the main shelter, relieved to find his stand and all his papers still intact where he had left them.

'Suppose it must have been,' he said, picking up his papers again.

'So this is how it is now, is it?' said the woman. 'Hiding away every time we hear that God-awful siren.'

'Well, thank goodness we're all still here, that's all I can say,' said the man, who was by now resting against the phone box and smoking a cigarette.

I left them to their speculation and continued to make my way across the city, in search of something much more important: something to eat.

After a while, I started to sense the mouth-watering smells of cooking as people got back on with their lives and started to prepare their Sunday roasts. I knew the smell well, and longed for a slice of nice beef topped with thick gravy, the way Annie used to prepare it for me as my favourite treat. But, although I could smell all this delicious food, it was all out of my reach.

I crossed the river. The sun was setting a bright orange. I found myself in a place where there were more houses than shops. I sniffed around and eventually stopped outside a small corner pub. I wondered whether I should risk going in to see if they had any spare food.

Inside, a group of men was standing at the bar, chatting. One said he swore he'd seen a German plane flying up the Thames, ready to drop its bombs right on St Paul's. He was drinking from a large glass and saying very confidently that he reckoned 'it was the blimps that stopped them in the end'.

Another man, who seemed quite drunk, began banging his hands on to his forehead. He said several times, each time progressively louder, that it was a plan to put the frighteners on us, so we'd 'do their bidding'.

'Shut up, you lot, will you? It's Bertie,' said a man behind the bar. I jumped for a moment and slunk back away from the door. Did he mean me? But how . . . ?

Then everyone went quiet and listened to a voice coming out of a large wireless on the bar. They sipped their drinks in silence as the man spoke about the 'dark days ahead' and our 'enemies'.

After a few minutes, the drunk man shouted out, 'Get on with it.' Everyone tutted.

'Have some respect for the King,' said the barman quietly, and they went on listening until the speech was over.

My hopes began to fade, and I gave up on the idea of getting any food from there. I left the pub and walked on, but pretty soon I gave up on getting any food from anywhere that night. As the sun finally set and a dark chill began to descend, I realized I was in for another night on the street, alone.

'George, your breakfast's ready, love. Georgie! Your egg's going cold.'

A woman's voice woke me from a deep and troubled sleep. I had no idea where I was or how I had got there. I opened my eyes. I was lying down. Above me was a tangle of cobwebs. A rusted garden spade was resting against a wooden bench. The floor was thick with dust. A spider began descending from the web. I stood up to move out of the way and wobbled for a moment, then sat back down and watched the spider run across the floor into a corner. I felt dizzy and confused.

I looked around for water or anything I could drink. There was an old tin in the corner. I sniffed it. It was sticky and made my head spin. I decided not to eat whatever was in the tin. I sniffed around the rest of the shed but there was nothing I could eat or drink, just bits of wood and sawdust. I started to remember how I had stumbled in there during the night. It had been almost pitch black, and I had found the shed after climbing through a hole in a fence. I'd finally fallen asleep after what seemed like hours of walking.

Through a small window with a large crack across it, I could see a young boy outside, running about with his arms out wide. He was yelling and making loud sounds. When the woman called out again, he ran into the small house and pulled the door shut. Once he had gone, I pushed open the shed door with my nose and walked slowly up the garden, towards the house. The window was open, so I positioned myself underneath it.

'Oh, do I have to?' I could hear the boy ask the woman. I assumed she must be his mother. 'Now the war's started, can't I join the Air Force?'

'Don't be daft, you silly thing. You'd never reach the controls,' she laughed.

A man was with them at the table, reading a newspaper.

'"Hitler! Wanted dead or alive!" Very good,' he said. 'Like the Wild West.'

'Well, he *is* a murderer. Think of all those poor Polish. The children. And it'll be us next, I'll bet . . .' The woman trailed off and changed the subject. 'Anyone for more tea? Darling?'

'Better be going,' said the man. 'Rent still needs paying, even with a war on.'

'What's a war cabinet?' asked the boy suddenly, with a mouth full of toast. He had picked up the newspaper. 'Is it like a bedroom cabinet for the war? Like what you make, Daddy?'

'It's the name of the cabinet during the war,' said the man, standing up. 'The group of men at the top of government is the cabinet. You'll be alright?' he asked his wife, kissing her gently on the cheek.

'I'll be fine,' she said. I could see her smile, but in her eyes I could see she was not really smiling. She was scared. A few minutes later, I heard the front door slam, and a while later the mother and the little boy, George, also left. He carried a bag and had a gas-mask box hanging around his neck.

When the house was empty, I felt freer to sniff around the garden a bit. Maybe there would be something to eat. I found a bucket of water and drank that up thirstily. Then I lay in the sun for a while on a patch of grass. Maybe they'll be nice, I thought, this family. Maybe I can live with them.

In their garden was a large pile of earth with a metal sheet across it. It had a small door in it. I started to dig around the sides of the earth mound. Perhaps there'll be some food in there, I thought. I dug and dug and made a huge hole, but found nothing except a few worms and some woodlice. I gave up and wandered around the garden a bit more. I day-dreamed that the little boy, George, could be my friend, and I could look after him, like I used to look after Annie. I lay there dreaming and dozing like that for hours, until the smell of more food made me sit up. They were back, sitting around the table. Where had the day gone? I was exhausted. Maybe I'll just sleep for ever, I thought. But I dragged myself up and slunk back to the shed and hid inside out of sight. The smells wafting over from their food were painfully delicious. I could tell it was lamb, which I loved, followed by something with custard. I longed for a plate of something like that. Or anything.

After they had finished their dinner, the little boy came outside to play. He ran about making loud noises with his arms outstretched again, which seemed to be his favourite game. A girl, about the same age as he was, leant over the fence from the next door garden.

'Hi, George. Did you go down your Anderson yesterday? We did,' she said proudly. 'Ours is completely finished already.'

'No,' he said quietly. 'We were at Granny's. Ours isn't completely done yet. Well, it is, but my dad's gonna make it more like a proper house when it's done, he says. It's got a real bed and everything but there are just a few things to finish off, he says.'

'Ours does smell a bit, though,' continued the girl. 'And there was a frog in it. I like frogs, so I didn't mind at all, but Mum went so green when she saw that frog, she looked like a frog herself.' Then she fell about laughing for a while, thinking about the frog. 'I tried to pick it up and show her,' she continued once she managed to stop laughing, 'but she screamed and made me throw it out. Poor frog.'

George looked more interested. 'Frog or toad?'

'Frog.'

'Bet it was a toad.'

'Oh, who cares,' said the girl, and she jumped over the wall into his garden.

'Anyway, wanna see my new beetles?' she said, producing a glass jar. 'I found two yesterday. One's a marvellous type of green colour.'

They tried to get the insects to race across the garden then lost them both in the undergrowth.

'Shall we play aeroplanes?' said George after a while, jumping up. 'I'll be the bomber.'

'You're always the . . . What's that?' she said, suddenly noticing me peering out of the window. 'In your dad's shed. George! I think it's a . . . puppy!'

They ran towards the shed. I was frightened. What would they do? I quickly crawled into a corner and pressed myself against the wall. Their big faces appeared at the door and they both got down on their knees and tried to get me to come out.

'Come on, little puppy,' said the girl, clicking her fingers. 'Here, boy.'

'He's not a puppy. He's a grown-up dog, I think. How did he get here, anyway, do you think?'

Perhaps they'll get me some food, I thought. They didn't look like they were going to hurt me. I began to crawl out cautiously. They petted me and stroked my head, but I got nervous again, and pulled back.

'He looks a bit scared. He's probably hungry. Shall I get him some milk?' suggested George.

'Milk? I don't know. Do dogs eat milk?'

I'll eat anything, I thought.

'My mum's got a pork pie in the larder,' he said, suddenly inspired. 'I saw it. I don't think she'll mind if we give him a little bit.'

My ears pricked up. Pork pie. Annie had given that to me before. So juicy. Yes, please, I thought. They both ran into the house and came back with a large pork pie and a saucer of milk, which I devoured in a moment.

'Gosh, he must have been starved,' said the girl.

'Pamela! Blackout,' a man called over the garden wall.

'I have to go and help Dad with the blackout. Good night, little doggy,' she said and kissed me on the head. 'Shall we keep him?' she whispered as they walked away.

'Definitely. Our secret,' said George.

A while later he came back to the shed on his own, carrying a large blanket. He led me out by my collar and into the earth house. There was a large step down into the darkness.

George explained to me that the Anderson was an air-raid shelter, that they all had them now on their street to protect themselves, and that theirs was going to be the best on the whole street.

'You'll be safer here,' he said, 'if Hitler comes. See, it's nearly finished.'

It was quite scary and damp in there, but there was a little makeshift bed with a thin mattress, which seemed like heaven to me at that moment. I jumped up and George

tucked me down into the blanket with just my head sticking out.

'What are you doing out there?' called his mother.
'We're doing the curtains.'

'Night night, little dog,' he whispered, ruffling my fur.
'Nothing, Mum,' he shouted and ran back to the house.

I woke up the next morning to the sounds of giggling.
George and Pamela were opening the small metal door to
the earth house and peering in.

'I got him some liver. I sneaked it into my pocket last
night,' said Pamela, producing a small piece of tissue
paper proudly from her pocket.

'Come on, doggy. Breakfast!' She placed the liver down
in front of me and I gobbled it up in a flash. George had
a little bit of bread-and-butter pudding for me, and they
had also brought me a dish with some lovely fresh water
in it.

'That's yours now,' said George, putting it on the floor.
'You can live in here as long as you like, but you have to
keep quiet, all right?'

I whined quietly as if to say I understood.

'Look at his collar. Is there a name on it?' Pamela
grabbed my collar and saw the copper token.

'Bertie.'

'Bertie the Wonder Dog!' said George.

'George! Have you seen that pie?' a voice called from
outside the shelter.

'Quick! Mum's coming. The door.'

'It was for your granny. For her lunch. I hope you
haven't had it, you . . .'

They looked at each other and then at me.

'I'll have to tell her eventually,' George whispered. 'We can't hide a whole dog.'

They ran out and shut the door behind them, leaving me in the earth shelter alone.

'Sorry, Mum. I was starved in the night,' said George as they walked back to the house. 'I thought you wouldn't mind.'

I bet he got into trouble for that, I thought to myself. I felt bad that he was taking the blame for feeding me.

Later that day, I sneaked back into the shed where there was more air and light. George came outside and began helping his mother in the garden.

'You're a good boy, really. Helping your mother like this,' she said, down on her knees, pulling out weeds from a flower bed. George was carrying the weeds over to a big pile of earth in the corner of the garden and getting thoroughly muddy in the process.

'Can I have a pet?' he asked out of the blue.

'What? Don't be silly,' replied his mother. 'What on earth . . .'

'But . . . a dog or something. It might help us. Sniff out gas and all that sort of thing.'

'Oh, I see,' she said, not seeing at all. 'Anyway, what's put this in your head all of a sudden? I heard on the wireless that you should have all pets put down. In case they run wild. That it's better for them. They were advertising these guns in the . . .'

'What, like dead?' asked George, horrified.

'Like asleep,' said his mother. 'Oh, I don't know. Anyway, we haven't got any pets and we're not getting any, so what's the matter? Granny says she's going to keep the cat, though, so that's all right.'

They carried on picking out the weeds for a while.

'So I definitely can't have a dog, then?'

'George!'

That night George came in and said goodnight again, but this time he had no food.

'I'm sorry, Bertie. I couldn't get a thing past the parents. But don't worry, I haven't given up on you just yet.'

The next day I was back hiding in the shed when George's father, Philip, came into the garden.

'What the hell's happened out here?' he shouted. 'George! Get over here right now.'

George came running out.

'What's this? Have you been digging into the Anderson? Are you mad?'

'Sorry, Dad,' he said. 'I was . . . er, looking for something.'

'Looking for what?'

I crouched down, listening. George's dad must have discovered the big hole I had made in the earth house when I was trying to find something to eat. He did not sound happy about it.

'George, do you understand? You could have got us killed. If anything happens and the Anderson's not secure . . . you tell him, Rose,' he said to George's mother.

'You must know it was wrong, love,' she said, exasperated.

'Sorry, sir,' said George.

'I'm going to have to punish you, though. No pudding for a week. And no sweets.'

After that, Philip was in the shelter most evenings, banging around and making a lot of noise.

Over the next few days, George continued to feed me with what scraps he could sneak from the dinner table, but he never brought anything again as filling and delicious as that pork pie. Pamela also managed to get a few bits for me from her house. But I was starting to feel cooped up and frustrated in that shed every day, and I was always hungry.

I also became worried that George was taking the blame for me too often. He'd got in trouble for the pie and now for the hole in the Anderson shelter. Maybe, I began to think, he'd be better off without me.

That night, as I lay in the shelter alone, that horrible wailing siren came again. I jumped up and leapt up the step, out into the garden, then ran back into the shed before they could see me.

'Georgie. Gas mask!' said his mother, urgently.

'I can't see anything,' said George as they stumbled down the garden.

'Hold my hand,' said Rose. 'That noise! It'll wake the living dead.'

'I've done the gas,' said Philip, running down the garden. They all piled into the shelter.

'It's so small!' said Rose. 'How are we all going to sleep in here?'

'At least I patched up Georgie's hole,' said Philip. 'What's this blanket doing down here? I don't remember bringing that in.'

I cowered in the shed, under the bench, waiting to hear what he said. But George kept quiet and they sat in silence for a while, waiting to see what would happen.

'He's been so good lately, though,' said Rose. 'George. I don't know what's got into him. What's got into you?' she asked him after they had been sitting there for a while. 'He did the washing up yesterday!'

'Still after a dog, are you?' asked Philip.

There was a sudden loud noise which shook the walls of the shed. I put my head to the floor and shut my eyes.

'What was that?' asked George.

'I don't know. Was it one of ours?' said Philip.

The noise stopped and there was silence again, which seemed to go on for ages.

'How long do you think we have to sit here like this?' asked Rose. 'I'd have brought something to do. Finish knitting that square for that blanket. Lucky it's only September. Can you imagine what it'll be like in winter?'

'Pamela's dad says Hitler's got a gun. And he's going to shoot himself with it,' said George, 'when we catch him.'

'Don't believe everything you hear,' said Philip.

After a while, a single siren sounded and then faded to nothing.

'All-clear, that means,' said George. 'We learnt that at school.'

'Come on, then, you,' said Rose. 'Let's get you into a proper bed.'

I watched through the window as they made their way in the half-dark back to the house. I shivered at the prospect of another night in the shed alone.

Over the next few days, I began to think more and more about whether I should move on and find somewhere else to stay. Every day I was more nervous of being caught, and every day I got a little hungrier. I was also getting bored, stuck in there on my own. I was even tired of watching the spider build yet another web, which I had found entertaining for a while. But she seemed to build a new web every day. I don't know what was wrong with all the other webs. As I was pondering all this, I heard loud footsteps suddenly approaching. I froze. Even the spider stopped moving. They weren't George's footsteps. The door latch clicked.

CHAPTER FIVE

A pair of big black boots stopped right in front of my nose.

'What the . . .'

A man bent down and picked me up. I barked and, out of instinct, went as if to nip his hand. I couldn't help it. I suppose I was in shock.

'You little blighter,' he said and dropped me on the floor. 'George. Did you know about this?'

George came skulking down the garden. I barked again and ran towards the shelter.

'It wasn't my fault,' said George, coming over to me and putting his hand on my head. 'He just appeared.'

I stopped barking and let out a short whine, then rested my head on his arm.

'Well, we can't keep him.'

'What was that?' said Rose, coming down the garden. Then she saw me.

'George, you didn't? We said no. You naughty boy.'

'I said he just appeared!' shouted George, suddenly angry, and he picked me up and ran into the air-raid shelter. He squeezed me so hard I thought I might burst.

'What shall we do? We can't keep it,' Philip said quietly.

There was some whispering between him and Rose. I couldn't quite make out what they were saying.

'Georgie. Come on out now,' called Rose after a while. 'We're not cross. We just . . . well, you know we said no, don't you? You were naughty to get a dog without our permission.'

'Where did he get it, do you think?' asked Philip.

'Well . . . I don't know. Maybe it did just turn up. People are putting animals out on the streets now, some of them. Jack down the road upped and left with his whole family. They went off to Kent and they just left their King Charles spaniel, Nipper, apparently, and no one's seen him since.'

After a while, Philip opened the door and jumped down into the shelter.

'What's his name, anyway?' he asked softly and squeezed in next to us on the narrow bed.

'Bertie,' said George. He had tears streaming down his face and was holding on to me so tightly I could hardly breathe.

'Hello, Bertie,' said Philip, taking hold of me carefully. He held me up to his face and smiled.

'Bit of terrier in him, I reckon,' he said. 'Bit of a mix, though. Looks like old Digger I had as a boy. With even more hair. Nightmare to keep clean, this one.'

I licked his nose and let out a single happy bark.

'Can we keep him, then?' asked George, wiping the tears from his eyes.

Philip looked at me. I licked his face. He smiled. I had a feeling I might be staying for a while after all.

Rose didn't take much longer to come around to the idea of keeping me, and she even forgave me for the pork pie when George explained how hungry I had been. And when Philip finally realized it was me who had dug a hole in the shelter, George was forgiven for that too, although I was warned in no uncertain terms never to do anything like that again.

Now that I was no longer a secret, I was allowed to play in the garden freely. Philip even made me a lead from a piece of leather so I could go out and about for walks to the shops and the local park, and run about and chase a stick. I don't know why they kept throwing the stick but I thought I ought to oblige them by bringing it back each time.

Not everyone approved of me, though. Rose's mum, Mary, lived in the next street with Rose's dad, Victor, who ran a clothing factory. They had a huge fluffy white cat; she never left the house and did her business in a tray, which I thought was strange. Her name was Wilhelmina, or Princess Wilhelmina.

They weren't dog people at all. Victor liked to say he wasn't really an anything person. He liked to say, often and loudly, that he thought pets were a flea-bitten, useless waste of space. He grudgingly accepted Wilhelmina as he said it 'kept the old woman happy'. I saw him petting the cat often enough, but he only did that when he thought no one was looking.

It probably didn't help that, the first time I went around to their house, Princess Wilhelmina jumped off a shelf and landed right in front of me, scaring me half to death. I barked and chased her across the room, thinking it was a funny game. But she turned and scratched me right on the nose. Mary screamed and I knocked over a small table. There was a loud crash.

'My shepherdesses,' she said, rushing over. She began picking up all kinds of delicate-looking things that had been on the table.

'You're not bringing that in here,' said Victor firmly, and he grabbed me by the collar and threw me into the garden and shut the door. I looked back through the glass and whined. I didn't know what I had done wrong. But they wouldn't let me back in.

Rose's younger sister, Nancy, came downstairs and saw me outside.

'Oh, a puppy!' she said and opened the door. She ran out and grabbed me around the neck excitedly.

'Not you as well,' said Victor, rolling his eyes. 'This house has gone half mad. Well, he can stay out here for now. But not in the house.'

The Princess was sitting by the kitchen window, staring at me. My nose was still stinging from the scratch. I wasn't in any hurry to go back inside.

The next-door neighbours liked me, though. George's friend Pamela had a little brother, Thomas, who pulled my ears a bit. Her dad, Bill, and her mother, Jean, let me into their house quite often and even gave me a bit of food. And on the other side was a postman called Frank and his wife, Maude. They had two grown-up sons who still lived with them. They both had a job with their dad in the postal service. They were twins, but they didn't look at all alike. Harry was tall, had a shock of blond hair and deep-brown eyes. Eric was shorter. He had brown hair and blue eyes. Eric wanted to be a painter, really, not a postman, and Harry was desperate to be a pilot, which he explained to me meant flying around in the sky in aeroplanes, which I thought sounded great fun, although a bit frightening.

Nancy came around a lot to see Eric, and they both played with me in the garden. Eric teased me sometimes by pretending to throw a stick over and over again to get me tired out, and then eventually he would throw it just when I had given up. It was a strange game, but I humoured him.

I was getting quite spoilt with all the attention I was receiving from my new human family, and was really beginning to feel that life was getting better again after losing Annie. I didn't stop missing her, and I thought about her every day, but it was a relief to finally have some love and comfort in my life again.

I had almost forgotten about the war, whatever it was. And despite all the panic at the beginning, and the need for shelters, it didn't seem to have changed daily life for people all that much. The thing they called the 'black-out' seemed to be the biggest and most difficult thing for humans to deal with. Rose and Philip had to put cardboard on their windows and hang up big thick black curtains every night. George explained to me that it was all about making sure no light at all could be seen from outside the house, in case this man, Hitler, who this war seemed to be all about, used the lights to guide his aeroplanes in an air raid to drop bombs or deadly gas on us.

One evening, our next-door neighbour Frank came around. He was wearing a new blue uniform.

'What's all this?' asked Philip.

'I'm on air-raid precaution now,' he said, proudly tapping his tin hat. 'I just wondered if the little dog wanted to

57

come along. I've got to do the rounds and could do with the company.'

'What do you think, Bertie?' asked Philip, looking down at me. I had no idea what it meant, but I liked the idea of getting out of the house, so I barked and wagged my tail.

'Looks like a yes!' said Philip, and he put my new lead on and handed me over to Frank.

It was quite a shock at first because the streets had suddenly become very dark. Whereas before I had been able to see the way by the street lamps and the lights from houses and shops, now it was almost impossible to see more than a few feet ahead, especially as there was no moon, because all the lights were out. Frank had a small torch with a slit in it, and that just about guided our way.

This was the first time I had been out at night since my time sleeping on the street, after that chaotic day when the war broke out and I lost Julia, Lou and Chico. When we stepped out into the dark streets, I felt nervous, but I was soon distracted by Frank and the job in hand. One by one, we went from house to house along our road, and Frank explained that it was his job to check there were no lights showing in any houses. If there was a chink of light showing, he had to knock on the door and advise people how best to cover it up, or to turn the light off.

'Like that, you see,' he said, pointing up at a light on in an upstairs window. 'That's just what we don't want.' He knocked on the door, and a small, unassuming man with a wispy beard opened his door.

'Mr Nibbett. I'm sorry, but you know the rules,' said Frank.

'They're not my rules,' he replied calmly.

Mr Nibbett told us that he didn't believe in the war, and explained that he'd been in prison for most of the last war for refusing to fight because of his religion, which was peaceful. He was an engineer by trade, he told us, and he was happy to work on anything in the name of peace, but because he didn't believe in killing of any kind, he wasn't, on principle, going to take part in anything to do with the war, and he said he didn't care if he got bombed.

In the end, Frank gave up with Mr Nibbett. Some other people on the street were a bit angry about being told what to do, while others were apologetic and happy to turn their lights off. It even seemed to help Frank that I was there, because sometimes, if they were a bit angry at being disturbed, they looked at me and started to pet me and would then soften a bit. A few of them even gave me a few tasty treats. By the time we arrived back home, I was exhausted but exhilarated.

Some nights I went out with Frank, but others I stayed at home with Rose and Philip. Nothing much usually happened on those nights, except sometimes when the doorbell rang unexpectedly late. This time it was Rose's sister, Nancy.

'Damn blackout,' she said, coming into the house. 'I couldn't see a thing. My ankle. A pothole. I think it's broken.'

She limped across the living room and straight away collapsed on to a soft chair.

'Why did you come over so late?' Rose asked. 'You know what it's like out there now in the dark.'

'I came to get that dress. The blue one you made. You said I could borrow it. I can't stay cooped up in there with them any more. Mother's got her jigsaw out all over the table. The one that's just sea. And she doesn't stop humming the whole blessed time. And Father. Constantly tapping with that pipe. It's driving me up the wall. I'm going up West. Well, I was, until . . . this,' she said, holding up her ankle and inspecting it. 'Do you think it's broken?'

'Let's have a look,' said Rose. 'Does this hurt?'

'Yes. Ouch. You're making it worse!'

'I think it's a twist. You'll be all right. Just don't put too much weight on it, that's all.'

The doorbell rang again. I followed as Rose went to answer it.

'Is Nancy here?' It was Eric, but he was all dressed up in a smart suit and a hat. 'We're supposed to be . . .'

'Oh, Eric. I've blasted gone and twisted my ankle, haven't I?' Nancy called out from the living room. 'You'll have to take me home.'

'Take Bertie with you. He can do with a walk,' said Rose. 'He's been restless all evening.'

I wagged my tail.

'All right, boy,' said Eric, patting my head. 'Let's get the walking wounded back to barracks.'

Nancy and Eric were what humans called 'courting'. But Mary, Nancy's mother, didn't approve of it one bit, and didn't hide it, either. Nancy was her baby, she said, and that scoundrel Eric, whose family were not even God-fearing and whose father spent all day in the public house on a Sunday instead of going to church, was not the kind of family she wanted her daughter involved with.

'She still thinks I'm about twelve or something,' said Nancy as she limped slowly along the street with her arm over Eric's shoulder.

'She just doesn't want to let you go, that's all.'

'I don't know why you're sticking up for her. She doesn't even like you.'

'She'll come around. Anyway, who knows what's going to happen. I probably won't even be here soon.'

'Don't,' said Nancy, holding on tightly to Eric's arm.

'Harry's keen as anything,' he continued. 'Can't wait to get up in a plane. If he gets into the RAF, that is. Wants to go as soon as he can. I don't much fancy sloshing about in mud or getting shot down, or having my head blown off . . .'

'Oh, Eric, please don't. I couldn't bear . . .'

'Your quarters, I believe,' he said as we arrived at the house. 'Will you be all right? Your ankle?'

'I won't die,' she said sulkily, and then kissed him gently on the cheek. 'Not with you here.'

The door opened. Mary was standing there in a pink dressing gown and slippers with the cat in her arms. When she saw me, Princess Wilhelmina jumped down and meowed loudly, her white fur sticking up on end.

'Not you again,' she said, looking at me suspiciously and keeping her distance.

'It's all right,' I said. 'I'm not staying.' I thought better of chasing her this time. I didn't want a scratch on the nose again. 'What's wrong with you, anyway?' I asked the cat.

She eyed me cautiously again, unsure whether to answer. 'Nothing's wrong,' she said. 'I just don't go outside much. I don't want dogs in here. It's my house. I don't like change. It's just the way it is. Mary doesn't like me to go out, anyway. Thinks I'll catch something. And I don't mean a mouse. I've never even seen a mouse, apart from once in the kitchen, and I jumped on to the chair and Nancy laughed.'

I was surprised by Princess Wilhelmina's sudden outburst of speech. She still seemed quite angry and hostile, but it also seemed as though she wanted someone to talk to. Even if it was a dog.

'You've never been outside, then?' I asked her, shocked to think she had spent her whole life just in one house, especially after my recent adventures.

'I like the house. The sofa. The fire. The kitchen is all mine at night, but I'm not allowed in the bedroom. I don't mind. I don't want to go out, really. Not much. I might get attacked, or eaten. By a dog or something. But I do wonder sometimes. What's it like? Out there.'

'We're not all cat killers!' I said defensively. 'Dogs, I mean. Out here. It's . . . all right, I suppose. There's a lot to see. Some people are nasty. You're probably better off here where it's safe.'

'I suppose . . .'

'Willie!' called Mary. 'Get back here. Away from that nasty dog. You'll catch something.' She bent down and scooped her up.

'You're back soon,' she said to Nancy. 'You're standing funny. What's he done?'

'Eric has looked after me like a perfect gentleman,' she said. 'I slipped on a blasted . . .'

'Nancy!' said Mary, leaving her mouth wide open.

'On a pothole. And twisted my ankle, and he brought me home. So I haven't even been up West, you'll be pleased, I'm sure, to know.'

'Well, good. I mean, not your ankle, obviously. But I do worry. In this dark. Come in, anyway. You're letting all the light out. I'll get you a nice cup of cocoa and we'll make it all better.'

With that, Mary pulled Nancy into the house and shut the door.

CHAPTER SIX

As summer turned to autumn, the days were getting shorter and the evenings chillier. I had my own bed now, in the sitting room, which was cosy, and Rose had started buying me in special dog food. It didn't compare to the cuts of meat and gravy I had with Annie, but I was very grateful for what I had and happy to be safe and loved by my new family.

It wasn't long before I was part of the household at number 47 Cherry Lane. During the week, Rose and I walked George and Pamela from next door to their school while Pamela's mum looked after Thomas. Then Rose went on to work at the clothes factory nearby for a few hours, before picking Pamela and George up in the afternoon.

I was allowed to stay in the courtyard of the factory building during the day, which was a bit boring at times because it was just concrete, and I was tied up out there in case I ran away. It also got quite cold, so sometimes they relented and let me sit on the factory floor, which was noisy and quite smelly. But it was better than being at home on my own. I also got petted by the factory workers during their lunch break, and they brought me out bits of their sandwiches.

Occasionally, Philip would take me into his work, but there wasn't any outside space there, so that wasn't very often. It was further away, so he rode there by bicycle along the river and I ran alongside him, which was fun. Philip made furniture in a small workshop near Tower Bridge under a railway arch. If the boss wasn't there, he let me sit in the workshop with him and the other lads as they shaped chair and table legs and then sanded and varnished them. It was very dusty, which made me sneeze sometimes, but it was a change from being at home, and it was interesting to watch them at their work.

In the evenings, sometimes I would go out with Frank on his ARP round, or if I was too tried, I would just sit in the lounge with George and Rose and Philip as they read books or listened to the wireless. Rose sometimes did her knitting, and Philip would often be whittling away at some piece of wood, shaping it into an animal or something.

George's new obsession was submarines, and when Pamela came over to play, she and George would often play at boats and subs in the lounge. They sometimes got me involved and tried to make me pretend to be a torpedo. I wasn't sure what that was, but it involved running across the room a lot while they screamed, shouted and rolled around. It was a strange game, but they seemed to enjoy it.

One day on the radio, the newsreader announced that something called the *Royal Oak*, a big ship, had been sunk and that many people had been killed. Everyone was sad and shocked because a lot of our boys had lost their lives. Then another battleship, a German one called the *Admiral Graf Spee*, was 'scuttled', whatever that meant.

People seemed happy about that one, so I wasn't sure whether battleships being sunk was a good thing or not.

Even though we still had the blackout, and air-raid warnings, people began to seem almost disappointed that there was nothing much else happening. What was all this trouble for, they asked, if life goes on nearly the same? People stopped carrying their gas masks as much as they had at first, although if he saw someone without theirs, Frank would always insist they still needed to carry them, and that the danger wasn't over.

We still had regular air-raid warnings, and the shelter was getting colder at night. But so far, they had always been false alarms. In fact, nothing much seemed to be happening at all with the war, and people started to think it was all for nothing and maybe it wouldn't last that long after all. But instead of the war ending, more young men were being told they had to 'join up'. Harry and Eric, the twins next door, were 'called up' first because they were the right age, in their early twenties.

Harry was quite happy about it, and he was even more happy when, on their birthday, he found out he had got into the RAF. Eric, who was also called up, but into the army rather than the RAF, didn't think it was much of a birthday present.

Frank and Maude threw them a surprise party. We all went next door and crammed into their living room.

'Happy birthday, you two,' said Rose in a sing-song voice as we arrived. She and George had made the boys a chocolate cake each.

Frank brought out a bottle of a red drink he called port, because it was a special day.

'There aren't enough glasses for everyone. We'll have to use these,' he said, handing out a strange array of cups and glasses of different shapes and sizes.

'A toast,' he said, 'to my boys.'

'Let's see the papers!' said George excitedly.

Harry showed us all his papers, and explained that he was going to a base for training just outside London. Eric was to be what was called a 'gunner'. George was very excited about it all, but Eric didn't seem very keen on the idea of leaving.

'Harry always was the active one. I can imagine you flying about up there in the clouds,' said Maude to her son. 'He was the first one out, of course,' she said to everyone else. 'You couldn't wait to be born, could you? Right there on the kitchen floor. Eric took his blessed time, though, lingering about in there.'

'Mum, please!' said Eric.

'Well, I'm jolly envious,' said George, and started reeling off the names of all the planes he'd learnt from his latest magazine and how to recognize them all by their silhouettes in the dark.

Pamela and her mum and dad turned up with her little brother Thomas, and they brought even more food – a plate of chicken and a big cooked ham – so there was plenty for me. It was suddenly a packed house.

At one point, Rose, who always got a bit more high spirited when she'd had a drink, got up from her seat and started singing a song which involved a lot of hand slapping and bumping into each other.

'Hands, Knees and Boomps-a-Daisy,' she sang. Everyone seemed to know the words and the actions, apart from me, but I ran around to join in. Rose tried to pull Philip up from his chair to get him to join in, but he was having none of it and stayed sipping his whisky in silence. She danced with Harry instead.

By the end of the song, Rose was swirling little Thomas around and around by his arms, and he was squealing with laughter. George and Pamela were running up and down in the hallway. Eric was trying to twirl Nancy around in the tiny space behind the sofa without damaging her ankle, and everyone else was clapping and Boompsing in time to the music. I even joined in with some appropriately timed howling.

'It's midnight!' said Rose, suddenly looking at the clock. 'We better be going.'

Everyone else had slumped on the floor or chairs. One by one, they got up and said their goodbyes. The children, who had by that time collapsed into a sleepy heap, were carried home.

When we got back to the house, Philip was unusually quiet.

'How many did you have?' he asked when Rose came down from putting George to bed.

'I don't know. Three, four,' she said. 'Why? It was fun, though, wasn't it? I can't help thinking about those poor boys being dragged off into this war, though.'

'You have to be so . . . loud. It's embarrassing.'

'How many did *you* have?' she asked, flopping down on the chair.

'That's not the point. It's not right. You know what you get like. It makes you ill.'

'Thank goodness it's not you. Going away. That's all I can say,' she said sadly. 'Anyway. Don't be daft. I feel fine.'

'Maybe I should go. Volunteer. It's only a matter of time, anyway.'

They looked at each other for a moment. Philip's eyes were tight and strained, and Rose looked suddenly tired. I was unsure what to do, whether to try and help. With Annie, I always knew exactly how to comfort her when she was feeling sad and how to make her feel better, or when to just let her be. With my new family, I wasn't sure how things worked yet. I didn't know whether to stay and try to make things nicer between them, or whether to leave them in peace. In the end, I went over to where Rose was sitting. Philip was standing by the fireplace.

'Good boy, Bertie,' said Philip wearily, almost absent-mindedly, and he stroked my head.

'Good night, Bertie, old thing,' said Rose, getting up to go to bed.

Philip followed her in silence.

In the morning, I was relieved to see everything was back to normal and there was no talk of Philip going any-where. Things were far from normal next door, though. It was time for Harry to join the air force, and Eric was heading off to that place called Wales, which seemed to Nancy to be the end of the earth.

Before they left, Frank and Eric and Harry all shook hands and slapped each other's backs. We all came out to say goodbye. Maude was in tears and kept hugging them both. She made them promise to come back in one piece.

They all hugged me, too, and I let out a sad whine so they knew I would miss them.

Nancy and Eric went for a quick walk to wish each other goodbye, and when they got back, Nancy's face was all red and blotchy, and she looked sad. But there was nothing they could do. It was the law. There was a war on, and no amount of crying was going to change that.

When the war broke out, some children from George's school had been sent away to live outside London in case of an attack, but a few of them had already started to come home because they missed their parents so much and it was nearly Christmas. Rose and Philip had been unsure about whether to send George away, but he didn't want to go, and in the end they had decided it would be better to all stay and face whatever happened together.

Most Saturdays, when she was off work, Rose took me to the market, which I enjoyed. It was on a long street full of stalls of every kind, and there was loads of food on the ground to have a nibble on. There were rows of fruit and vegetable stalls, meat and fish and freshly baked bread, and men and women shouting out, and people jostling to buy the best bargains. Rose did complain a bit, though, because things were getting more expensive. I knew that humans did their jobs to make money, and money was how they bought food. And I started to feel guilty because I knew she was having to buy extra food for me to eat. But she assured me that she was managing all right.

By December, though, I could tell she was starting to get worried. It was becoming more and more difficult to get hold of any decent vegetables in the market; the weather was getting colder and the market traders told her that the ground was so frozen the farmers had barely been able to dig, which meant that vegetables were hard to come by and expensive.

It was so cold, in fact, that one morning, the water pipes froze and then burst and water came gushing all down the street and into the houses. Even the milk froze on the doorstep a few times, and Philip complained as he had to have water with his porridge and bitter black tea.

Then the coal ran out. That was because the coal man's horse and cart couldn't get down the road, which was slippery with ice. There were a few cold nights that week, until Philip managed to bring some wood home from his workshop to burn on the fire.

Despite the cold, everyone was still excited for Christmas, which was just around the corner. Rose wanted to make it especially fun this year because of the war and, she said, 'because who knows what might be happening next year'.

I got excited about it, too, even though I didn't really know what Christmas was for, except that people always seemed to prepare more food than they could eat, which I thoroughly approved of because I got all the scraps. With Annie, it had always been quite a quiet affair, just the two of us. I usually had a special dinner and an extra treat wrapped in paper, something like a ball or my special collar. But Christmas with my new family seemed to be full of chaos and colour and laughter.

The day before Christmas, Nancy and Rose were in the kitchen, rolling out the mince pies, with George helping to scoop in the filling, when a face appeared at the window. Rose screamed, and Nancy jumped up and ran outside, letting in a blast of cold air.

Nancy jumped into Eric's arms. He picked her up and spun her around, and they couldn't stop laughing.

'Surprise,' he said, putting her down and leading her back into the kitchen. 'Didn't think I'd make it,' he said, taking off his coat. 'Snow on the roads. Managed to get a lift with one of the lads in the end.'

'Shut the door, and then you can help us with these,' said Rose, smiling. She gave him a big hug, handed him a rolling pin, then went to the larder and pulled out a big ham she had bought that morning. 'And I'll get on with this.'

'Why did you get so much food?' asked Philip, coming in. 'We'll never eat all that. Eric!' he said. They shook hands. 'How's the army treating you?'

'Can't complain,' he said. 'Taught me how to fire a gun, anyway.'

'You look taller,' said Nancy. 'And your hair. It's all short!' She ruffled his head.

'Oh, I bought something for Georgie. And,' he produced a small package from his bag, 'this, for Bertie.'

I wagged my tail when I heard my name. I was so excited by it all, I jumped up at Eric and started sniffing at the package. I couldn't tell what it was, but I was slightly disappointed because, from the smell, I could tell it clearly wasn't food.

'Bertie, get down, you naughty dog, it's not Christmas yet,' said Philip.

'Oh, lovely! We can put them under the tree,' said Rose.

'It's a shame Harry won't be here,' said Eric. 'They've got him up in some God-awful place with no trains. But he sends his love. And this, a special treat for George.'

George ran over and inspected the package, trying to work out what it was.

'Is it a book?' he said lifting it up and putting it to his ear. Everyone laughed.

That night, George wanted to leave something out for Father Christmas, who he thought would bring him more presents, so he left a glass of milk and an apple for the reindeers by the back door. He said that, although Pamela insisted they would come down the chimney because they were magic, he was of the firm belief they would have to come in through the door, because the hot coals would burn Father Christmas's boots. I didn't see why anyone would choose to come down the chimney instead of through the door, whoever they were, so I was with George on that one.

Every Christmas, humans brought a tree into their house, which was strange. George had great fun putting bits of sparkly stuff on the family's tree, and he had made a big black spider out of cardboard to go on the top, because he said it was better than a boring star, which was what Pamela had made for next door's tree.

On Christmas morning, George was up before it was even light, and he was already under the tree, poking about, when I woke up.

'He came!' he said, running over to me. I didn't know how Father Christmas had got past me, because I didn't hear anything. George then produced a big sock, which he said he found at the bottom of his bed, along with an orange peel, an empty chocolate wrapper and a model submarine.

'There's other stuff under here,' he said, poking about. 'There's one for you, Bertie!'

I sniffed that one, and it did smell like food, which I was pleased about.

When Rose and Philip came down, they all had eggs on toast, and jam, and I had half a tin of meat as a treat. Then we sat around the tree to open up our presents. Well, I didn't actually open mine; George helped me with that. But Rose opened hers, which was a bottle of perfume. She dabbed it on straight away and smelt strongly of roses. Philip got a gramophone record, some cigars and a blue hat Rose had been secretly knitting. He put it on even though we were in the house.

'For you on that bicycle in this cold,' said Rose, and gave him a hug and a kiss.

George also got a hat and a book about the British Isles. But he was most pleased with a pilot's uniform, which was the special present from Harry. He put it on and immediately began zooming about the house. I got a rubber bone to chew on and a bag of special edible treats. All in all, Christmas was turning out to be very jolly indeed, despite the war.

Philip put on his gramophone record and, unusually for him, tried to get Rose to dance around the room with him, which she did for a bit. Then Rose suddenly started panicking and told everyone they all needed to stop messing about, even if it was Christmas, because we all needed to get ready. We were going over to Victor and Mary's because they had a dining room, and could fit everyone around their big table.

I was dreading going there because the last time I was in their house I had knocked something over. I was also a bit nervous of seeing Princess Wilhelmina. I know it sounds silly, because she was only a cat, but since I had found out how nervous she was of dogs and how she had never left the house, I felt anxious about being there. And it wasn't helped by knowing that Mary wasn't keen on me at all. But George had insisted I should be allowed to go with them, saying that otherwise he wouldn't be able to enjoy Christmas one bit, and eventually they had relented, as long as I didn't cause any trouble. I thought it would probably be more fun than staying at home on my own, anyway.

'Oh, you're all dressed up posh,' said Rose to Nancy as she opened the front door when we arrived. I looked around for Willie but she was nowhere to be seen.

'Look what Eric's gone and got me,' she said, lifting her hand up.

'Not you as well! Everyone's gone wedding mad lately,' laughed Rose, who knew at least three people who had been married just before the war started. She gave her sister a big hug.

'Congratulations, love,' said Philip when he heard.

'Mum's not very happy about it, though,' she said in a low voice. 'Think it rather ruined her morning.'

'When?' asked Rose. 'Have you got a date, I mean?'

'Don't know. It only happened last night. Whenever he can get away again, I suppose. It was quite a surprise, to be honest. I haven't quite taken it all in yet.'

'Can you two girls come in and start bringing out the dishes?' Mary called from the kitchen. 'Georgie, you can come and help your granny stir the gravy.'

Victor was sitting in his chair, smoking a pipe in front of a roaring fire, which looked very inviting.

'Oh, you've brought the horrible mutt,' he said. But he was smiling, which I found a bit confusing. 'Bring him over here, out of trouble. The cat's sulking in the kitchen, anyway.'

Philip led me over to the corner, and I was quite surprised that Victor put me down by his side and patted me and started stroking my ears.

'Fancy a quick snifter before lunch?' he said to Philip. But before Philip could answer, he jumped up and went over to a big cabinet with several glass bottles on it. 'Before *she* comes back in,' he said and touched his nose conspiratorially.

The dining room was next door, but there was a gap in the wall between the two rooms, so when they all sat down for dinner, I could smell all the delicious smells wafting through. Brussels sprouts (though I wasn't that keen on them), chicken, sausages, gravy and potatoes. It all made my mouth water.

'For what we are about to receive, may the good Lord make us truly grateful. Amen,' said Mary, bowing her head and clasping her hands. There was a mumble of Amens, and then everyone dived into the food.

'Calm down, you gannets,' she said, tucking her napkin into her blouse. 'Such a beautiful sermon this morning. The true spirit of Christmas, didn't you think, darling?' she said to Victor as she sliced a sausage down the middle.

'I thought he went on a bit,' said Victor. 'That part from Galatians 4. I don't know. Slaves, illness, and I'm afraid he completely lost me with that bit about childbirth.'

'Didn't see you in church,' said Mary, looking over her glasses at Rose.

'Mmmm,' said Rose. Then there was a scraping of plates and some awkward eating sounds.

Mary broke the silence. 'Has Nancy told you her *news*?'

'Mother. Must we now?'

'Yes, she chose Christmas morning to make her pronouncement. She's to wed that boy from down the road. Ernie . . . ? What's his name? She's barely out of school and . . .'

'Eric. And I'm eighteen!'

'I just think you should be certain, darling,' she said, touching her arm. 'And consider your options. I always thought that Chipping boy, Dennis. He's so tall.'

'Eurgh. He's awful. He's such a snob,' said Nancy. 'Where did you pluck the idea of him from, anyway?'

'His mother's a school governor, and you know Mr Chipping stands a very good chance of being elected counsellor next year. You used to play together, dear, don't you remember?'

'When we were five!'

'Oh, I don't know,' sighed Mary. 'You could have anyone, with your cheekbones.'

'Didn't you buy some crackers, dear?' said Victor, changing the subject.

'Oh, gosh, yes,' said Mary. 'I knew I'd forgotten something.' She pulled out a big box from under the table.

Then there were a load of loud bangs, which made me jump every time, even though I knew from Christmas with Annie that those crackers were harmless, even though they gave off a loud and scary noise.

After dinner, everyone came back into the living room, and George ran over and gave me a cuddle.

'Oh, Bertie, you've been such a good boy, sitting here all this time,' said Rose. 'Can we give him something, Mother? There's loads of meat left.'

Christmas Day seemed to have softened Mary, perhaps because I hadn't knocked any of her precious ornaments over yet. Eventually, she relented and said I could have some giblets.

When I went into the kitchen, Princess Wilhelmina was sitting in her basket. She was asleep by the stove, so I crept past her to get to the food and tried to eat as quietly as possible. I know she had spoken to me last time, but I didn't know how she'd be today, and I didn't want a row or anything. I obviously wasn't quiet enough. She opened one eye and looked at me for a moment. I tensed up and looked at her. She must have decided she was too comfortable where she was to move, though, and she shut her eye again and went straight back to sleep. That was something of a relief.

When I had finished eating, Philip took me for a quick run around the garden, but it was freezing, so we soon went back into the house, and I sat by the fire again at Victor's feet. I was almost beginning to feel, with all the Christmas spirit, that I was becoming truly one of the family.

'Are you eating the chocolates already?' Rose asked George, who had discovered there were some hanging on the tree.

'Granny,' he replied with his mouth full, 'said that I could.'

'Granny spoils you,' said Philip.

'The King's on at three,' said Victor, turning the dial on the large wireless in the corner of the room.

A man's voice came crackling from the speaker and everyone went quiet.

With all the festivities, I think we had almost forgotten about the war just for a moment. But the King's talk about sacrifice and dark times ahead made everyone go quiet and thoughtful, especially Nancy.

I could see Rose starting to look worried, too. When he ended with a bit about putting your hand into the hand of God, I could see tears welling up in Mary's eyes. Even Victor's were starting to glisten a little bit.

When the music, the national anthem, they said, came on at the end, they all stood up and Victor put his hand up to his forehead in a salute. Despite all the Christmas fun and good cheer, this war must be a pretty serious business, after all.

CHAPTER SEVEN

January 1940 was the coldest month I could remember ever having experienced in my life. The whole house seemed to have a chill running through it all the time, no matter whether the fires were lit, and I never seemed to feel warm.

To make things even worse, Rose began to talk about how the government had started to 'ration' things. People were only allowed a certain amount of food and everyone was given a little blue book. Rose took ours with her to the market where she got the allotted amount of food, and no more.

At first it was bacon, butter and sugar, which wasn't so bad. But then other things started to be rationed as well, such as eggs, cheese, jam, and even tea, which horrified Philip, who loved his morning cup. But most importantly for me, they started to ration meat.

People also began to argue about whether food should be given to 'useless' animals such as dogs and cats. Eventually, they were told by the government that no food humans were able to eat should be given to pets, because of the shortage. That meant fewer tasty meaty treats for me. I was still allowed tinned pet meat when we could get it. But it did mean Rose had to go to more and more difficult lengths to feed me enough food, and I started to feel hungry most of the time.

That was when I really witnessed the fine art of queuing. These humans seemed to queue at every opportunity; it was almost as though they enjoyed it. There were queues for bread and queues for meat, but the longest queue of all was at the fish stall at the end of the day. When we arrived, there was already a long line of people stretching all the way down the street and around the corner into the next street. There were dozens of people there, chattering away, all hoping to get something cheap and tasty for themselves, but also for their pets. Eventually, after several hours of waiting, we got a small paper bag of fish heads and tails. Fish scraps were among the few things we were allowed to eat apart from dry food. They were a lot better than nothing, but not really enough to fill me up. The next week, we joined another queue for about an hour and a half outside the butcher's and left with just a small bag of kidneys. I felt bad that Rose had to queue for so long to get enough food for me. I began to have doubts. Was I really a 'useless mouth'?

Things got worse when a letter arrived. Philip opened it and his face looked serious. Later on, I heard him and Rose whispering together in the living room. I was worried and desperate to know what was going on. I crept in and lingered by the door, unsure what to do. They were holding hands. I saw the opened letter on the sideboard.

'What'll we do? For money?' asked Rose. 'If you're not earning any more.'

'There's an allowance. For wives. It's not much. Can't you get more hours at the factory?'

'I'll have to,' she said. 'George isn't getting any cheaper, you know. And with Bertie now, too. And Mr Gaunt's put the rent up again. Everything's just getting more expensive all the time, and they expect us to live on nothing and sacrifice everything.'

'I know. But it's the same for everyone,' he said. 'I know that doesn't make it any easier, though. I don't want to go. You know that. I'm not much of a fighter. Never have been. Spent most of school in the workshop while the other lads were out tearing into each other on the field. But, my conscience, if . . .'

'I know,' she said. 'But what's it all for? Can't those men at the top, Chamberlain and Hitler and all that, just settle it between them, with an arm wrestle or something? Where, anyway, will they send you, do you think?'

'Can't say. France, most likely in the end. It'll be next now, they're saying. But we'll be training first,' he said. 'You can visit me, I'm sure. I won't be going far.'

I decided not to interrupt them this time and crept out of the room again before they saw me. As I was leaving, Rose put her head on Philip's shoulder.

'I don't think I can bear it,' she said quietly. 'Without you.'

Over the next few days, Philip began to get ready to leave. Although George had seen Harry and Eric go off to war, that had all seemed rather like a big adventure. When Rose told George his father was also leaving, he became quiet and sullen. He even stopped eating much, which was very unusual for him. And when I saw George sad and confused, it made me sad, too.

'Where will you go?' he asked his dad quietly one evening.

'I'm going to join the army,' said Philip. 'The regular army.'

'Will you get shot?'

'No, I won't get shot,' said Philip, taken aback by his forthrightness. He looked at Rose, who looked down.

I didn't think humans could know what would happen in the future, but then I remembered that, in the heat of the panic, I had told Chico it would all be all right when I had no idea what would happen. Perhaps this was what they were doing with George, telling him a little lie to make him feel better.

'Pamela's dad's going too, you know,' said Philip. 'He's been accepted into the Navy.'

Philip seemed to be hoping to get George excited about it all again, but he remained quiet and thoughtful. Although the war had seemed like an adventure, now that it was affecting his family directly, it was starting to become a bit too real.

The day soon came for Philip to leave, and everyone was quiet as we walked with him to the railway station. It was a bitterly cold but clear day, and the sun was shining directly into my eyes almost the whole way, which seemed somehow wrong for the mood.

Rose and Philip took it in turns to try and remain upbeat for George's sake, but there was none of the slapping of backs and hearty goodbyes we had seen when Harry and Eric had left.

The railway station was full of crowds of people moving in all directions. I had to keep dodging between them to avoid being trodden on. There were groups of men getting on to different trains. Some were on their own, or with other soldiers. Others were kissing girlfriends and wives with shining new gold rings on their fingers. Some were with their parents, who were waving goodbye, while others were waiting, just staring up at a large board with writing on it. One couple was sitting on a bench together with their heads on each other's shoulders in silence.

Rose didn't say much, I think because she knew that, whatever she did say, it would make her sad.

'Have you got the ticket?' she said after a while.

Philip patted his pocket and smiled. 'You'll look after your mother, won't you?' he said, bending down to look at George and ruffling his hair. 'You're the man of the house now. You and Bertie, that is. Be a good lad, won't you?' he said and shook his son's hand.

'Yes, sir,' said George quietly.

'Write as soon as you can, won't you?' said Rose. 'Let me know you got there safely. Have you got enough warm clothes? I don't want you getting ill before you've even started.'

Before he could answer, the train pulled into the platform. Philip kissed Rose and hugged George tightly. He held on to Rose's arm for a moment before giving her one last kiss. Then he pulled himself away, jumped up on to the train and the door slammed shut.

A whistle blew. We stood on the platform as the great engine began to move, and I began to whine a little to say goodbye too. The air filled with great puffs of steam and the noise got louder. Philip opened a window a bit further along and leant out. The train began to move. He mouthed something to Rose but I couldn't tell what it was. She smiled. Eventually, the train built up enough steam to move away, and we watched as it snaked off into the distance until, finally, we couldn't see the train or Philip any more. Everything was suddenly quieter, with just the announcements in the background and the buzz of people waiting for the next train.

Rose and George stood there for a while and looked along the tracks. Eventually, George bent down and hugged me and put his head into my fur. Rose put her hand on his shoulder.

'It's just us now,' she said, and we made our way slowly back to the house.

CHAPTER EIGHT

Things felt empty and quiet with Philip gone. Although Rose tried to keep things normal for George, he spent a lot of time in his bedroom and became very quiet. He began to read more and more books about the war and all the different planes and boats. I lay on the floor next to him as he read. Sometimes he talked to me and told me about what he was reading. Other times he was quiet and hardly spoke at all. I wondered what he was thinking about but could never ask.

Rose also seemed to rely on me more for company now that Philip had gone. She started chatting away to me more as she did the work around the house, especially on washing day, which seemed to take an entire day at least once a week. They now included me in the conversation at dinner time, as though I was really becoming another member of their family.

In some ways, it felt good to be needed more by George and Rose, and to be able to comfort them. But Rose was coming under pressure from some of the neighbours about having a dog, a 'useless mouth' to feed, when there was a war on. She also said that we had less money now that Philip wasn't earning from the workshop, and it was definitely getting harder to get enough to eat. I was feeling hungry most of the time, although she kept on queuing to get food for me.

One blessing, though, was that winter was nearly over. When spring finally arrived, a few birds came and settled in our tiny garden and cheered the place up. The little apple tree began to sprout small green leaves and blossoms, and before long, the days were getting warmer and longer. When the hard frost on the ground finally thawed and the soil became soft again, I could enjoy being in the garden more, instead of being cooped up in the house in the cold and dark.

That is until, horror of horrors, Rose and George started to dig the garden up.

It was one Sunday afternoon, when the sun had really begun to shine and give off a warm heat again. I was lying out and enjoying it warming up my fur after so long. The pair of them came outside, chatting together. George was holding a little spade and Rose had a larger shovel. Bit by bit, they began to dig up the small bit of grass at the back of the house by the Anderson shelter, near where I was lying. George had a packet of something and began sprinkling it all along the ground in long rows.

'Dig for Victory' was the slogan; I had heard people saying it, but I thought they just meant dig holes like I always liked to do. I soon realized it was because of the shortage of food; people were being encouraged to grow their own. Rose loved gardening, so I thought it could be a great solution. The only problem was, I wasn't that keen on vegetables, and I was a bit upset at first when I saw that tiny patch of garden, where I loved to run about, disappearing in the name of carrots and turnips. But Rose told me in no uncertain terms that this area was now out of bounds to playful dogs. It was hard to resist digging about in the newly turned earth, but I knew it helped them to have more food, and I soon got used to keeping away. I even started getting a taste for vegetables when I realized they were among the few remaining options.

Rose was very excited. She had a letter in her hand from Philip. We all gathered around as she read it. He had been posted overseas, but he couldn't say where for security reasons. He said he was fit and well and missed us all terribly. There was a big hug for me, and kisses all round. He longed to see us all again and told Rose to keep her chin up, though I'm not sure why.

'I wish he could say more,' she sighed as she put the letter down. 'It doesn't sound like it's really him. Not really.'

Although many of the men on our street had gone to war, those of us who were still at home began to wonder whether it would ever really affect us much, apart from the rationing and missing Philip. The much-anticipated air raids hadn't happened yet, although there was still a blackout to abide by. Most people didn't even bother to carry their gas masks around any more. And when the air-raid siren did go off, sometimes people didn't even bother to go into their shelters, although we always did, as Rose insisted.

The newspaper men began to shout 'Forget Hitler – take your holiday'. There was a lighter feeling in the air, and with summer approaching, people started to think again that it might be over soon after all.

Another thing that happened around that time was Clive.

It was a rainy, humid day, and I was sprawled out in the living room while George played with his submarines.

Rose had spent all morning in the rain, trying to get food for me at the market, but all she could find were some dry dog biscuits, which were barely edible. I ate them anyway, I was that hungry.

The doorbell rang, and Nancy was standing there, all smartly dressed up with lipstick on, and a hat, and smelling very strongly of perfume. Next to her was a tall, thin man in a suit, a bright-red tie and a brown overcoat. His hair was slicked back against his head and he was chewing on a toothpick. He smelled of stale cigar smoke and, for some reason, cheese.

'This is Clive,' said Nancy, nervously. 'He can get us all sorts of things. He's got lots of things . . . Meat. Butter. You name it.'

'Get them from where? Hello, Clive,' said Rose, shaking his hand. 'And how much are these *things*?'

'Oh, not much. Well, you know, bit more than usual. But it's things we simply can't get now any more. Meat . . . bacon!' she whispered.

My ears pricked up. It had been so long since I had eaten any proper meat. I wandered over and sniffed at a large, green canvas bag at Clive's feet.

'Hallo, boy. What's his name?' he said, pulling at my ears. 'Cheeky chops, bet you want some, too, don't you? Where d'you find this one?' he asked Rose, and pulled at the sides of my mouth playfully.

'It's Bertie. He was a stray. Found us, actually,' said Rose. Then she whispered to Nancy, 'Is this stuff . . . legal? I mean, where's it come from?'

'No one's completely legal these days,' said Nancy. 'Not if you want to survive. Don't worry. Everyone's doing it.'

'Look, do you want the stuff or not?' asked Clive, his tone suddenly changing. 'Cos there's plenty of people around here that do.'

Nancy let out a nervous laugh. 'Well, do you?' she hissed at Rose. 'I said you would and we came all the way from Bethnal Green.'

'All right. Come through,' she said. 'But no promises.'

I followed eagerly into the kitchen to see what was in the bag. I could definitely smell meat.

'So, let's see what we've got here,' said Clive, pulling out several packets and laying them on the table. 'Rack of beef, some best pork chops, bacon here, Irish butter, finest sugar from the West Indies and, the pick of the crop, bananas.'

'Gosh, I haven't seen this much food in months,' said Rose. I could tell she was tempted.

George came wandering in to see what all the noise was.

'Is this all for us?' he asked, excitedly picking up a banana and sniffing it. 'Does this mean the rationing's over?'

Rose looked confused as she tried to decide what to do. Part of me could sense she thought it was wrong. Food was restricted and there seemed to be a good reason, though I hadn't quite worked out what it was yet. But the growl in my stomach was hoping desperately that she would buy the extra stuff.

'All right,' she said. 'This once. As a treat, you two,' she said, looking at me and George. 'But don't get used to it, all right?'

I gave a whine of assent and George whooped.

'How much for a bit of bacon and the beef . . . and the butter, and the sugar?' she asked Clive.

'And the bananas. Pleeease?' begged George.

'All right. And the bananas,' sighed Rose.

They agreed a price, which I sensed, from the look on her face, was a lot more than she would normally pay at the market.

'I'll have to put in a few more shifts at the factory to pay for this lot,' she said, taking the money from a box on the mantelpiece. 'Here you go,' she said, and counted it out into Clive's hand. 'It's all there.'

'You won't regret it,' said Nancy.

'I hope not,' said Rose.

'Come on, girl. Let's get moving,' said Clive, stuffing the money into his inside pocket. 'I've got Canning Town to do before it gets dark and that prig comes around with his lights-out nonsense.'

'Bye all,' said Nancy as they left. 'Enjoy the food!'

They disappeared, leaving behind them the smell of perfume, stale cigar smoke and cheese.

That week, we enjoyed some delicious meals courtesy of Clive. I got slivers of beef, which melted in my mouth, and I even got a bit of bacon. George and Rose enjoyed two meat pies, and had bananas and even real custard for pudding. After we had gorged ourselves, though, I could tell Rose began to have doubts about buying all the extra food.

When our next-door neighbour Maude came around, Rose went through the kitchen, hiding the extra sugar and the bananas. Then, later, while she was washing the dishes, she confided in me.

'I feel sick about it, Bertie,' she said. 'Others are going hungry. It doesn't seem right. I want the best for you and George. He's still growing and I couldn't forgive myself if he got rickets or . . . scurvy or something, and there was something I could have done about it. But it just doesn't feel right.'

The next time Clive came around, Rose resisted buying anything, which he wasn't too happy about. She told him she didn't have the money and that we would do just fine on what we had. Other women were being inventive, using carrots and beetroots to make up for lack of sugar, she said, so why should we be any different.

Clive told her she was daft if she didn't realize that everyone was doing the exact same thing. In the end, she looked more confused than ever and didn't know what to believe.

By June, though, we did start to reap the rewards of the new vegetable garden, which meant Rose could add some new flavours to the food at no cost to anyone. Not buying from Clive did, of course, mean going back to the long queues at the fish stall for off-cuts, and waiting hours at the butcher's for scraps no human would eat.

In June, another letter arrived. Rose read it out.

To my darling Rose, little Georgie and Bertie,

I hope you are all well in Blighty and that you're keeping up your spirits. I hope you're managing on the allowance? I do hope so. How's George doing at school? Tell him to keep it up from me. And I trust old Bertie is looking after you all.

Just to say, I've safely arrived here. The weather is marvellously warm, and there are wild flowers all around us, which makes me think of our little garden and miss you even more. We're staying in huts on the outskirts of a small village, but exactly where, I'm not allowed to say. I've two new chums, one a Scots lad and another from London who is quite the joker, and we all have a good laugh together. I do hope I can get some leave soon but I don't know when. I miss you all.

Love,

Philip

Rose folded up the letter and put it in a wooden box she had, with all her precious things in it, on the mantelpiece. Not long after that, we heard on the wireless that France had 'surrendered to Germany'. I didn't know what that meant, but it seemed to worry everyone, especially Rose now that she knew Philip was right there in the middle of it.

A few days later, I was in search of something to eat, and I found Rose in the kitchen, sitting on the floor, surrounded by things from the kitchen cupboard.

'Hello, Bertie,' she said. 'Have you heard? They want us to give up all our metal. To the government for war supplies. So we can help our boys. Do our bit. George!' she called out. 'Come and help me sort through all these things.'

George came running in and together we helped her turn out the rest of the kitchen cupboards. We had to put aside anything made of a metal called aluminium.

'Make a pile there,' said Rose, and before long we had a whole selection of objects made of the metal. I even got quite good at carrying stuff to the 'in' and 'out' piles in my mouth, and by the end of it all there was a pile of saucepans, a round thing with holes in it called a colander, an old kettle and even the bath tub from when George was a little baby.

We took them in George's old pram to a local hall where they had set up a collecting point, and discovered that loads of other people from all over London were doing the same thing, bringing all their kitchen stuff, so that the stocks could be built up.

'They're going to make aeroplanes out of them,' said George, getting very excited about the prospect. He even offered some of his own toy soldiers into the mix.

'I'm just glad I can do my bit,' said Maude, who was helping to unload and sort the items.

She had even brought her old jelly moulds. One was in the shape of a fish, and it amused everyone to think that it might one day become part of something as grand and deadly as a Spitfire.

'Do I just leave the things here?' It was a woman's voice. I recognized it but I couldn't think where from. Then I heard a familiar meow. I spun around. There, by the table piled high with saucepans, was a basket, and inside it was Chico.

'Oh, what a sweet little cat,' said Rose. Chico arched his back and let out a long cry.

'I had to bring him,' said Julia, who was standing there holding a pile of saucepans, some of the ones I had seen in the cafe. 'He's so nervous these days, I can't leave him on his own any more, and with my husband ill. We're so afraid he'll run off.'

'Chico,' I whispered. 'Over here.' I had hidden under the table and poked my nose out. The cat turned around and peered through the bars on the basket.

'You!' he said. 'You left us. We had to spend the whole afternoon at Gerald's, and he never stops talking. Not ever.'

'I didn't leave you. I got lost,' I said. 'I spent the night on the street. You should have seen where I ended up sleeping. It was awful.'

Chico turned his head away. I wondered if he would ever forgive me.

'It all went wrong after you left,' he said eventually. 'Lou's got this mystery illness. We don't know what it is. He went yellow. Julia's had to do everything. She's going out of her mind.'

I started to feel guilty. Perhaps I should have gone back to the cafe that day, tried to find them, instead of just running off.

I peeked out from under the table. Rose and Julia were chatting away. For some reason, I was really hoping Julia wouldn't notice me. It would be so awkward. I just wouldn't know what to do if she decided she wanted me to go back with her.

'I've got my dog here too,' said Rose and she tugged on my lead. I dug my claws in and stayed under the table.

'Come back with us,' pleaded Chico from inside his basket.

I looked at Julia. She looked tired. Then George came tumbling over and got under the table with me and clung on to my neck.

'Bertie,' he squealed. 'They're going to make a Spitfire out of our saucepans.'

I remembered his face when Philip had left. I couldn't leave him as well.

'I've got a new family now,' I said to Chico. 'You'll have to look after things. Be the man of the house.'

Julia looked at her watch, and without looking down, she picked up the basket. Chico let out another howl, and a moment later, they were both gone.

When we got back to the house, Maude was standing on the doorstep, looking distressed. She had a letter in her hand.

'Frank's out at some ARP thing,' she said. 'I didn't know what to do.'

'It's all right. Come inside,' said Rose, taking her arm gently. 'What's wrong?'

'It's all happening, on the wireless. It's all starting.'

Rose switched on the radio, and there was a man's voice shouting out of it, over the top of loud buzzing and firing sounds.

'It's a dog fight!' yelled George, getting excited.

A dog fight? I couldn't hear a single dog. All I could hear were loud roaring sounds in the background and, every now and again, loud cracks one after another followed by more roaring sounds going off into the distance. I hid behind the sofa, hoping these strange loud noises would stop and wondering what on earth kind of dog it was.

'They're here, Bertie,' said George, excitedly running over to me. 'Don't worry. They can't hurt you here, you silly old thing. Our Spitfires'll finish them off!'

As the noises continued, Maude and Rose were sitting on the sofa, looking at the pieces of paper.

'It's Harry,' said Maude. 'Says he's now a pilot proper. They've sent him up there already. I can't believe it. He might be up in one of those planes. And then Eric's on the anti-aircraft guns. So, they might both be right there, right now. And there's nothing I can do. I feel so useless, just sitting here listening. My boys, right in the middle of it all.'

The awful noise on the wireless was getting louder, and the man talking was getting more and more excited as he described what I realized must be a fight between the two planes and not two dogs, after all.

Rose put her hand on Maude's shoulder and tried to reassure her that it would be all right, that we were doing all we could, and that they were both brave boys and she was sure they would do what was needed.

But I had the feeling she was far from sure it would be all right. This war everyone had been talking about for so long suddenly seemed a lot closer to home.

CHAPTER NINE

Over the next few weeks, some of the neighbours got in quite a panic that we were going to be invaded by the Germans. I started to wonder what a German would look like and how I would know if I saw one.

'They'll parachute in,' said Mr Pickard from up the road as he stood and chatted to Rose on the doorstep one afternoon. 'You can't tell who's the enemy now. People say they'll go to any length to slip past us. Even dress up as nuns. Anything just to get here. Everyone, even kitchen maids, might be a spy these days.'

'What would you do, though? If you saw one?' asked Rose. 'I mean, how do we know? If they're such masters of disguise.'

'They're sure to slip up eventually,' he said. 'The odd word in German. Things like that. You can just tell.'

'The odd Nazi salute,' said Rose, who was getting a bit tired of all the spy panic.

Mr Pickard lowered his voice to a whisper. 'Did you know, there's one on this very street,' he said. 'Living right over there. I saw them arrive a few weeks ago. Surly lot.' He pointed to a house with a green door opposite.

'Oh, I'll have to go and say hello,' said Rose. 'Make sure they have everything they need.'

He tutted and walked slowly away down the street, muttering to himself.

The fear got worse, though, and many people were now absolutely sure we were about to be invaded, that is, if the Germans weren't already here and about to over-run the Houses of Parliament. A few days later, I was tied up outside the shop, waiting for Rose to buy some vegetables, when there was a commotion inside.

'It's Mr Pickard. He's been attacked by a German spy,' said a woman clutching a box of strawberries. Mr Pickard was lying on the floor on top of another man, who looked very confused. When I saw the other man, I thought I recognized him. I was sure I had seen him on our street.

'I've got him,' said Mr Pickard. 'Don't worry. It's all under control.'

The man was wriggling under Mr Pickard's weight and trying to get his leg free, but he did not appear to be putting up much of a fight.

'I'm not a spy,' he said, trying to get up. 'I'm buying a marrow.'

Mr Pickard released his hold on the man slightly, and when he saw he wasn't going to run away, he stood up warily and began to look a little bit embarrassed.

'What's going on?' asked a policeman, who had been summoned by someone in the crowd.

'I was attacked by this . . . German,' said Mr Pickard, brushing himself down.

'You came at me!' said the man. He did have a strange voice, not like the voices in London I had heard before, but he didn't seem very scary.

'Well,' said the policeman. 'Are you a German?'

'Well . . . yes. But . . .'

'See, Officer. What did I tell you? They're coming over here in droves and we're just standing idly by. They need to be locked up. Why are they still coming in? That's what I want to know.'

'But I'm Jewish,' said the man. 'We've escaped from the Nazis. I'm hardly likely to be a spy for them. I just want to be somewhere safe with my family.'

Quite a crowd had gathered, and there seemed to be a division of opinion among the people as to whether the man was a spy or just going about his daily business, buying a vegetable, as he claimed.

'Well, they're just as bad,' said Mr Pickard. 'The Jews. Not all of them, obviously. But some of them are just pretending. Spies under cover. You just can't tell, that's all I'm saying. Better to be safe, Officer, in my opinion.'

He seemed to be tying himself up into knots when faced with the obvious fact that the man in front of him was not in any way threatening.

'Well. Did the fellow actually do anything, Pickard?' asked the policeman with a sigh. 'Did he attack you?'

'He pushed past me,' said Mr Pickard, 'with malicious intent. I could see it in his eyes.'

'I brushed past you in the queue. I tried to apologize,' said the man, getting quite desperate and flustered.

'Shall we put this down to a misunderstanding, then?' said the officer.

'Yes, a misunderstanding. I understand that,' said the man, holding out his hand to Mr Pickard, who, after some deliberation, reluctantly shook it.

Once it was all over, people dispersed and got on with their shopping. The man picked up his marrow and walked away down the road.

It made me sad that people didn't trust each other now, that someone buying a marrow could be accused of being the enemy. I didn't know what the enemy would look like if it did come, or if it even existed any more. I had a lot of time to ponder this and other things, because Rose couldn't always take me to work, especially if it was raining or too cold, and more often than not I would find myself on my own in the house for most of the day. I started to hear strange, scary noises from within the house and would get quite frightened. One day, I don't know what came over me, but I was so restless I didn't know what to do with myself, and I thought I heard a noise coming from the larder. I managed to get in. I couldn't find the source of the noise, but instead I did find a load of delicious food. When Rose got home she was very angry with me because there was nothing left for their dinner. I had been so hungry and bored, I had eaten a whole chicken and a fish pie, and left the carcass and pie plate on the floor because I didn't know what to do with them. I just didn't feel like myself any more, and no matter how hard I tried to be good, I never seemed to be able to control myself. Especially when it came to food.

Nancy had given up working at the factory and was helping Clive full time now with selling things. But Rose was worried about that, too.

'Is it safe? Where does he take you, anyway?' she asked her sister one day.

'It's fine. It's fun!' said Nancy. 'Last week I actually met Ma Finch. Did I tell you about her? I didn't realize she had such thick white hair. She's tiny but you wouldn't mess with her. She's in charge of everything, Clive says. Where to get the stuff from. Where to sell it, how much. All that.'

'It sounds like quite an enterprise,' said Rose warily.

'Ma Finch is Clive's stepmother, sort of. I don't know. She kind of adopted him when his parents died when he was eight. He'd do anything for her. Then there's Mad Carpet Tony.'

'Carpet Tony?'

'I don't know why they call him that. He's Ma's real son. Older. Doesn't like Clive. Something about when they were growing up and Ma got him a catapult for his birthday and Tony wanted it . . . All very silly, but, you know, these things stick.'

As Nancy told her more about her new adventures, Rose had an idea which would solve two problems at once.

'Listen, why don't you take Bertie with you? When you go out. He's not much of a guard dog, I know. But it would be good for him and he might help if anything gets . . . difficult.'

Nancy agreed it was a good idea, and the next time she went out with Clive I went with them.

It was so exciting to be out of the house again. We walked along streets I didn't even know existed and went through alleyways and crowded backstreets where dozens of people all seemed to live in one house.

We went down to the docks by the river where all the boats were and walked through huge open buildings, where Clive would collect things from a small group of men wearing suits and hats. It all felt very serious and secretive, and exciting.

One day, we arrived at one of the buildings – they called them warehouses – and could see a tall, thin man standing at the far end with his back to us. The men at the door told us we were seeing Tony directly, because there was a big delivery and he wanted to deal with it himself and for Clive to 'do the drop'.

As we walked in, the man was just kind of standing, staring into space. Next to him was a rather large, fearsome-looking black-and-white dog. As soon as she saw me, she started barking. So I started barking back, and Clive pulled at my lead.

'Calm that animal down. He's frightening Jane,' said the man, who I assumed must be 'Mad Carpet Tony'.

Jane! I thought. That's a strange name for a dog. I didn't think she looked particularly frightened of me, either. She was barking right at me, basically telling me that I was in her territory and that if I didn't leave right away she might have to sort me out.

'Shush, girl,' said Tony, bending down and looking at her right in the eyes. She calmed down straight away and let out a friendly whine. I breathed a sigh of relief.

When Tony looked at us, his tone changed immediately. 'You better not mess this one up,' he said to Clive.

Tony didn't look at Nancy at all, and she kept her head down. Clive looked nervous, which was unusual for him. Normally, he was very confident and had a kind of swagger. But that was all gone when Tony was around.

'I won't mess it up,' he said, fiddling with the buckles on his bag.

Tony stepped aside. In the corner, on the dusty floor, were two large brown boxes. Clive tied me to a post near where Jane was standing and they all went over to look at the boxes.

'Bring it all straight back here. No funny business. By two sharp,' grunted Tony.

'Straight back here by two,' said Clive.

As they were talking, I kept my eye on Jane, but she was just sitting down, licking her feet and fastidiously cleaning between each claw, one by one. She didn't say a word so I kept quiet too. Then, after a while, she made me jump.

'Want some water?' she asked quite casually, out of the blue.

'What? Er, yes, thanks,' I said.

While the humans were talking, we both drank together from a nearby bucket. She had a sip and then I had a sip. She didn't say anything else to me. It appeared Jane wasn't much of a talker.

'Come on, Bertie. Here, boy,' called Nancy. 'Let's go.'

I don't know why, but I kind of wanted to stay there. I didn't much like the look of Mad Carpet Tony. He frightened me, and the warehouse was big and cold, even in the height of summer. But Jane had this calmness about her, in spite of her barking on our first meeting. It was obvious she was fiercely loyal to Tony, and it looked like she would do anything to protect him, but it was as though we had a kind of understanding. An unspoken connection.

'Come on, Bertie, old boy,' said Clive with a whistle. 'We've got a job to do.'

I said goodbye to Jane quietly. She looked at me with penetrating eyes, which were hard to read, and remained quiet. When we got to the door, I looked back, but she and Tony had gone.

Nancy carried one of the boxes and Clive carried the other one as we made our way towards the nearest underground station. We crammed on to a train, but there was hardly anywhere to stand as people squashed on at every platform until the train was full. It felt like being in a sardine tin, and I was panting for breath in the heat by the time we arrived.

'South Ken. This is us,' said Clive.

They struggled off with the boxes, and I followed behind, trying not to get stepped on by the other passengers. We made our way up the escalator and back outside, where the cool breeze was a welcome relief.

The houses here were much bigger than where we lived. Some had four or even five windows going upwards, and more windows going downwards below ground. Many had large imposing doorways with huge pillars on either side. There were also lots of loud and smelly motor cars all around, big shiny ones that nearly knocked you down if you stepped out into the road without looking. I wasn't used to it because we had hardly any of those down our way.

Clive stopped outside a large painted white house. It was about six floors high with several windows across and a large front garden. He pushed open the large black gate. On either side of the main entrance there were two huge creatures with long tails and wings. I jumped back and barked at them loudly, thinking they were about to attack us. 'Don't worry, I'll protect you,' I said to Nancy and Clive, although they probably couldn't understand me. But the dragons didn't move, so I barked some more. They still didn't move. I soon realized they were completely still and not going to move any time soon.

'They're made of stone, you silly thing,' said Nancy, laughing. 'He thinks they're real dragons. It's so posh. Who lives here again?'

'I don't know his name. Sir something . . . Bonham-Flips or something. We've got to be on our best behaviour, right? No giggling when we get inside. And, Bertie, you be good, too. No barking or jumping or scratching at anything.'

'Yes, sir,' said Nancy, trying but failing to look deadly serious. I barked and then immediately regretted it when Clive looked at me with a cross face.

We walked up to a huge red door and Clive managed to free one hand from behind the box he was carrying in order to bang a gold metal ring, which was in the nostrils of what looked like the head of a lion.

There was no reply. We waited. Clive knocked again, harder. After a while, I could hear the faint sound of slow footsteps from inside and could smell the strong scent of pipe tobacco. Eventually, the door opened just a few inches, and a small, balding man wearing round glasses peeped around. He was wearing a grey knitted jumper with holes in the cuff and a pair of battered red velvet slippers.

'My darlings. You're here,' he said very quietly, opening the door up fully and waving us in. 'Have you got them?'

'All here,' said Clive, showing him the boxes.

'Do you mind him . . .' said Nancy, pointing at me with her nose.

'As long as he's all right with other dogs,' said the man and gave a small chuckle.

He introduced himself as Kenneth and ushered us into an enormous entrance hall with a large staircase and a black-and-white floor, which dazzled my eyes.

All around the hall were more statues – humans with wings and humans with no clothes on, standing in various poses. There were all kinds of animals – a man with a human face and goat's feet, and a man with a bull's head and human legs. It was all very confusing. But none of them moved, so I began to relax.

'I travelled a lot. As a young man. Digging all over Greece, Mesopotamia, North Africa,' said Kenneth as we walked down a long hallway full of more statues.

'I just couldn't help picking up bits here and there. I can't resist a market, you see, wherever I go. Can't take the journey now, though,' he said sadly. 'The boat. With this hip. But I have all these. My friends, I like to think of them.'

'They're . . . lovely,' said Nancy, staring warily at a large statue of a horse with a human torso and head.

Through the doorway at the end of the hall, I could hear a strange noise. There was squealing and what sounded like barking. As we walked in, I couldn't believe my eyes; there was not one or two dogs, but what must have been about ten dogs of different sizes and shapes, and a few cats, too.

'I didn't mean to end up with this many,' he said. 'We take them up to the house every couple of weeks. The old ancestral, you know, manor. We've had a lot brought in this week for some reason. My sister, Joyce, takes care of it all at that end. Abandoned, poor things, most of them. When the war broke out. People panic, you see. And then there was that radio broadcast, "get rid of your pets". I ask you. So we've turned the old family seat into a kind of . . . home for the cats and dogs, I suppose it is now. She's got about thirty of the things now, Joyce. And a couple of goats. And a few llamas from a zoo somewhere. Two, or three is it now? I can't remember.'

'Oh my goodness!' said Nancy, rushing over and picking up a little tabby kitten with a white nose. 'He's adorable. Clive, can we keep him?'

I ran across the room and barked hello at a couple of shepherd dogs who looked friendly enough. They barked back and we ran around together a bit. They told me their owners had fled to the countryside and one day just turned them out into the street. They had been picked up by a van and taken to a scary kennel, but Kenneth had rescued them and brought them here and fed them and they were feeling much better.

'Quiet, boy,' said Clive to me as I barked with the dogs. 'No, we can't keep the kitten.'

'Anyway,' said Kenneth loudly over the din of all the barking and meowing. 'Shall we get to business?'

Clive and Nancy heaved the boxes over and put them down on a large table. Next to it sat a brown leather suitcase.

'The money's all there,' said Kenneth, pushing the suitcase towards Clive. 'If you want to check it.' Then he immediately tore into the boxes.

I jumped up on to the table for a look. Inside there were what looked like a lot of wood shavings, but he soon pulled out two large vases. He lifted them up carefully, squinted, and appeared to read something on the bottom. They were painted with all kinds of swirling patterns and creatures that looked like exotic birds or something from faraway lands.

'It's them,' he said quietly. 'Thank you. Not many people know what these are worth, you know,' he said, tapping his nose. 'Just me and a few others who might just be interested in purchasing them.'

Clive counted out the money in piles. Then he smiled and snapped the suitcase shut.

'All present and correct.'

'I wish I could say I was keeping them,' said Kenneth, looking at the vases sadly. 'I'll sell them at auction, though, of course. My sister, Joyce . . . we need every penny we can get now, what with the sanctuary. And I can't sell anything from my own collection. It's all far too precious. Too many memories.'

Most of the other animals had calmed down. Some were lying asleep, and a couple of spaniels were tugging a piece of cloth between them and growling playfully. I wanted to join in but I was trying to be good for Clive and Nancy. A small kitten wandered over and pawed at my tail and then rolled over on to its back. Nancy picked that one up, too, and had two kittens wriggling in her arms. Clive looked at his pocket watch.

'We better get this back,' he said, 'before Tony sends out the armed guard.'

'Thank you again, my darlings,' said Kenneth. 'And you must come and see the house. Benley-on-Clough, Wiltshire. The Denham-Phipps. Ask anyone. We'll have afternoon tea and you can meet my sister Joyce and the menagerie.'

He whisked us back to the door and out on to the street. When we were back outside, it was almost as though we had never been in there at all.

'What a strange man,' said Nancy as we walked back to the underground station. 'Fancy taking in all those animals like that. I wonder where they all sleep.'

Clive was walking quickly and kept looking at his watch.

'What's wrong? What's the hurry?' she continued, jogging along behind him, with me alongside.

'Tony hates it when I'm late,' he said. 'I don't know why, it's just a thing of his. Even just a minute.'

When we got to the platform, a train had already pulled in and we only just managed to jump on. My tail nearly got stuck in the door but I flicked it away just in time.

Clive was clutching on to the suitcase tightly and looking around warily. The train stopped in a tunnel for a while, which felt like it would never end. When we got off at the other end, we broke into a proper run, all the way back to the warehouse. I didn't have time to stop and sniff anything along the way or mark my territory on a single lamppost.

This time we were shown into a small room at the back of the warehouse. Tony was sitting on a large leather chair behind a desk. There was nothing much else in the room except a large cabinet with a big padlock on it. There were two very tall, stocky men I had never seen before, and a small, wiry man who looked a bit like a rat. The smaller man was standing in front of the desk, looking nervous. He seemed to be begging Tony for something, or for him not to do something, but I couldn't tell what. As soon as we arrived, Tony waved them all out, and one of the tall men took the ratty man by the shoulders, and I never saw him again.

'You're late,' said Tony quietly when they had left. 'Have you got it?'

Clive took out the money and laid it in piles on the table. For the first time, I saw Tony smile . . . well, half his mouth smiled, anyway. The other half stayed where it was. He gave Clive a wad of notes. But then, almost immediately, the half-smile disappeared and he waved us away. Jane was asleep in the corner so I didn't get a chance to see her, but that time I was actually quite relieved to get out of that dark warehouse.

To celebrate the success of their mission, Clive and Nancy stopped off at the local pub on the corner of our road, the Dog and Whistle. When we walked through the door, there, sitting at the bar, was Eric.

I had almost forgotten about him in the excitement of the past few days. He was on his own and staring down into his glass of beer. Nancy hadn't had a letter from him for a few weeks, and with all the time she'd been spending with Clive, she seemed to have put him out of her mind.

Nancy saw Eric before he saw us, and I could tell she wasn't sure whether to sneak out straight away, or go over and say hello. In the end, he looked up from his pint and saw us. She ran over and put her hand on his arm.

'When did you get back? I haven't heard anything for ages. I was so worried.'

'Yesterday. Haven't you heard?'

'Heard what?'

'It's Harry. He's . . . his plane was . . .'

'Oh my God. Is he . . . ?'

'They haven't found him. I don't know. Mum thinks he's still alive. Thinks he's going to come walking through the door any minute. But I don't know why they put him up there in the first place. He wasn't ready. He'd hardly been up in a plane.'

'Oh, Eric. I'm so sorry,' said Nancy, her eyes beginning to glisten with tears.

Clive came over with the drinks and I followed. Nancy looked awkwardly between the two men. Although she and Clive were only friends, or so she always said, it suddenly seemed all a bit difficult to explain.

'Eric, this is Clive. He's a friend of mine. I mean, we work together, selling things, and things. Oh, I'll explain later. Clive, sorry. This is Eric. My . . . fiancé. His brother, Harry. His plane. Oh. This is all so awful.'

Clive shook Eric's hand and said he was sorry to hear about his brother, and that he had a job to do. Eric finished off his pint in one gulp, and he and Nancy walked home. They hardly spoke to one another and I kept quiet too as I trotted along beside them.

When we got back home, Nancy broke the silence. 'Shall I come in and see your mum?'

Eric opened the front door to his house. 'Not now,' he replied. 'I don't want to upset her.'

'Good night, then,' she said sadly, and leant over to kiss him. He flinched slightly; it looked to me like he did it almost unconsciously. But then he let her kiss his cheek.

'Good night,' he said and went inside, leaving me and Nancy on the doorstep.

CHAPTER TEN

I understood what death was now, sort of. Since Annie had gone, I knew that, when someone was dead, it meant they were gone. But with Annie I had actually seen her lying there, cold, and I knew that she wasn't here any more and that I would never see her again. But with Harry, it was different. Although the officials had told the family he was 'missing in action', Eric and Frank quite quickly took that to mean that he would be gone for ever. But Maude could not accept it and kept saying he would come back. She said she was sure that he had bailed out in a parachute and swum to shore, that he had probably lost his memory and couldn't get back home, and he was all alone somewhere in Kent or somewhere, just wandering around, lost.

In the end, I didn't know what to think. I was so lucky to have found George and Rose and Philip, and all the other new people in my life, and even Princess Wilhelmina. But now Harry was gone. I desperately wanted him to come back and throw me a stick like he used to, and play games with me and George in the garden. Perhaps none of us are safe any more, I thought. Perhaps anyone could vanish at any time.

Eric came over the next day and told us that he was stationed somewhere nearer London now so he might be able to pop back more often. But he wasn't very happy about Nancy's new 'job'. He wanted to know who these people were, what they were selling, and he said he was concerned that the whole thing might be dangerous, not to mention illegal. I was sad because that meant I might not see Jane again, or have any more adventures.

Later that day, I was out in the garden sleeping in the late afternoon sun when the air-raid warning went. We'd heard it many times before, of course. It sounded much louder for me than it did for humans and hurt my ears, but at least I knew what it was now. But this time, there was something else. A low buzzing from above. Then, all of a sudden, across the sky swept dozens of dark shapes, and the buzzing became a growling, followed by rapid gunfire. Then hundreds of them came sweeping right overhead. The sky went dark.

'They're here,' shouted George, running outside and pointing upwards. 'The Luftwaffe! Must be thousands of them.'

Rose came out of the house and squinted to look up. Then came an awful sound from somewhere right nearby.

'Anti-aircraft fire,' said George, who had heard all about it from Eric, who had told him about the guns that he fired up at the aeroplanes to try and stop them dropping their bombs on us.

'We better get in the shelter,' said Rose, trying to stay calm but clearly distressed by this sudden, dramatic turn of events.

'Can't we stay and watch?' asked George excitedly. He couldn't stop looking up at them as the small silver planes swept over in perfect formations across the sky.

'Come on, George. Let's get inside,' said Rose, and she pulled him in. 'It'll probably be over soon anyway, but better safe than sorry.'

From inside the shelter, we could hear the planes still buzzing over, like huge, angry bees. We sat and listened as they flew this way and that. The sound of guns got louder and was, every now and again, punctuated by a loud explosion which shook the earth around us.

'Will they land near here?' asked George, half nervous and half excited.

'I hope not,' said Rose.

After a couple of hours of waiting and hoping nothing bad would happen, the all-clear sounded, and we came out and went back in the house.

'Thank goodness for that,' said Rose as she made us some food. 'That wasn't that bad.'

She was about to put George to bed when the air-raid siren rang out again with its ghostly wail. 'Not again,' she said. I looked out of the window. Through the darkness, I saw more and more planes were filling the sky.

As we walked across the garden, back to the shelter, the ground was wet with dew underfoot. I could see searchlights flashing across the sky, and already, great clouds of smoke had started to fill the skyline. There was a horrible bitter smell of burning in the air.

The following few hours were filled with the most terrifying noises I have ever heard: explosions and bangs and sounds the like of which I had never heard before. It hurt my ears. Some were close by, some further away, but they all seemed to reach right down into the pit of my stomach. At one point, the whole ground shook and bits of earth fell through the shelter on to our heads. I jumped up on to the bed, and Rose hugged me and George tightly.

'I'm frightened,' said George. Rose told us it would be all right; we were safe there all together. She tried to distract us by telling stories, but she was having trouble stopping her voice shaking, and after a while, her voice just tailed off and she went quiet. We had no choice but to listen to the awful sounds going on all around us – explosions, gunfire and what sounded like breaking glass, then bells ringing followed by more explosions and gun fire. On and on it went, relentlessly.

We huddled together, unable to think about anything other than when it would all be over.

Then, suddenly, it stopped. I opened my eyes.

'Is that it?' asked George, lifting his head out of Rose's lap.

'I don't know,' she said, stroking his hair. I whined, and she stood up and cautiously opened up the doorway to the shelter. I was desperate for some fresh air, so I scratched at the floor. Rose waited for a while. When it seemed safe, she pushed the door open fully and I jumped up.

'Be quick, Bertie,' she said. 'We don't know if it's over yet.'

When I got outside, the air was fresh and cold and a relief after being in the stuffy shelter. The sky was all lit up and there was smoke rising high and thick all across the city. But I hadn't been outside for more than a minute when a plane flew right overhead. There was an explosion nearby. I dashed back inside, and the gunfire began again, even more loudly than before. Rose began to sing George a little song, but I could hear that, with every minute that passed, her breathing was getting faster and faster. I could feel the panic rising. I nuzzled up to her. I wanted to do everything I could to help. She stroked me and whispered, partly to us and partly to herself, that it would be all right, which seemed to calm her and George down, though I could still feel them both shaking next to me. I don't know how long we sat there, listening to the explosions. My whole body was tense, and I could hardly move. George was lying in Rose's arms on the little bed with his hands over his ears. I closed my eyes again and wondered if it would ever end. My ears were aching from the noise and my nose was twitching. I felt sick from the new and horrible smells which filled the air. Eventually the gunfire stopped, a lone aeroplane sounded, then got quieter. We opened our eyes and sat up.

'Is that really it now?' asked George. 'Are they going home?'

The all-clear finally sounded.

'I think so,' said Rose, and she opened the door again. I poked my head out cautiously, daring to hope it was really over.

It wasn't quite light yet but the early-morning birds had already begun to sing, perhaps confused by the lights in the sky and the noises above. On the horizon, I could see a line of light, glowing orange and red and flickering in the wind. Columns of thick, dark smoke were rising up into the sky, forming a new layer of clouds. Bells were ringing all around.

'Fire engines,' said Rose quietly, then she wrapped George up in the blanket and carried him back to the house.

CHAPTER ELEVEN

Everyone was in shock after the night's dramatic events. It was only by the light of day that we saw the extent of what had happened. News soon began to get around our street about the damage caused all over London. Rose read in the newspaper that the docks had been very badly hit by bombs. That's what all those explosions were, I thought. Then I remembered Jane. When we had met, it was in a warehouse right by the river. I remembered that Clive had called it 'the docks'. But we hadn't seen Clive since Eric came back to London, so I didn't have a chance to find out whether she was all right. I felt sick to think she might have been caught up in all that smoke and fire.

That morning, we walked over to Mary and Victor's house to check they were all right. As we approached their road, I noticed that, where before there had been two houses on the end of the row, their house was now on the end, and the next-door house had been almost completely destroyed. The inside of the house was now visible. Part of the bathroom, with most of the floor missing, and a child's bedroom were on show. You could even see the pictures still on the wall, which had been half destroyed, and part of a piano, all covered in bits of brick and dust. It looked like a doll's house that had been left out in a storm.

Frank was standing next to the ruined house in his ARP uniform. He had been talking to a group of neighbours who had gathered around to see what was going on.

Rose's father Victor was also out there with a large spade, and he and Frank were shovelling bits of rubble as though they were looking for something. Mary was consoling a young woman who looked very distressed, and there were two men in hats with a long hose, spraying water on a fire which had started in the middle of where the kitchen had been.

'Oh my goodness,' said Rose. 'Mrs Jenkins. Is she all right? The whole house. I can't believe it. I didn't know her well, but only last week we were chatting at the market.'

'We're trying to find out,' said Victor. 'Her daughter Caroline was out with a friend last night. She came home this morning and . . . what a thing to come back to.'

'She's in here. I'm sure she's in here,' said a young woman I assumed must be Caroline. 'She always hides under the stairs . . . insists on it. I should have been here. It's my fault.'

The area where the stairs had been was completely destroyed. Victor began pulling away large bits of wood and plaster. I pricked up my ears. Suddenly, very faintly, I thought I could hear a sound, something like crying. I ran over to the spot and started barking urgently. Victor came over to see what it was, and everyone started digging. After a few minutes, we saw something ginger, and then a face all covered in dust and plaster. I started to help, digging through what I could with my paws, carefully. An ambulance arrived and eventually it was possible to pull what was down there free.

'Fluffy,' said Caroline. It wasn't her mother after all. It was a cat, a little ginger kitten, all covered in dust, but alive. A woman in a green dress then appeared, walking hurriedly along the street.

'Mother!' said Caroline, running over to her. 'We thought you were inside. Oh, thank goodness.'

'I made it to the shelter. I popped out to the cinema. Last minute thing. But I couldn't get back in time . . . had to stay there. Oh, thank the lord. I thought you were here too. And the cat . . .'

Little Fluffy let out a croaky meow, and Caroline handed her over to her mother.

We left them all to their reunion, and walked over to Victor and Mary's. I didn't really know what I had done, but they all kept patting me and calling me a good boy, and saying I had probably saved little Fluffy's life. I was even allowed some scraps from the table at lunch for being such a good rescue dog. Then, from the kitchen, came a distressed cry. Mary came running in. Their own cat, Princess Wilhelmina, was missing.

'I can't find her anywhere. She was here when we left. She never goes out. Not ever,' said Mary. 'Willie!' she called out the back door. But there was no sign of Wilhelmina anywhere.

'It must have been the noise. Last night,' Mary said, 'when the big one dropped next door. We were out . . . went to the church shelter in the end. Didn't get back until early this morning. But I didn't even notice when we got home that she was gone.'

'How did she get out?' asked Victor.

'I don't know,' said Mary, exasperated. 'Perhaps I left a window open. I don't know! My poor Willie, out there all alone. I can't bear to think of it.'

She immediately went into action and organized a search party, giving us all areas to comb, looking for any signs of her precious Princess.

Rose and George and I had to check the area over by the park, and we walked up and down for hours, calling out and checking under bushes and in bins, and even down drains. But there was no sign of her. I was worried about Princess Wilhelmina and wondered whether I was somehow responsible for her escape. Had our conversation about going outside encouraged her to leave? Or had I driven her away by just being there? She seemed so nervous of me. Even though we weren't exactly the best of friends, I didn't want anything bad to happen to the poor cat, who had barely ever left the house before.

Back on the road, we stopped outside another bombed-out house where a crowd had gathered. There was a man with a black hat and a walking stick, looking concerned and talking to people. They were telling him about how two houses on that street had been almost completely destroyed. A young family stood on the street beside the ruins of one of the houses, all in tears. Rose gasped.

'That's Winston Churchill,' she whispered. 'What's he doing here?'

It turned out he had come to our area to have a look at the damage that had been done the night before. Once he had finished looking around, he moved away with a group of men and police officers.

'Well, I never. Never thought I'd see him down here,' said Rose, shaking her head as we walked on. Then our thoughts turned back to the missing cat. All the way home, we checked for any signs of animal life. But, as the sun began to set and London prepared itself for another night of blackout, Princess Wilhelmina was nowhere to be found.

CHAPTER TWELVE

Life was getting harder for Rose and George, as they had less money than ever with Philip away in France. With the attacks on London, Rose also began to worry about their safety and to wonder whether she should have sent George off to be evacuated to the countryside.

When lots of other children had gone a year earlier, they had agreed it was best to stay together, but with real damage being done, and lives being lost, she wasn't so sure now. George was still adamant that he wanted to stay with his mum and me, and for the time being she agreed to let him.

We did all wonder, anyway, whether the attack might just have been a one-off. Sure enough, the next night began as a beautiful, sunny evening, with no early air raid like there had been the previous day.

Rose put George to bed and gave me what scraps she had managed to get from the market the day before. She was just starting to write a letter when the air-raid siren went again. My body tensed. There was the sound of aeroplanes overhead again, the penetrating buzzing of the German planes, followed by a far-off boom, boom, boom, and then the rapid firing of our own anti-aircraft guns.

Rose ran upstairs and gathered a sleepy George up in a blanket and carried him downstairs. My instinctive reaction was to cower under the table, but Rose called me out to the air-raid shelter with them. It was terrifying, listening once again to the sounds of bombing all around while we huddled together in the cramped and damp shelter. It was all the more terrifying now that we had seen at first hand the damage the bombs could do.

'Will they hit our house, Mummy, like they did the Jenkins'?' asked George.

'I'll look after you. Me and Bertie will always be here,' she said soothingly. She rocked him until he fell back to sleep and then lay him down on the narrow bed. In the background, the bombing continued. Once again, it went on for most of the night until the all-clear sounded just before it got light.

Rose had to go to work, but George was so exhausted he refused to go to school for what was supposed to be the start of the new term. In the end, Rose had to pop around and ask Nancy to come over and look after him because he looked quite ill. He immediately perked up when Nancy arrived, though, particularly when she said we were going 'up west' to get some ice cream from a friend of hers who owned a cafe.

On the way, we met up with Clive, who was carrying two large suitcases. He was on his way somewhere, where he said he could do a 'swift trade'. He asked Nancy and George if they wanted to earn a bit of extra cash by helping him. Nancy had agreed not to work with Clive any more, to put Eric's mind at rest, but some extra money would not go amiss, especially as they were saving for the wedding. She agreed, just this once, to help out.

I remembered some of the main roads in London from my time out walking with Annie. Before long, we were on the long road I had found myself on the first day of the war. It was quite a shock to see that, already, some of the buildings there had been badly damaged. There were sandbags piled up high and, every now and again, a gap where a shop had been destroyed. I was relieved when we passed the cafe where Lou and Julia lived, but I felt a churning in my stomach when I remembered what Chico had said about Lou being ill. I was even more relieved when I saw him in the cafe, laughing with some customers and handing out cups of tea. I could see he was thinner than before, but he looked like he was getting better. Julia was at the counter, smiling, as determined as ever to carry on, and finally, sitting outside in the sun, there was Chico. I thought about going over and saying hello. He licked his paws and seemed to be smiling.

'Come on, Bertie,' said Clive, pulling at my lead. 'We're late.'

I turned away. I was more sure than ever that I had found my new life now and there was no going back. But I was happy to see them all alive and well.

We finally arrived at a busy market, bustling with activity. Clive seemed to know everyone there, including a crowd of women gathered around a stall. When they saw him, they all began to gather around us.

'Hallo, Peggy,' he said to one woman who had her hair in tight brown curls. 'How's Arthur? His knee any better? And I must say you're looking as lovely as ever.'

'Ooh, Clive, you charmer, you,' she said. Then he moved on to the next woman and enquired after her children, and her brother who was in the army. He seemed to know them all by name, and every detail of their lives.

Nancy, George and I had been charged with looking out for any policemen. I found it all very exciting, as Clive explained to us that there was a special signal which meant a policeman was nearby, and another to signal that he had gone. I wasn't sure exactly what it all meant, but I was happy to play along.

Clive opened up one of his suitcases to reveal a pile of what he called 'silk stockings', and he laid them out on the road. The women seemed very keen to get hold of them and started inspecting them and picking them up and putting them back down again. Over the next half an hour he sold nearly all of them. All the while, George and I were keeping our ears and eyes open and on Nancy, waiting for her signal. She raised her hand, just as Clive had told her, so, quick as a flash, I ran over to George and barked, and then he gave another hand signal to Clive, who quickly packed up his suitcase and hid it behind one of the stalls, and then leant with an innocent look on his face against a lamp post. He pulled out a cigarette from his pocket and lit it up. A policeman came sauntering up the road.

'Mr Finch,' he said to Clive. 'Not up to anything, I hope.'

'Of course not, Officer,' said Clive, smiling a most innocent of smiles.

'Hmm, well, I hope that really is the case this time,' he said, and he wandered down the road and started talking to the other stallholders.

I ran back to Nancy and waited for the next signal. Eventually, she raised both hands. I ran back to George and gave him two barks, and he signalled to Clive, who got out his other suitcase and continued his trade in silk stockings. It was all very elaborate, but it seemed to work.

Why women were so keen for silk stockings, I didn't know, but the war didn't seem to have dampened their enthusiasm for them. By the afternoon, Clive had sold every single pair, even the ones with holes in them.

After that, we took George for his treat of ice cream at a local cafe where Nancy knew the owner, a woman called Angelina. She said she was having to work extra hard to make the ice cream with rationing, and she made it all by hand in big ice buckets at the back of the shop. She took me and George out and gave him a go at mixing up the big buckets of cream and then gave him a large scoop of strawberry flavour. He had the biggest smile on his face for the rest of the day.

While George was eating his ice cream, Nancy spoke to Angelina quietly about how she was getting on since her husband and two sons had gone. One of her sons was in the army, and the other two were 'imprisoned by the British government,' she said, because Italy had joined the war on Hitler's side and Churchill thought they might be spies. Which was ridiculous, she said, because they had been there for nearly twenty years, and her eldest boy had been there nearly his whole life, and the youngest, the one in the army, was born here.

When George had finished his ice cream, Angelina gave me a treat too, a big juicy bone from a stew she had been making. My mouth watered as I chewed into it and sucked out all the delicious flavours.

Nancy said goodbye, and we decided to get the underground home because we'd had such an exhausting day.

But it had been exciting to get out into the centre of London again and see all the different people. When we got back, Rose was already home from work and looked relieved to see us when she opened the door.

'Where have you all been?' she asked. 'I was so worried!'

'We went up west for ice cream,' said Nancy. But she didn't mention Clive or the silk stockings.

'George, you've got it all over your nice shirt. And I suppose you won't eat your tea now. Oh well, you look happy, anyway!' she sighed, realizing she was on a losing battle when it came to George and ice cream.

The bombings continued on a nightly basis after that. They usually began just after dark and continued until morning. It was always terrifying, but we did begin gradually to get more used to it, or at least knew what to expect and so didn't panic quite as much, although I never got over my initial fear at hearing the sound of the air-raid siren. A few weeks after the air raids had started, Frank came over in his ARP uniform. He said he could do with some extra help now that things were getting busy.

'I don't know,' said Rose. 'I'm not very happy about Bertie being out there while all those bombs are being dropped. What do you think, Bertie?'

All I could think was that I wouldn't be cooped up in that air-raid shelter all night, listening to the dreadful sounds but not being able to do anything about it. I thought I might have a chance for some more adventures if I was allowed out, so I wagged my tail enthusiastically and gave a loud bark.

'I think he wants to,' said Frank, laughing. 'We'll be careful, Rose. You know, they're using dogs now to help with the search. And he's already done so well with that Jenkins cat. We need all the help we can get.'

The first night I was allowed out, it was just after midnight when the air-raid siren went. I felt bolder now that I had a role to play and hardly flinched at all when the siren sounded. Frank came around to collect me and said we were heading down towards the docks where they'd been badly hit.

'I know a short cut,' said Frank, and we ducked under a fence near the house and on to a patch of wasteland. I was excited about being in a large open space and ran on ahead, feeling brave. But I stopped suddenly. Right in front of me, the path was blocked by a large crater in the ground. I peered over the edge. At the bottom I could just make out a large cylindrical object in the moonlight. It was even bigger than me. It had a curved end. I barked and looked back.

'What's up, Bertie?' asked Frank, running over with the torch. 'What is it, boy?'

I barked again and then growled a little. Something didn't feel right.

'That's a bleedin' unexploded bomb,' said Frank when he saw the metal object in the crater. I couldn't hear anything except the sounds of a few anti-aircraft guns further away, so I moved a bit closer. I stopped and arched my back and barked more urgently.

'What's going on out here,' came a voice. 'What's all the noise?'

A small man approached. As he got nearer, Frank flashed his torch in the man's direction. It was Ted Nibbett, who lived on our street. The one who didn't agree with war or the blackout.

'Don't worry, Ted. You get back inside,' said Frank. 'We're dealing with this.'

I didn't know what an unexploded bomb was, but Frank's voice was quivering.

Ted didn't go back. Instead, he came closer and stood with us as we looked at the object.

'What's this, then?'

'Hitler's left us a present,' said Frank. 'A UXB.'

Frank could not hear it, being only a human, but I could hear that this UXB, whatever it was, was making a strange noise.

'When did it come down, do you think?' asked Ted as we stood and looked at the metal object in the crater.

'Anyone's guess. Could have a timer on it. Could have been tonight or last night. Might just not have detonated when it landed, or anything might set it off.'

A group of passers-by, coming out from their shelter, had stopped by the fence and were peering over to look at what was going on.

'Nothing to see here,' called Frank and waved them on. 'What should we do?' he whispered. 'Shall I get a sign up, do you think?'

'I think I might know something I can try,' said Ted. 'Wait here.'

Frank moved some sandbags to block the way to the area, to stop anyone approaching the bomb, although of course, for some, that made it even more appealing.

In a few minutes, Ted arrived back, carrying a small blue bag.

'You might want to stand back,' he said to Frank, and he began to approach the crater. I followed cautiously.

'Keep back, boy,' he whispered. I stood a little way back and watched as, very carefully, he made his way down inside the hole.

'Are you all right?' called Frank after a while.

'Yes. My torch's bust. Can you get the dog to bring yours over?'

Frank put the torch in my mouth, and I carried it over and inched my way down into the crater. I couldn't see very well and nearly slipped on a loose bit of earth. I eventually reached Ted and he took the torch and put it in his own mouth. Then, very carefully, he climbed on top of the bomb and began to remove parts of it.

I could feel his breath stop almost completely as he worked. He paused for a while deciding what to do next. Then he worked away again on a load of wires and bits of metal which were inside the bomb. It felt like time kind of stopped, and even I stopped breathing as I waited. Then I heard the quiet noise begin to change. He made a final adjustment.

'You hear that, boy?' he asked quietly, with his ear to the bomb. 'Nothing!'

The noise had completely stopped. We both finally breathed out and I barked happily. Whatever he had done, it seemed to have been a success. We waited for a moment, and then he got down off the bomb and we both climbed back up out of the crater.

'Well done, boy,' Ted said. But it wasn't me who had sat on top of an unexploded bomb that night.

Ted Nibbett was what they called a conscientious objector, but there was no doubt he had taken his life into his hands to save the street from being blown up. He had heard the noise, too, and knew there was a timer on the bomb, which meant it had to be deactivated before it exploded. He had saved a lot of lives, and Frank made sure to tell everyone about Ted's bravery that night.

But it wasn't over yet. We still had our air-raid duties to attend to. By the time we got to the docks, the bombing was in full swing, and although I had heard air raids from the safety of our shelter before, I had never seen anything like this. It was like hell on earth. There were huge piles of bricks and twisted metal sticking out all over the place. Fires were still burning and the whole place was thick with a bitter smell. Everything was louder and scarier this close up, and with every explosion my whole insides trembled. But, at the same time, it was kind of a breathtaking spectacle as black objects streaked across the sky in formation and the fires lit up the horizon. Then, one by one, they began to drop and land, not very far away from us, with huge booms which made the ground shake under our feet.

As we got closer to the fires, Frank met up with other ARP men and firefighters.

'We're trying to keep this factory from burning down,' said one of the men, holding a long hose in his hand. 'We need all the help we can get with the water.'

They had pumps connected to buckets of water and other pumps that were connected to the ground.

Frank got stuck in, and he soon had me running back and forth, finding out who needed water next. The heat from the burning factory was intense and like nothing I had ever seen or felt before. It burnt my paws, and my eyes became dry and painful. Just when it looked like we might not be able to save the building, there was a huge explosion from inside. Then I felt water on my nose. First a few droplets, then a torrent.

'Thank God,' said Frank, looking up at the orange inferno. And sure enough, as the rain began to fall, the fires began to dampen down. As the rainfall got heavier, the sky lit up and a huge lightning bolt streaked across the sky. A moment later, thunder cracked and then rumbled all around the docks. But when I looked up, Frank was smiling. I started to smile too, inside. Water was splashing into our eyes and into our mouths and up our noses, and before long, we were completely soaked, but we didn't mind a bit.

'Have you ever been so happy to see a storm, Bertie?' said Frank, as the black soot from the fires ran in great streaks as water trickled down his face.

Rain had never felt as lovely or as welcome as it did that night on the docks.

CHAPTER THIRTEEN

Not long after the Blitz started, George made a new friend on the street. His name was Alfie. At thirteen, Alfie was a bit older than many of the other children who lived nearby. The younger children in the neighbourhood looked up to him and were a bit in awe of him. Most dangerously, they also believed everything he said. With Rose at work so much now, and Nancy getting busier again on jobs with Clive, George and I began to spend more time with Alfie. George wasn't allowed out on his own without an adult, but because Rose thought he was at Alfie's house, and Alfie said it was all right if they went out on to the streets because his mum let him, we ended up hanging about the streets quite a lot anyway.

On my nightly trips around London with Frank I saw all the fires and the bombings, but with George and Alfie during the day it was almost like a different London. It became much more like a game.

Alfie would march us around the neighbourhood, looking for secret ways to get on to the sites of buildings that had been bombed. Alfie's main aim was to find as many of what he called his 'souvenirs'. He had quite a collection, and it was much envied by George. He had several bits of 'shrapnel' of varying shapes and sizes. And a long stick. I didn't know what it was, but George was especially covetous of it.

Sometimes our next-door neighbour Pamela wanted to play with us too. She always liked a good adventure. But Alfie had a rule in his gang that no girls were allowed. She would hang around and try to follow us, but they would leave her behind and run off to play at their own games in the bomb sites without her. When Alfie and George played air raids, after they had collected their souvenirs, it was quite different to the old game of air raids Pamela and George played, which just involved getting into the Anderson and hiding.

With this game, either George or Alfie would zoom around the bomb site pretending to be the German planes and the other one would pretend to be a person in the house, asleep. Then the bombs would start falling and the person asleep would pretend to get hit and pretend to be injured. Then the person who had just been the aeroplane would become an Air Raid Warden or a fireman and would come back and rescue the other one, often calling on me to help. Then they would go back to searching through the rubble for more objects.

Although I enjoyed the games, I didn't much like Alfie. Once or twice, he pulled my tail until I yelped and then he laughed. He also seemed to take a bit of delight in teasing George by hiding for ages and then bursting out on him. But George was so keen to be out with a bigger boy that he seemed quite prepared to tolerate Alfie's teasing.

When George got home, he would pull out all the things he had collected and lay them out on his bed to show me. He had four pieces of shrapnel, and even a pocket watch he particularly treasured that he had found amongst the rubble of a house. He couldn't let Rose see any of it, of course. He still didn't have one of these long sticks that Alfie was so proud of, though.

One day, we were walking back from playing with Alfie, just before it got dark, and we saw not just one but two of the sticks on the ground right in front of us. George ran over and picked them up.

'Yes!' he said. 'Wait 'til I show Alfie these, Bertie!' He stuffed them into his pocket.

Round the corner, a policeman was walking up the road. He saw George running with the sticks poking out.

'What's that you've got in your coat, lad?' he asked.

'Nothing. I'm just on my way home,' replied George. 'And I've only got these old sticks,' he said, proudly showing them to the policeman. 'My friend Alfie's got six of 'em already and . . .'

The policeman stopped him in his tracks, put his hand up and approached us with caution. I barked, as I wasn't sure what he was going to do, and I remembered from our time in the market that policemen were probably best avoided.

'I'll have to ask you to keep your dog under control,' he said. 'And you had better give those sticks to me, lad.'

'You can't have 'em,' said George, tightening his coat. 'I've waited weeks for these and Alfie says . . .'

'I don't care what "Alfie" says. You know what those are, don't you?' said the policeman. 'They're firebombs. Incendiaries. And those particular ones, if I'm not mistaken, haven't gone off yet. So I think it's best you give them to me. Carefully now.'

The policeman did not sound angry; in fact, his voice was sounding quite nervous as he tried to coax George into handing over the sticks. George wasn't used to arguing with people in authority, so when he heard the policeman's voice change, he gave in immediately and handed the sticks over.

As soon as he got hold of them, the policeman placed them carefully on the ground and stepped right back. He motioned us away and a few seconds later there was a bright spark and the sticks burst into flames one after the other.

I barked and tugged on George's trousers to get him to move further away. But he just stood there, kind of transfixed as the flames leapt into the air. The policeman ran to a nearby lamp post and picked up a sandbag which was on the ground.

'Get back, boy. You want to know what to do when a firebomb goes off?' he said. 'Well, you're about to get a lesson. Smother it like this.' He ran back and dumped the sandbag on the fire. George ran over and handed him two more sandbags, and eventually the fire was out.

'So that's why you don't collect those sticks, all right, son?' he said. 'And you certainly don't put them in your pocket. Under any circumstances. They're definitely not toys.'

'Yes, sir,' said George sheepishly.

When we got home he decided not to tell Rose about the incident with the exploding sticks. I was just relieved they hadn't gone off in his pocket.

A few days later he was in the garden when he saw Pamela in her kitchen. He called over the garden fence and Pamela came outside.

'What do you want?' she said. She had clearly not forgiven George for abandoning her in favour of Alfie.

'Wanna play air raids?' asked George. 'I got myself into a right situation with those damned sticks . . .' He started to tell her about his adventures. But he stopped when he realized that she was dressed up in a smart blue jacket and had her gas mask around her neck in a box.

'Going out?' he asked.

'Well. Yes, sort of. Anyway. I couldn't play even if I wanted to,' she said. 'We're leaving in just a minute.'

'Leaving where?'

'To Auntie Peggy's. Well, she's not my real auntie but she's got this farm with hundreds of sheep. So Mum says I'm to go there instead of here, so I don't get bombed.'

At first, George didn't seem to take in the sudden news that his best friend was leaving. He looked down and started to fiddle around in the earth, looking for worms.

'So when will you . . . be back?' he asked.

I got the feeling he didn't quite know how to take it. Pamela began to soften after her anger about Alfie.

'I don't know. I'll send letters. About what adventures I get up to. You'll write to me too, won't you?'

'Maybe,' he said. 'If I've got time.'

Pamela was about to jump back over the wall when she looked back at George as though she wanted to say something. But before they could say another word to each other, her mother appeared at the door.

'Come on, love. The car's here.'

'Goodbye, Bertie,' she said, bending down to give me a hug. 'Goodbye, George,' she said, standing up. George looked down again and plucked a large wriggling worm out of the ground. By the time he looked up, Pamela had jumped back over the wall and gone inside.

A few moments later, a car door slammed and they drove away.

Summer gradually turned to autumn. The nights got colder, and the leaves began to turn a golden orange. It was funny to see the seasons changing as they always had done, to see nature going on as it always had done, in spite of the war. It soon became clear that air raids were to be an almost nightly occurrence, so Rose decided that on the nights when I wasn't out helping Frank, we should all go into the shelter before the air-raid siren started. She would tuck George up in the little bed in the shelter. Then she'd finish off things in the house and join him later, and try and get some sleep before the raid.

One night, I was upstairs waiting for Rose to call me down to go to the shelter when I heard the sirens in the distance. I was about to go and warn Rose they were on their way, when something fell through the roof and on to the floor in front of me. It was one of those sticks George had tried to put in his pocket. I barked at the stick. Then, a few moments later, it burst into flames. I panicked. I didn't have any sandbags, and I couldn't pick the stick up now that it was on fire. I tried to touch it but it burnt my mouth so I backed off. I ran downstairs to find Rose. I was barking as loudly as I could.

'What's all the barking, Bertie?' she called up from the kitchen. 'You seen a ghost?'

I was on the stairs still when smoke began billowing out of the bedroom.

'Oh my God. Run and get George! The pump!'

She went to the cupboard under the stairs and pulled out a bucket and a long pipe with a pump attached to it. I ran outside to the shelter and barked and barked, trying to wake George up. Eventually, I had to jump down into the shelter myself. I pulled on George's sleeve with my teeth.

'What is it, Bertie?' He was still half asleep. I barked more and pulled his sleeve harder. He fumbled around for the torch and finally woke up.

'Is it the Germans?' he asked, half excited, half nervous. 'Are they here?'

I barked and ran out of the shelter, and he put on his slippers and followed me out. Then I heard a loud explosion, and the upstairs window burst out and glass fell down all over the floor below.

'Where's Mum?' asked George, getting anxious. 'What's happening?'

I thought I had to be brave. I knew Rose needed George if they were to put the fire out, so I pulled him into the house even though it meant shards of glass got into my paws on the way in.

'Mummy, Mummy!' George shouted. 'Where are you?'

'Up here, love,' she called from upstairs. Then she started coughing. We both ran upstairs. Flames had started flickering out from the bedroom and on to the landing.

'Be a good boy and help me with the water, will you? You need to run downstairs to the kitchen tap and fill this bucket when it gets empty. And pump this pump here. OK?'

'OK,' said George, sounding very grown up all of a sudden.

George ran downstairs and filled up the bucket, which was almost as big as him, then carried it back up again. Rose was in the bedroom, hiding behind a chair, spraying water on the flames to try to put them out.

I stayed in the bedroom with Rose and tried to flatten myself to the floor to avoid breathing in the smoke. Whenever I saw something start to smoulder or catch on fire, I barked to let Rose know where to spray next. The flames eventually died down and there were just the odd puffs of smoke here and there.

'My best rug,' said Rose, looking at the damage. 'But thank goodness you're both OK.' She ran over and gave me and George a massive hug.

'I couldn't have done it without you two,' she said, and she kissed George's head and almost smothered him with cuddles.

Then I thought I smelt something still smouldering under the rug. I barked at Rose and she brought over a metal hatchet. I could tell it broke her heart, but she had to hack away at the rug to get underneath it as quickly as possible. Sure enough, underneath there was a large piece of glowing wood, and the rug began to catch fire again as we watched. This time, Rose just stamped on it with her shoe, and the fire was finally out.

She flopped on the bed with George in exhaustion, and we were all quiet. The blackout curtains, which had been pinned up permanently, were all burnt away and you could see out of the window and on to the street below. Most of the rug and a pile of clothes on the back of a chair had burnt completely away, and a chest of drawers had been burnt black.

A loud, ghostly siren filled the air followed by the distant sounds of an aeroplane.

Rose jumped up and headed for the door.

We ran down the stairs. Then I heard what I dreaded. The whistling of the bombs as they fell, getting higher and higher pitched. I had a feeling what it meant. They were heading directly towards us.

CHAPTER FOURTEEN

There was the most terrific explosion, and the walls of the house seemed like they were about to cave in. It felt like my head was exploding with the impact. We all dived on to the ground. Rose covered George with her dressing gown and I crawled under there too and started shaking. Rose was breathing faster and faster, and George began to cry. A few minutes later, I heard more aeroplanes overhead, and the next time I heard the whistling sound, it was moving away. I opened my eyes. I wondered if I was dead and this was the next life. But, as I looked around, I saw that the house was still standing. We had not been hit after all.

'Everyone all right?' said Rose, standing up and brushing herself down.

'Mummy, I'm scared,' said George. 'I know I'm not supposed to be scared and that I'm supposed to be brave, but my tummy hurts.'

'It's all right to be scared,' she said, 'and we're all still here, aren't we? Anyone injured?'

'I don't think so,' said George. But his nose had started to bleed.

'Oh my goodness, let me get a handkerchief,' said Rose. But she couldn't find one, so she pulled him back up and dabbed away the bleeding with the corner of her dressing gown. 'I think it's just the shock of the explosion. I hope.'

My ears were ringing. That explosion had definitely been closer than anything I had heard before. But the house was still standing. We finally got to our feet and went to the back door to see what had happened. At the bottom of the garden where the Anderson shelter had been, there was now a large hole. The roof had completely caved in. The shed had been flattened. Next door's shelter was caved in too, and the wall between the two gardens had crumbled to pieces.

'Oh, George,' said Rose. It was finally too much for her, to think that just moments earlier George had been in there on his own, fast asleep. She started to laugh, almost hysterically, and sat right there on the kitchen floor.

'What is it, Mummy?' asked George.

'That firebomb saved your life!' she said. 'I can't believe it. Thank you!' she screamed. 'If there's anyone up there. Thank you! Who could have believed it? Saved by a firebomb.'

The doorbell rang and a voice shouted through the letter box. Rose smoothed down her hair, pulled herself together and stood up.

'Frank!' she said, opening the door.

'Everything all right in here?' he asked. 'That was a near miss. Thank goodness the neighbours are away; otherwise they would have been in their shelter. And I felt sure you would have been too, but thank God you're all right. Let's get you down to the Dog and Whistle. They've got space in the cellar.'

Rose was still in her dressing gown and slippers, and George was still in his pyjamas as we all trooped down the road to the pub. When we arrived, it was closed, but Frank banged on the door, and eventually the landlord came up and let us in.

'Room for a few more?' asked Frank.

'Come on,' said the landlord, ushering us all in and closing the door quickly. When we got down to the cellar, there were so many people, I could hardly breathe. There was a heavy smell of sweat and, I thought, also the smell of what I can only imagine was fear. We found a corner and squeezed in, and Rose began to tell everyone about the firebomb and the shelters being hit. Then, out of nowhere it seemed, a woman appeared with a cup of hot drink. When Rose took a sip, she coughed.

'It's brandy,' said the woman, smiling. 'May as well, 'ey? Who knows when it'll be your last.'

Then I realized who it was. It was Frank's wife, Maude. It was the first time I had seen her since Harry had gone missing. I was amazed; the last time I had seen her, she had a shock of brown hair, and now it was almost completely white. If it hadn't been for her voice, I'm not sure I would have known who it was.

Maude sat down next to us and put her arm around George and me, and we sat there all together in the damp cellar and curled up and tried to get some sleep. All around us, we could hear the sounds of explosions. Some were far away, some others close by. But I never again, that night at least, heard the whistling sound that meant the bombs were heading our way. Someone's elbow was digging in my back and someone else's foot was right by my head. But it felt somehow safer than anywhere else I could have wished to be at that moment. Eventually, I put my head in my paws, and in spite of it all, I fell asleep.

*

It very quickly became clear that the cellar of the Dog and Whistle was not a long-term solution for us. For a start, there was Neville. Neville was a softly spoken man who had nothing against dogs, but every time he came near me, he started sneezing.

Rose tried moving away from him, but then there was Gillian. She wasn't allergic to dogs. She just didn't like dogs. In fact, the only animal she did like was a tortoise. She told us in great detail about her two rescue tortoises she had living in her garden, about how she had dug a huge trench for them, protected by corrugated iron and bricks, because there was no way she could bring them to the shelter each night.

As the Blitz raged overhead, she sat in the cellar, nervously speculating about what might be happening to them. But, despite her love for her reptilian friends, she wasn't at all keen on mammals, and especially dogs, and she said that if she couldn't bring her tortoises in, then really she didn't think there was room for dogs or other hairy pets.

So, what with Neville's sneezing and Gillian's complaints, Rose was eventually forced to think of an alternative. It wasn't very comfortable down there, anyway, and it smelt quite bad and sweaty and damp. To be honest, I was quite relieved when we decided to look elsewhere for a shelter.

Victor had an idea.

'We tried the Anderson for a night and my back seized up so badly I could hardly move,' he said. 'Then when it filled up with water, that was the final straw. So we tried the church. The crypt holds about fifty people. And the vicar was so welcoming.'

'They even served sausages and tea,' said Mary. 'You should take George and Bertie down there. I don't want to see you sitting under the stairs or anything daft like that.'

So Rose decided we would give it a try. She packed everything up that George would need for the night, his books and his toy aeroplanes, all in a little knapsack. She put a blanket in her bag, and just before it got dark we headed towards the church. She also took with her a little box in which she kept all the important things, like documents and precious photographs that she didn't want to lose if the worst happened.

Before we got to the church, the air-raid siren had already started up.

'We don't have time to make it,' she said. So instead of turning left at the end of our road and going towards the church, we turned right instead.

'The underground station, then. It's the only other option,' said Rose, breaking into a run. 'I only hope we find a spot.'

When we got to the station, there was quite a line of people already going down the steps. We crowded down with them, and by the time we got on to the platform there were hundreds of people – families, elderly people, children and even a woman with her cat.

Although, strictly speaking, pets weren't allowed in public shelters, the people down there seemed pretty relaxed about it, and no one was really checking up. As we pushed our way through, it soon became obvious that everyone already had their own special place to sit or lie down, and there was very little space left.

'Do we get to ride the trains?' asked George.

'I don't think so,' said Rose. 'Can you see anywhere we can go?'

We looked up and down the platform. Some people had what looked like camping beds set up. There was one family having a kind of picnic with a blanket spread out and everything, and further along, a young girl and her father were playing the accordion together while a little boy was dancing on the platform and laughing. It seemed as though a mini London was forming right under the streets. It was so full of the people and noises and smells of the real city above.

There was so little space on the actual platform, Rose ended up finding a tiny corner at the bottom of the stairs where we managed to squeeze in and lay out the blanket.

As we settled down, I could hear, very faintly in the background, that the bombing overhead had started. At one point, there must have been one land almost directly on top of us, as there was quite a loud noise, and then plaster began falling from the ceiling on to the people below. Someone screamed and put his head into his hands. But it soon passed, and everyone went back to chatting and tucking up their children into their makeshift beds.

After a while, people started dropping off to sleep. The accordions stopped and there was a strange quiet all across the station. Every now and again, there was a whisper, or a baby began to cry and was comforted by its mother. As the hush fell, I soon drifted off to sleep myself, snuggled next to Rose and George.

When I next opened my eyes, a pair of shiny black shoes was right in front of my face. A man wearing a bowler hat and carrying an umbrella was stepping around us. The first train was pulling into the platform for the morning commute. He hopped on the train, and after that a steady stream of people began to flood on and off the platform on their way to work.

'Up you get, you two,' said Rose, bleary eyed. It didn't look as though she had slept much.

All the way back home, we played the now-daily game of pointing out what had been destroyed in the previous night's raid.

'Oh dear,' said Rose. 'That dear couple. He's a doctor, I think. The whole front of their house, just gone.'

We stopped to talk to the firemen who were clambering all over the rubble of the house, looking for any signs of life.

'Were they at home, do you know?' Rose called out to the firemen standing on top of the ruins of the house.

'We're not sure yet,' shouted back one fireman, who was spraying water at the smoke wafting from the bricks.

Along the next street, there was a similar scene at the house of another family we didn't know by name but who we had seen around the neighbourhood. They had a young daughter aged about three years old. The mother, who had survived the blast, was distraught because she couldn't find her.

'Aggie,' she was crying. 'Have you seen Aggie?'

She was being comforted by a woman in a blue uniform with letters on her tin hat. I sniffed around the rubble, wondering if I could be of any use, and I thought I heard faint crying.

I barked at the woman in the uniform and started to dig away with my paws. The cries got louder but nobody else seemed to be able to hear them. After a few minutes, I saw a small hand, all covered in dust, then a head of brown, curly hair and then a little face all screwed up and very faintly whimpering. I barked loudly and licked the child's face clean of the dust. She began to choke and cough. Her tiny arm was trapped underneath a large piece of brick and she couldn't move. Rose and the mother and the woman in blue came running over.

'Aggie,' cried the mother, 'my darling! Are you all right? Is she all right?'

Together they carefully began to shift the precarious pile of rubble to make sure nothing else fell on the child. Eventually, the woman in the blue uniform lifted her out and carried the little girl carefully across the pile of bricks, back to the mother, who took her into her arms. She was crying and her arm was all floppy, not like a normal human arm. She seemed to be in a lot of pain and had gone quite white.

'Better be careful. It looks broken,' said the woman. 'We haven't been able to get an ambulance all night, it's been that busy. I've got my van. Let's get her to the hospital and get that arm checked out.'

'Thank you,' said the mother in relief, and then she bent down to me. 'And you, you brave soldier. You saved the day.'

'Bertie, you're becoming quite the rescue dog,' said Rose as we walked back to the house.

I barked, mainly out of relief. But the image of that child's tiny hands and tiny face, all covered in dust, confused, shocked and in pain, would not go away, and even though she had been found alive, it haunted me. It had been too close for comfort.

CHAPTER FIFTEEN

When we got back to the house, we were relieved to see it still intact. There were some people on the doorstep. Victor was peering through the letter box.

'Oh thank goodness,' said Mary, running over to Rose. 'We thought . . . you said you were going to the church crypt and . . . Oh, it's so awful.'

'What happened?'

'Took a direct hit last night,' said Victor, looking serious. 'Whole thing collapsed. Just caved in.'

'And we were so sure you'd gone down there,' said Mary. 'At our suggestion, too. I've been sick with worry. I'm going over now to see what I can do to help.'

'Oh my God,' said Rose. 'No. We went to the tube station in the end. Why don't you take Bertie with you, if you're going?'

My hackles went up. I knew Mary didn't like dogs very much. And since Princess Wilhelmina had disappeared, she had hardly looked at me. I think she thought I had chased her beloved cat away or something. But at this point, she didn't have much choice. Rose and Victor had work to do at the factory, and I really didn't want to spend the day on my own.

Rose managed to persuade George it was best to go to school, and he was too exhausted from the morning's excitement to argue. Mary and I dropped him off, and then, the most unlikely of duos, we headed over to the church.

When we arrived at the scene, a crowd of people had gathered around the ruins of the building. There were large pieces of stone, including a huge gargoyle's head, which had fallen right across where the entrance to the church crypt must have once been.

The crowd was a mix of anxious friends and relatives and passers-by who knew the church, or looked like they must have been part of the congregation. One man whose entire family had been down there, including his four young children and his wife, was sitting on the ground in tears, shaking, while a member of the fire service, a great burly man in black boots, knelt down with his arm around him.

Several ambulances had arrived but no one, as yet, had been found. Neighbours began to bring shovels and started to work together with the fire crew and the local ARP men and women to remove the large stones from the entrance.

Among the rubble, a man picked something up and scraped it clean. It was a sign saying 'public shelter'.

'So much for shelter,' he said, then threw it aside and continued digging.

I started to dig about with my paws, and gradually we began to see a black hole leading to a steep drop. I suppose it was what had been the entrance to the crypt, but the staircase had disappeared.

One of the firemen got a rope from his van and put it around his waist.

'Lower me down, boys,' he said, and his colleagues lowered him gently down into the hole so he could assess the damage. I began to bark. I thought, if I could get lowered down there too, I might be of some use.

'I think he wants to help. That dog. Quick, pull up the rope, John,' said one of the fire crew.

'We can send him down with Bob. Is that all right, missus,' the man asked Mary.

'I, er . . . I suppose. I mean, he's not my dog, but . . .'

I barked again, and Mary said they could let me help but told them to please be careful with me as I was her daughter's dog.

I stood still as the fireman tied the rope around my middle and I braced myself as he very slowly lowered me into the darkness below.

It was dark and dusty, but I knew I had to continue. I looked up at the fireman and he called down at me.

'All right, boy?'

I barked back and he continued lowering me into the darkness, right down to the bottom where I could wriggle out of the rope and look around. I could hear Bob a few metres ahead of me, inching his way along a narrow space, his torch lighting up the way. I followed the dim light.

'Hallo, lad,' said Bob. 'See what you can find.' He moved to let me pass.

Because I was so much smaller than a human, I was able to wiggle my way further into the space, and I began to burrow my way ahead, looking for any signs of life.

Then I saw something in the bricks. I barked for Bob to shine his light and burrowed my way over towards the thing I had seen. There was a finger sticking up out of the dust. Then another one, and then a human thumb.

The hand was slender like a woman's hand. There was a ring on one of the fingers. I ran over and sniffed it, but when I pulled gently it moved far too freely and I realized it was a hand and only that. There was no arm or anything else attached to it. I dropped it in horror and howled out.

'What is it, lad?' called Bob. He had managed to remove enough debris to reach me. 'Oh, Christ,' he said, seeing the hand resting on the floor by my feet. 'Come on. Let's keep moving. This one can't be saved.'

We had no choice but to leave the hand where it was and keep moving in search of people who might be alive. After quite some time, we had worked our way past the worst of the rubble and into a small opening where the main crypt was located.

'If anyone's made it through this, they'll be in here, no doubt,' said Bob.

All around, I could smell humans but I couldn't work out where they were. Eventually I started to hear some noises. The faint sounds of a man calling out for help, a young child crying and even the sounds of scratching. After a few minutes, two more of the fire crew made it through the path we had made through the rubble, and the four of us spent the next few hours locating the survivors.

We found four children under there. They were all alive but dazed and very confused. One had a large cut on his head, which one of the firefighters bandaged up. The fire crew began very carefully to carry the people through the darkness and lift them back outside with the ropes.

I saw things that day I would rather forget. There had been around forty people down there, the neighbours reckoned, and by the end of the day we had only rescued twelve. The four children, plus six women and two men. I had found several limbs without bodies, and saw people who had already died and who could not be saved. It broke my heart that there was absolutely nothing I could do. One man had been so badly burnt in the explosion he was partly stuck to the wall and he could not be removed by us at all.

All I could do was to help locate the people as best I could, but I knew there must have been people we couldn't get to at all, as we definitely did not find forty whole people. Eventually, Bob decided we had done what we could without specialist lifting machinery to remove the large masonry, and one by one, we were lifted back out into the open air.

It took quite a while for my eyes to get used to the daylight again. There was, by now, a very large crowd of people, ambulance crews, nurses and volunteers tending to the injured. Once all the survivors were out, a new group of people arrived. They began the grim task of removing the bodies and body parts for identification by the relatives. An official-looking man was undertaking the task of bagging up the body parts and those who had not survived. Some, I imagined, it would be difficult to identify.

Mary was standing with a group of people in uniforms, helping to tie up wounds with pieces of white cloth to stop the bleeding. She was talking to the survivors to make sure they didn't pass out as they were put on to stretchers.

Three of the children we rescued had not been able to find their parents, so they went with the Red Cross as a group in one van together. The other child, a small boy, found his mother, who had concussion and a badly cut leg, lying on a stretcher. The two of them had a momentary happy reunion before both being bundled off in an ambulance together.

The man who had been waiting to hear news of his wife and four children was sitting on a large piece of stone step from the former entrance to the church. There was an undrunk cup of tea next to him. He was not speaking or moving but just staring into space with a stunned look in his eyes. His family had not been found among the survivors. All we had found was that hand. The woman's hand with a wedding ring on it. When he was shown the wedding ring, the stunned man broke down in tears. They didn't need to show him the hand.

By the time I got home that evening, I was still shaking from what I had just witnessed. Mary had gone to the hospital with the man whose family had been killed, and she dropped me off on the way. But I couldn't stop thinking of his face. The stunned sorrow. The absolute grief.

As soon as I got home, we left for the underground. Rose wanted to get a good spot. But we were already too late. All the floor spaces were taken, and we ended up sitting on the stairs. Incredibly, there were even people sleeping on the tracks that night when the trains had stopped.

All night, I was pressed up against a man who spent most of the time moving between a loud and stuttering snoring, and a strange and ghostly talking as he slept. At one point, his leg came flinging out and he yelled out something I didn't understand and nearly kicked me. Rose hardly slept a wink, either, as the angle we were lying at was very awkward. In the morning, the commuters came streaming back down and all the people sleeping on the tracks had to jump up before they switched the electrics back on.

The following day, Nancy came over and helped us finish clearing up the house, which was still a bit of a mess after the fire and the bombing of the shelter, while Rose went to work. There was still a lot of broken glass, and there was plaster hanging from the ceiling.

'We'll get this place spick and span in no time,' said Nancy, who always seemed to somehow manage to remain cheerful.

After that, she said we were going to see someone about something. I felt like I could do with a walk, so I jumped up eagerly.

As we walked, it soon became clear we were heading back down towards the docks. As we approached the river, in the daylight, I could see the damage that had been done over the past few weeks. There were huge skeletons of buildings, charred and burning. Twisted metal and broken glass and bricks everywhere, along with the smell of chemicals and burnt wood and metal. There was also a strange smell of perfume in the air. Nancy said a perfume factory had been hit; the smell was a strange and flowery contrast to the bleak and broken scene. When we arrived at the entrance to one of the main docks, I heard a noise. It was quiet but unmistakably made by an animal. I stopped moving.

'What is it, Bertie? We'll be late. No time for marking your territory today,' said Nancy, pulling on my lead.

I whined and gave a low bark. Wait, I was saying. I'm trying to listen. There it was again. I sniffed the air and tried to follow the scent through the smell of perfume in the air. I was sure it was a cat. Then I saw a tail and then two scrawny whiskers. I hardly recognized her at first, quivering in the corner, not quite as fluffy and not quite as white any more. She had lost a lot of weight. You could see her rib cage, and her formerly luxurious fur was matted and thick with dirt.

'Oh, a kitty,' said Nancy. 'Here, puss.' She hadn't recognized who it was yet. Princess Wilhelmina gave a weak, croaking meow. Nancy picked her up and wrapped her in her coat.

'She's so light,' she said. 'All skin and bones, poor thing.'

Then she noticed her distinctive blue-velvet collar that Mary had bought her as a treat for Christmas.

'Hang on. Bertie, it's . . . it can't be. But she's so thin. It's Willie! It's Princess Wilhelmina! Oh, where have you been, you naughty. Oh, thank goodness. We'd almost given you up for lost.'

Nancy smothered the cat in kisses and hugged her so tightly I thought she might snap her in half. Then the Princess lifted her head and licked Nancy gently on the hand. I was so relieved to see her alive, and was curious to know what she had been up to all this time. But for the time being, we had a dilemma. Clive had told Nancy that Mad Carpet Tony had a very important job for them, and that she really needed to be there. Nancy very much needed the money.

But she couldn't leave Princess there all alone, looking like she was at death's door.

'I'll have to take her home, Bertie,' she said. 'Can you help me out?'

She wrote a note with her eyeliner on a piece of paper.

'Take this, will you? To Clive. You remember the way, don't you? We're nearly there. Just around the corner, that way. He'll bring you back. I simply can't . . .'

I barked and took the note carefully in my mouth to indicate I would be fine. Nancy turned and ran off in the direction of home with Princess tucked up inside her coat.

I carried on towards the old warehouses, hoping I would be able to find the way. The landscape looked very different with half the buildings now gone. After searching for a while, I noticed some smells and sights I did remember, and a building on the opposite side of the river I had seen before. Eventually, I found the place with all the boats. The warehouse was still standing. There was a bustle of activity all around. Men in flat caps were rolling barrels from the dockside into the warehouses, and Clive was shouting orders at them.

'Bertie,' he said. 'You're late. Where's Nancy?'

I shoved the note into his hand with my mouth.

'Oh, damn that girl,' he said as he read it. 'For a blasted cat! Well, we'll have to do it on our own. We can't wait. You up for it, Bertie?'

I didn't know what I was supposed to be up for, but I barked anyway.

I heard another bark from inside the building. Then a gravelly, quiet voice, which sent a chill down my spine. Jane the bull terrier came trotting out with Mad Carpet Tony not far behind.

'You ready?' he growled at Clive. I went over and greeted Jane. I said hello and we sniffed each other. I was pleased to see she wagged her tail when she saw me. She was quiet as ever, though, and I wasn't sure whether she was shy or just not that interested.

'Jane,' shouted Tony. 'Get here. Don't sniff that dog, you dirty animal.'

She whined and ran back to her owner, loyal as ever.

'Come on, Bertie,' whistled Clive. 'Here, boy. Let's go.'

Where we were going, though, I still had no idea.

CHAPTER SIXTEEN

Clive always looked quite smart, but today he looked even smarter than usual. He was wearing a stripy grey-and-brown suit, which looked and smelt new, and he had on a brown felt hat and very shiny brown shoes, which smelt of polish. He was twitching with a kind of nervous energy as we walked.

'I wish that stupid girl was here,' he said, rubbing his fingers together. 'A cat. I ask you. What next? A home for injured pigeons. I don't know. This day of all days. What's going on, 'ey, Bertie? World's gone stirring mad.'

We took the underground and came out on the other side in a posh area, not with big houses this time, but official-looking buildings with people walking urgently in and out. There was a flag flying outside one of the buildings. We walked through the main entrance.

'Why Tony couldn't do this job, I don't know,' muttered Clive under his breath, 'if it means so much to him. Delicate, he said. I'll give him delicate.'

A man in a bowler hat stopped us before we could go any further. 'Sorry, sir. You can't bring that in,' he said, looking down at me. Clive handed him a piece of paper. The bowler-hatted man read the note and immediately became, or pretended to become, a lot nicer. He smiled a fake kind of smile and bowed very slightly.

'Right, sir. Yes, of course. In that case, you'd better come this way.'

The building smelt of furniture polish and shoe polish and newspaper and was ever so grand and imposing. We walked through a series of big doors, and the bowler-hat man signalled for Clive to sit down on a large green leather chair in a long corridor with wood everywhere. I waited at his feet and tried not to make any noise, though I was quite excited to find out what was going to happen. Eventually, a tall, thin man in a grey suit with a moustache and wispy grey hair opened the door.

'Mr, er . . . Finch?' he said, looking at a piece of paper.

'Yes, sir,' said Clive, standing up and banging his knee sharply on the edge of the chair. He winced and tried not to cry out.

'Right, in you come.'

'Do you mind if . . . my dog,' said Clive, looking at me.

'As long as he doesn't chase the cat. We've sort of adopted her by accident. Turned up during an air raid one night. In a puff of smoke, we all said. So we named her Puff. Looks like one, too. Fur-ball of a thing. Can't miss her. Livens up the place, though. Damn good ratter, too.'

A flash of grey fur whizzed past us, down across the corridor in hot pursuit of a small mouse.

'As I said,' the man said with a smile and motioned us into the room.

He sat down behind a large wooden desk with paintings all along the walls behind it. They depicted men in funny clothes, sitting on horses or in grand poses with dogs by their side. I didn't know who they were but they looked important.

'So we've agreed . . . terms,' said the man, drumming his fingers on the desk, 'but your man was very insist-ent we meet in person to transfer half the money. Quite irregular, I must say.'

'That's correct, sir. He, er, likes to make sure. You know. No funny business. Not that we don't trust . . .'

'Right. Well, never mind. Just be sure to bring the stuff tonight. My man'll let your people in through the trades-men's entrance. And you'll be . . . discreet.'

Clive nodded. 'Absolutely, sir. Discretion is the name of the game.'

He had relaxed and seemed almost to be enjoying the secretive transaction.

The man with the moustache went over to a sealed box in the corner of the room, and after some fiddling around he produced a black leather bag. Inside it were smaller cloth bags, each with money inside. He handed them over to Clive to count. Puff the cat came running in through the door, looking very excited. She had caught a mouse and had it in her mouth, still alive, but it was hardly moving.

'She'll tease that now for a while,' said the man proudly. 'And then eat it when she gets hungry. Like a little lion, she is.'

Puff took the mouse into the corner of the room and dropped it on the floor.

'What will you do with it?' I asked, curious to know why cats were so keen on catching mice.

The mouse twitched a little then went completely still.

'They ask me to do it,' said Puff. 'It's why I'm here. To keep the mice down. I just play with them a bit for their amusement. Don't know why they're not keen on mice. I don't mind them myself. But it's all part of the plan.'

'The plan?'

'The plan for getting fed. If I catch mice, they feed me extra food, so I get to eat the mouse and I get more free food.'

'Is it your job, then? Catching mice?'

'Yeah, I suppose so. Chief mouse catcher, they call me around here.'

Puff looked at the mouse with a wild look in her eyes, waiting for it to move, then she poked it with her paw, before realizing it probably wasn't going to be much fun after all.

'This one's boring,' she said, and ate it.

I felt sorry for the mouse but I knew that Puff had to eat it in order to survive, especially now that animals were seen as surplus to requirements unless they did something useful.

Clive counted the piles of money and shook hands with the man. I could tell he was relieved things had gone smoothly, and I was pleased I had been there.

On the way back, we stopped for fish and chips, and Clive gave me his scraps and quite a few of his chips. That was my reward, I thought, for going with Clive, like Puff's food for catching mice.

I thought he would take me home after that, job done, but instead we walked up another grand street past some very posh houses.

'We've to go straight to the Palace. To meet Tony and the lads and unload before the guests arrive.'

I thought for a moment maybe we were going to visit the King. I heard he lived in a palace.

Eventually, we stopped at a very large house with a grand entrance. Men in hats were standing out the front, greeting motor cars as they came through and helping people get out, but there was no sign of any royalty. There was a sign on the front.

'Grande Palace Hotel,' said Clive, reading it out. 'This is where all the toffs stay. All right for some, ain't it?'

We went around the back and waited on a step by a small door. Clive lit a cigarette. It was starting to get dark. I wondered whether Rose would be worrying about where I was. Around about now, she and George would be heading for the underground station to find their spot. I wondered if they would get a bit of floor or if they would end up on the steps again.

It was a clear night, but as the sun had gone down, it began to get cold. Perhaps there won't be any air raids tonight, I thought. Perhaps we'll get the night off.

A van pulled up. Tony and a group of men jumped out. Clive handed over the bags of money, and Tony stuffed them into his large inside pocket. He ordered the men to carry a pile of wooden crates and barrels out of the van. The back door opened and a man in a hat appeared in the darkness. He whispered for them to hurry. In less than ten minutes, all the cargo had been transferred into the hotel.

'All the best stuff,' Clive said to the hotel man and touched his nose.

'Let's just get it all out, shall we?' said the man with a sniff. 'You're late as it is.'

I followed as they went through into the hotel with the boxes and watched as the man in the hat opened them up and counted them. Tucked inside, nestled in beds of straw, were glass bottles of all colours, shapes and sizes.

'Whisky, champagne, wine and brandy and the cigars. It's all there,' said Clive. 'There's a big do on,' he whispered to me. 'Those toffs need their booze, see. Some party for a big cheese ambassador or something.'

When the last of the boxes had been brought through and unpacked, we went back into the kitchen. The guests started to arrive in the main room next door. I peeped through the door and saw ladies wearing sparkling dresses and shining head pieces, and men in black suits and shiny shoes, with white scarves and white gloves.

The hotel staff had just managed to lay out the champagne and were pouring it into glasses for the guests as they arrived. In the corner, a group of musicians was setting up, and they soon began to play. A man with slicked back hair and a smart suit began to sing.

'They start out so civilized. But you should see them at the end of the night.' The voice was coming from the corner of the kitchen.

A man in blue-and-white clothes appeared out of the shadows. He was covered in bits of food and had sweat all over his face. He put a tea towel down on the side bench and sat on a small wooden chair in the corner of the room.

'My job's done now, at least,' he said. 'Been preparing "canapés" all day for this lot.'

'Canapés?' asked Clive. 'What's that when it's at home?'

'Posh cheese on toast cut into bits, basically. French, it is. But they seem to like it. Anyway, at least we get to eat what's left over, so long as the boss isn't looking.'

Tony and the lads had gone off in the van with the money, and nobody seemed to mind that we were still there, so we hung around. Clive chatted to the chef, who introduced himself as Eddy.

Every now and again, the waiter would come in with an empty tray and fill it up with more of the canapés. Once in a while, he came back with a tray with a few left over, and Clive and I got to eat them. Once the food was all gone, or had been brought back in, the music started up again and the guests started dancing. The band played a fast song, then a slow song, followed by another fast one, and the guests were getting more and more excited by the music. The singer said a few words and everyone laughed, and then they played another fast number, and people whirled about the dance floor. One of the waiters came back with a bottle.

'Managed to sneak this out,' he whispered, waving it in the air.

'Oh, you brilliant man,' said Clive. 'Give us a swig.'

Clive, Eddy and the waiter sat down and started drinking. Before long, they had drunk the lot.

Humans were funny when they drank from those bottles. First they were quite normal, then they were laughing, and after a while they all started to dance in the kitchen, imitating the guests. Then Clive put on the chef's hat and, for a while then, he and the waiter were arm-wrestling on the kitchen counter. There was the sound of footsteps. I barked.

'It's the boss,' said Eddy.

Clive took the hat off and they all sat down, trying to look innocent. But none of them could suppress their smiles, and then Clive burst into a snorting giggle.

'What's that animal doing in here?' said the boss, ignoring their snorts of laughter.

It was the same man who had let us in earlier. 'It's a health hazard. It's probably got fleas or who knows what. Rabies or something.'

Before Clive could answer, the air-raid siren sounded.

'Well, anyway, just get this dog out of here,' he said and hurried out to check on the guests.

'Here we go again,' said Eddy.

'Where do you lot go, then?' Clive asked him.

'We stay here, generally. The ballroom's used as a shelter most nights anyway. People come from all over when there's not a do on like there is tonight. Pretty safe, actually, they say, as it's partly underground. We get the odd fire-bomb on the upper floors. The spotters are on the roof, though. They'll let us know if anything heads our way.'

Eddy opened the door and I could see all the dancers again. They seemed untroubled by the air raid. Among those whizzing across the floor was a tall, grey-haired man. I recognized him as the one who had paid us the money earlier. He was dancing with a lady in a blue silk dress. On her head was a shiny kind of crown thing and around her neck was a row of very shiny stones, which were glistening in the light. Everything about her was shiny, even her silvery-white hair.

I assumed she was his wife from the way they looked at each other, as though they had known each other for ever.

She was a graceful dancer. In fact, I was quite mesmerized as they spun across the room together. When the music stopped, they looked at each other and laughed. The man took the woman's hand and kissed it, and she curtsied slightly. They went to sit down together.

The air-raid siren had stopped, and everyone seemed to have forgotten about it already. After that dance, the waiter went back out to collect up glasses and empty trays. Eddy put on some coffee to boil and I sat down next to Clive. We sat there, listening to the music and the sounds of laughter from the ballroom.

Through the din of the music, from somewhere outside, I heard a distant explosion, followed by the sounds of anti-aircraft fire. I knew the sounds so well by now. It was nothing new and seemed quite far away. The next time I heard it, my ears twitched. No one else could tell, but it was slightly louder. I sat up and barked.

Clive and Eddy had found a pack of cards, and they were drinking coffee and playing a game for money on a small table by the door.

'Quiet, Bertie. We don't want the boss back down here. I don't fancy getting kicked out now. I'm just getting comfortable.'

I whined and sat back down. The next time I heard the noise, it was even louder and the building shook slightly.

'Hitler's getting busy, then,' said Clive, selecting a card. But he didn't seem overly concerned. Then I heard the whistling, high-pitched noise that rose up at the end and meant only one thing.

CHAPTER SEVENTEEN

A huge cracking sound split through the building. There was a ringing in my ears, and at the same moment, it felt like the air was being sucked out of my eye sockets. Without thinking, we all dived under the kitchen counter, and Clive put his coat over me. Plaster was falling from the ceiling. I heard a horrible screaming sound. Then I blacked out.

I don't know how long it was before I woke up, but when I did, the air was full of smoke and it was dark. I could hardly breathe. Clive was lying next to me and Eddy was curled up in a ball next to him. The counter we were hiding under had protected us from the worst of the blast. I barked quietly.

'You all right, boy?' asked Eddy, feeling around in the dark. My hearing was still muffled but I could make out what he said. He uncurled and pulled himself over towards me. Clive wasn't moving, but I could tell that he was breathing.

'Mate,' said Eddy. 'Wake up.' He wiped Clive's face with his handkerchief, and tapped his face lightly.

Clive groaned slightly. He had a large gash in the side of his arm where something had flown over and struck him. It was bleeding badly.

'You're in shock, mate,' said Eddy, and he tore off a bit of his white coat, turned it inside out and wrapped it tightly around Clive's arm.

'Can you stand up?'

'Think it's just the . . . my . . . arm,' said Clive, wincing in pain. Eddy lifted him to his feet and we crawled out from under the counter into the darkness.

When I looked up, I could see a bit of sky. There was a spotlight casting across it, and anti-aircraft guns were firing out loudly somewhere very close by. The aeroplanes had passed over and I could hear them moving off further away.

'There's a torch in here somewhere,' said Eddy, feeling around in a drawer.

He found it and shone the light around the room. I could see that part of the wall and ceiling had been blown right through. The cupboards were all gone and their contents had been spilled out on to the floor. The cooker had been blown off its wall completely.

'The gas,' said Eddy, and he felt around in a cupboard out the back to turn the gas off to avoid another explosion.

There was glass everywhere, and I tried to pick my way carefully through so as not to cut my feet. It was impossible, and in the end I had to resign myself to a few cuts because otherwise I would not have been able to walk anywhere at all.

The music from the ballroom had stopped. It was pitch dark. There was an odd smell and an unnerving quiet interspersed with the occasional moan, and the intermittent sound of someone, I couldn't tell whether it was a man or a woman, crying out in pain from near where the band had been playing.

There was a sudden commotion on the other side of the room. A group of people appeared in the shadows, moving very nimbly. They were all carrying torches, and as they moved about, they lit up the room in brief flashes.

'Who's that?' whispered Eddy.

'I think I know who,' replied Clive quietly. 'And if I'm right we're better off keeping our heads down.'

'What are they? They're not . . . ?'

'You don't want to get involved with that lot,' said Clive. 'Believe me.'

So we had to just sit there in the dark and watch as the men worked their way around the room, poking about among the ruins, and the people. They were very quiet as they went about their work, and they ignored those who were crying out for help.

'Hurry up, you bastards,' said a man with a gravelly voice that I recognized. It was Mad Carpet Tony.

After about ten minutes, they had swept through the entire room and the bells of the fire brigade and ambulance began to ring out. One by one, the members of the rescue team made their way into the ballroom. They looked around at the damage. On the other side of the room, the group of men slipped away quietly through a hole in the wall before anyone spotted them.

Eddy, Clive and I made our way through the rubble and began to help look for survivors. Eddy found the remaining bottles of champagne and brandy and began pouring the liquid on to the wounds of those who were still alive, to protect from infection, he said.

I couldn't see everything in the torch light, but I could tell the explosion had killed many people. Over where the band had been, there was a large crater and a leg, but no body. I couldn't see the singer anywhere.

'Unbelievable. Bloody looters. Been in already,' said a fireman, shifting a huge piece of wooden table out of the way as he looked for the bodies. 'Picked the poor buggers clean like vultures.'

He shone his torch on the face of a woman in a blue silk dress. Her silver hair had fallen across her face and it was streaked with blood. Next to her was a man with a grey moustache. He was covered in dust, and one of his legs was trapped beneath a table. The other was going off at a strange angle. The man's eyes were open but there was nothing behind them. He and the woman in blue had clasped their hands tightly together. Beside them was a single diamond earring among the plaster and dust.

'Missed this, at least,' said the fireman, and he tucked the earring gently between their hands.

'Too late for them,' said a woman ambulance driver, coming up behind him. And they moved on together in the darkness.

By the time we left the ruins of the hotel, it was just getting light and there was a chilly drizzle of rain. Clive was silent as we walked. He had a bandage on his arm with a spot of blood already seeping through, but he hardly seemed to notice or care. When we got to the underground, it had only just opened and there were people still sitting, bleary eyed, all along the platform. We picked our way between them and jumped on the first train of the morning along with the city's early workers, men and women in blue and green, some heading for factories, others for their volunteer posts, as well as shop workers and business people in their suits.

When we got to our stop, I began to look out for Rose and George. They weren't on the platform, but as we walked up the steps towards the exit, we found them curled up together in a patchwork blanket, both fast asleep. Above them was a woman with a crying baby, who she was trying to quieten down. Below them, a couple of young women in blue suits were chatting and applying their make-up for the day. The first of the commuters were already pushing their way down the steps, so everyone was now waking up and collecting their things.

'Bertie,' said Rose, waking up and setting George carefully on to the step beside her. 'My back's stiff as a board this morning. Hello, Clive,' she said. 'We thought Bertie must be with you. Heavy night, wasn't it? Glad we got down here when we did.'

'Heavy,' said Clive quietly.

'Are you OK? Did you and Bertie find somewhere to shelter? It was raining incendiaries like nobody's business. But we got here all right. Didn't we, George, sleepy head?'

'Found a hotel,' said Clive, staring into space. 'Bad situation.'

'Your arm,' said Rose, seeing the bandage. She stood up and looked at it.

'It's all right,' he said. 'It's fine.'

The images of the bodies in the hotel came back into my mind. I couldn't shift them. I wondered how it was that we had survived, and I started to feel guilty. Perhaps I could have done more to stop the looters or find survivors. But Clive had said those men were not to be messed with.

'Come on, let's get back home. Have a cup of tea,' said Rose, rolling up the blanket and putting it in her bag. George woke up and started stretching out his limbs.

'Bertie!' he said, and I licked his face and he gave me a huge hug. 'We were worried about you. We had a right time getting down here. Mum had to push her way down just to find this spot.'

'Want to come back for some tea?' Rose asked Clive. His face was white, and he didn't seem to be quite there. He said he had to get home.

'Well, you take care of that arm, won't you?'

He walked away down the street without saying another word.

When we got outside, George ran on ahead and played the game of pointing out which buildings had been hit the night before. The little bookshop and the butcher's shop had both suffered a small blast. But they were opening up anyway. A young boy sat on a pile of rubble by the bookshop. He was reading one of the books intently, surrounded by a pile of books which had been blown off the shelves.

A few doors down, the butcher was sweeping up the glass from the floor and his assistant was laying out the meat on what they could salvage from the counter. Rose picked up her rations and even managed to get some offal for me.

When we passed the post box at the end of our road, I took one look across towards our house and felt immediately sick to my stomach. I'd seen this sight so many times before. But now it was all of a sudden very real, like a knife going right into my heart. I barked.

'Bertie. What is it? Oh, God . . .' said Rose, and she saw what I had seen.

Where yesterday our house had been, now there was just a pile of bricks and rubble.

The whole front of the building was gone, and all that was left of the living room was the fireplace. I could see scattered objects dotted here and there – one of George's shoes, part of the gramophone sticking out. Towards the back of the house, the inside of the kitchen was partly intact, with the sink still in its place, and the doorway leading out to the garden was somehow still standing. The upstairs bedroom wall was still almost standing, with the wallpaper still visible. The carpet was hanging over the edge of the floor into the void below.

Rose said nothing. She stared at the house for a few seconds, unable to absorb it all. Then she fell down to the ground on her knees and clasped George in her arms.

'Did Hitler hit our house last night, Mummy?' George asked. 'Can I go and get my aeroplanes out? Is my bedroom still there, do you think? Can we go back in?'

Rose wiped the tears from her face and stood up and breathed in.

'We're all alive. That's the main thing,' she said. But I could tell she was struggling to hold it together.

Incredibly, the houses on either side were undamaged apart from their windows, which had been broken, and a few bricks and roof tiles that were missing here and there. Pamela's family were all still away, and Frank and Maude would most likely have been out somewhere, doing their air-raid duties.

An elderly woman from across the road, who I had only ever seen but never met, came across to speak to us.

'I'm Mrs Oliver, from number sixty-three,' she said, holding out her hand to shake Rose's.

'We're so relieved you weren't in there. You and the boy. They were just about to go in and look for you. We heard it last night. We were in our Morrison in the living room. It shook the whole house. We thought we were all for it.'

'No, we weren't in there,' Rose said in a daze, pulling George closer to her.

'How about some tea?' said Mrs Oliver.

'Can you spare it?'

'Can't we go in and get my things?' asked George, tugging on Rose's arm and pulling her towards the house. 'Or go and help the firemen.'

'It's not safe, love,' she said. 'We should wait and ask Frank when he gets back. He'll know what to do.'

When they saw us, the firemen clambered down from the wreckage of the house with their hosepipes snaking behind them. They were needed somewhere else where there might be people trapped. As they packed up and left, we followed Mrs Oliver across road.

'Let's have that cup of tea, shall we?'

I never understood tea because I didn't drink it. But for humans, it seemed to be able to solve a lot of things. Although it was rationed, along with milk and sugar, people seemed to be drinking more of it than ever.

Rose and Mrs Oliver sat down at her kitchen table. Rose's hands were shaking and she had gone quite white. Mrs Oliver petted my head and gave me a biscuit as a treat. Then she gave George a book to read that belonged to her grandson, and he went and sat in the living room on his own.

'I just don't know,' said Rose quietly as she sipped. 'I thought he was better off here with us, I really did. But now, I don't know. And with his father so far away anyway.'

'Well, my Sarah's little ones, Ronnie and little Katie, they went with their school. The whole class went, practically, even the teacher, set up a little school there, you see. It was just awful when they left, though. Saying goodbye. Their little suitcases . . . I miss them every day. Seeing them grow up. The little changes.'

'That's what we thought. And he was so insistent on staying with us. It would have been impossible,' said Rose, staring into her teacup and frowning. 'But this . . . this is too much. What if we'd been in there? What if he'd been in there? I can't take much more. It's the worrying.'

'If you like, I could ask my Sarah. There might be a family who'd take the boy in. They're in . . . Wiltshire it is, right by this big forest, all wild horses apparently, walking about on the road and everything.' She paused for a sip of her tea, then continued. 'We've had some lovely cards. Katie's even learning to ride a horse! Can you imagine? She'd never be able to do that here. I won't lie, though. Ronnie's found it hard to settle. He's a naturally shy boy. Doesn't mix. Not so adaptable. Being that he's from the city and they're all country people.'

'Well, George is quite a lively boy. Doesn't mind new people . . . so maybe he'd be all right. I don't know. I thought it would only last a few weeks and it would be

Christmas in a month and . . . but I just don't think I could live with myself if anything happened to him.'

Mrs Oliver put her hand on Rose's arm. 'How about I ask my Sarah, just to see what might be possible in their village? Can't hurt, can it?'

George wandered into the room and jumped up on to Rose's lap with the book in his hand. It had pictures of animals in it, like lions and fishes from the sea.

'You're getting nearly too big for my lap now,' said Rose. 'What's this book all about, then?'

'Animals from all around the world,' he said. 'Places I'll probably go one day. When I'm in the air force.'

The events of the past few months had simultaneously made George seem both older, almost grown up, but also like a little boy again.

'How do you fancy a holiday?' Rose asked, smoothing the hair out of his eyes.

'What, to the seaside? Will Dad be there?'

'Not with me and your dad. With some other children. Like Mrs Oliver's grandson, Ronnie, and his sister, Katie.'

'And horses and lots of green land to run about in,' said Mrs Oliver.

George stiffened. He knew about evacuees. He had said he didn't want to go last time, and he knew all about it from when Pamela had left.

'What, and miss the war?' he snapped. 'And then you'll all die and I won't be here and I'll never see you again.'

'George!' said Rose. 'I'm so sorry, he's not normally like this. It's . . . well, what with the house now and everything that's happened and his father away.'

'It's not because Dad's away,' he said. 'It's you, and this and . . .'

He jumped off Rose's lap and made for the door. I ran over and barked and wagged my tail to encourage him to stay. He took his hand off the door knob and knelt down next to me and put his head in my fur.

'You won't let them send me away, will you, Bertie?' he whispered.

I let out a comforting whine and tried to reassure him. But in my heart I knew there was nothing whatsoever that I could do. I'd never been to Wiltshire, or anywhere apart from London, but I'd seen pictures of the countryside, and it looked nice and green, and children were safe there from what the posters seemed to say. So maybe it wouldn't be such a bad thing. After everything I had seen over the past few weeks, all the death and horror and people mourning those they loved, I didn't think I could bear to lose George on top of everything else.

'I'm taking Bertie for a walk,' he said after a while. 'Unless you don't think it's safe for me to be outside at all. Except, where am I supposed to go, anyway, now that we don't even have a house and I'm not even allowed in to get my aeroplanes out?'

Rose seemed defeated and too tired to argue.

'All right, George,' she said. 'And we do have a house. We'll go and stay at your granny and granddad's until we sort things out. And we've got Bertie and . . . George.'

He paused by the door and looked at her.

'Yes,' he said quietly.

'Whatever we decide to do, I love you and all I want is for you to be safe.'

Seeing the love in Rose's eyes at that moment, I made a promise to myself. I would never forget that they had taken me in when I was most desperate. I didn't know how to repay them, really, but I swore to myself then that I would do anything I could to look after Rose and George, and that whatever happened, I would protect them.

CHAPTER EIGHTEEN

Christmas was approaching and there was a strange mix of excitement and sadness in the air. This would be the first Christmas since the Blitz started. Many people had now lost relatives. Many men were still away, although some had written to say they could get leave for a few days. Philip had written to say he hoped we were all doing all right in the bombing, and he worried about us every day. He was fine, but couldn't say much about where he was. He would try and get leave as soon as he could.

Nancy was very excited because Eric was given leave for Christmas. It was easier for him because he was based near London. But there was a sadness, too, because Harry had not been found. Maude was still holding out hope that he may have survived.

Rose had also made a decision about George. Mrs Oliver had heard back from her daughter that there was an 'auntie', as they called them, who might have a spare room. They were waiting to hear back from her.

'And miss Christmas!' he said, horrified, when he heard it might be on the cards. 'You can't mean it.'

'But, George, darling. We've been hit twice,' Rose said. You could have been killed. I just can't protect you here. And Hitler's not going to stop just because it's Christmas.'

She had made up her mind that she simply couldn't live with herself if she did nothing. Seeing their house destroyed had been the final straw.

'There'll be other Christmases,' said Victor. We were all squeezed into his and Mary's sitting room. 'And I'm sure you'll find a nice family who will look after you there and have a nice tree and it might even snow and you can make a proper big snowman in the countryside.'

'But . . . what if they don't get me any presents? What if they lock me in a room and they hate children and . . .'

'George,' said Rose. 'This is one thing I will not argue with you about. You are too young to know. It's not a game. I'm sorry but that is the end of it. We'll be taking the train next week.'

'We could all go up there for Christmas, maybe, if it happens,' said Mary when George had gone to bed that evening. She was sitting in her chair, doing a jigsaw puzzle, which was mainly sky with a large flock of birds swooping across it. She liked the difficult jigsaws. 'Stay in a lodging house. So we can be together,' she said.

'I couldn't afford it,' said Rose.

'We can help,' said Mary, and they agreed it was probably their best bet at convincing George.

The next day, we went around to the ruins of our old house. It was a sad sight. The rubble had been cleared up a bit, but most of it remained just as it had been when we first saw it. Rose didn't want to let George climb on the remains, but he found some pieces of shrapnel in the garden and picked them up as a memento. It was too dangerous to collect much of our stuff, so we went next door to see Frank and Maude.

'Come in, my loves,' said Maude. She had a tired look in her eyes, but she still sat us down and comforted Rose and gave George a bit of a special cake that she had made.

'What will you do?' she asked Rose.

'George is going away, we hope. And I'm doing extra shifts at the factory. And I might even get another job. I really feel like I've got to do something now. Anything.'

The doorbell rang. Maude went to answer it, and I ran along beside her to see who it was.

Through the frosted glass in the door, I could just make out the shape of a tall man with a shock of blonde hair. When the door opened, a man in a Royal Air Force uniform was standing on the doorstep.

'Mrs Baxter,' said the man. He looked a bit like Harry, and for one moment I'm sure Maude thought it was her son, come back after all. But when I looked at the face, I could see it definitely was not Harry's. He had a longer face and different eyes.

'Oh, I thought . . .' said Maude, stammering. 'Yes. I'm Mrs Baxter.' She sounded confused.

'I won't keep you,' said the man. 'I'm so sorry to turn up like this without writing first. I just wanted to meet you. Face to face.'

'Yes, of course. Come in,' said Maude.

They sat down and Maude put the kettle on. Frank came through and shook the man's hand.

'I was right behind him when the . . . when it happened,' he said. 'I just wanted you to know he went down fighting. He was a hero.'

'And you're sure he couldn't have . . . swum to shore?' said Maude. 'Because I was so certain. I could sense it. I really thought I could feel him . . . communicating . . .'

'I wish it was true. I really do. But I'm afraid there is no way he could have . . . not the way he was . . . No way he could have made it to shore. But I can assure you it was quick. He wouldn't have experienced any pain. He did everything he could.'

Maude, who had for so long held out hope that Harry might come back, sat down and put her tea cup on the table.

'Is there anything . . .' said the RAF man, putting his hand on her shoulder. 'Can I help in any way?'

She took his hand.

'No, thank you, dear. Thank you for coming . . .' Her voice began to break and she looked up at the young man who had seen her Harry fall from the sky. 'Thank you for coming all this way.'

Two days later the doorbell rang again, and Nancy answered. It was Frank with a letter.

'Thought I'd bring this one straight over,' he said. 'Post-marked Wiltshire. Given you're all waiting for news from there, for the boy, and all that.'

'I hope you're all doing . . .' said Nancy. 'I'm so sorry to hear about Harry.'

'Maude's taken it bad. It's hit us all hard, especially with Eric away, too. We spoke to him on the telephone yester-day. It's worse for him. Because they were twins, they had this connection. But at least we know now. We can grieve for the lad.'

Frank left for the rest of his round, and Rose came into the hall. Nancy looked at her, and she took hold of the letter. The three of us stood there for a while, just looking at the envelope.

'Who was it, dear?' called Mary from the living room.

'Nothing, Mother. Just Frank with some post.'

She breathed in deeply and then slid the letter open with her finger. It was on light-blue paper, written with a scrawling hand.

'What does it say?' asked Nancy.

Rose read it out slowly. 'I'm writing to tell you we would be delighted to take in your little boy, George, in order that you can evacuate him from London. I spoke earlier this week to your neighbour, Mrs Oliver, whose grandson and granddaughter are already living in our village. I informed her that we have a spare bedroom which I am certain would suit the child. I have no children of my own, but would do all I could to make the boy comfortable here. There is a small train station some four miles' walk from the cottage.'

There was a small hand-drawn map of the local area. It was signed 'Miss Brenda Eagle'.

'Lord,' said Rose, partly to herself and partly to me and Nancy. 'It all feels very real all of a sudden. I wonder what she's like . . . Miss Eagle.'

She folded the letter up and stuffed it into her cardigan pocket.

'Now comes the tricky bit,' she said to Nancy. 'Persuading George that it's really for the best that he gets out of London.'

I was still having a hard time convincing myself of that, although any time I started to wish he wasn't going to leave, I just remembered that night in the ballroom at the Palace Hotel, and then I knew in my heart it was for the best.

That evening, Rose made sure she and Mary cooked a very nice dinner, George's favourite, cottage pie, with real minced beef and thick gravy. For pudding, Rose made a custard from some real eggs she managed to get hold of from a woman down the road who was keeping chickens, and there was sliced apple with sugar.

'What's all this in aid of, then?' said Victor as they finished the unexpected feast. 'Real egg custard. I was quite getting to like the powdered stuff.' He tapped his nose and winked at George as if to say that he was definitely not getting to like the powdered stuff.

Rose seemed nervous, and her hands were shaking slightly.

'Oh, I managed to get some eggs, for Mother,' she said. 'Anyone for more? George?'

'Delicious,' said George as he put down his spoon. 'I'm so full I couldn't eat another thing.'

'You got custard all over your face,' said Mary, wiping it off with her handkerchief.

'Granny!' said George, pulling away and laughing. 'I was saving that for later!' He grinned.

Victor stood up and started collecting the plates. Mary went to work on her jigsaw puzzle.

'Please may I get down?' asked George.

'Just a moment,' said Rose. 'There's something we need to talk about. You know, after the house and everything, we talked about you maybe going away for a while.'

George didn't say anything but his face twitched slightly.

'For a holiday of sorts,' Rose continued. 'Well, I've had some wonderful news. That lady in the same village as the Olivers, she has a spare room and says you can stay with her.'

'Some stranger's house. She's probably a witch or something,' said George.

'Love, please. It's not easy for me, either. I don't want you to go away. But I can't take any more. My nerves. I just want you to be safe.'

'But what about Christmas?'

'We can come and see you at Christmas, make it a family holiday, all of us, Granny and Granddad, your Auntie Nancy. It would be fun.'

'How long, though, would I be there?'

'I don't know, darling. Not long. Just until the bombing stops,' said Rose. 'I'll write to you every day. I'm sure there's a telephone in the village. And we'll take you up there on the train, Bertie and I. We're not abandoning you, Georgie, it's just . . .'

'You'll be there for Christmas? You promise?' said George, softening slightly.

'Scout's honour.'

Over the next week, George laid out all the things he wanted to take with him. Although they had lost many of their belongings in the bombing, they had managed to salvage a few items, such as books and some of the heavier furniture. George had also collected two new pieces of prized shrapnel from the blast. He was very proud of them and carried them everywhere with him.

Mary and Victor bought him a leather-bound writing pad and a new pen for writing letters to them. Even Clive came around with a warm jumper and gloves he had got hold of from Berwick Street market.

The afternoon before George was set to leave, we all went around to see Frank and Maude so George could say goodbye to them.

'You'll be grand, son,' said Frank, pulling his ear gently. 'You'll see all kinds of new things. Have adventures. When I was a lad in Suffolk, we made this cart with these huge wheels on it. Fit all four of us. Went breakneck down the hills. Fell off and broke my arm once, but it was worth it.'

'Don't encourage him,' said Maude 'We bought you this, love. For the journey.' She handed him a large bar of Cadbury's chocolate.

'Don't eat it all now. At least wait until you're on the train,' she said. 'I know what you boys are like . . .' She stopped and her eyes began to glisten.

The sun was just setting as we made our way to the underground shelter for what would be George's last night in London.

Mary and Victor and Nancy all joined us. As we arrived, a local charity was cooking up some sausages and soup in a large saucepan, which meant the whole place was thick with the smells of food. There was a long queue of hungry people snaking along the tunnel at the bottom of the stairs.

Although most people were still fine with me being down there, there was always the odd character who was determined there should be no pets, so Rose carried me under her coat most of the way in, with my nose just peeping out.

Mary was also sneaking in her own forbidden cargo in the form of Princess Wilhelmina, who she was much more protective over now, ever since the cat had gone AWOL for several weeks. I had noticed some changes in Princess, too. She had a slightly wild look in her eye now, as though she had encountered something dreadful in her weeks away. Her fur had lost something of its glossy sheen. Sometimes she would just sit on the windowsill and look outside, and every now and again she would let out this long, wailing meowing sound. When I asked her about it, she clammed up and wouldn't tell me a thing.

Victor and George queued up and got some sausages while we went and found a spot on the platform. Mary managed to bustle her way into a tiny flat area just before the entrance, and she and Rose laid out their blankets. Mary put down Wilhelmina's basket gently on the ground next to her, and the cat let out a thin wailing sound. Only Mary singing quietly to her would calm her back down.

When the lads came back with the sausages, I had to restrain myself from grabbing them straight out of Victor's hand. My mouth was watering; they smelt so delicious. Eventually, everyone pulled off a little bit for me and Wilhelmina, even though it was strictly against the rules. As the people around us began to drop off to sleep, George was quite restless so Rose chatted to him quietly about what he might see in the countryside, all the animals and the fresh air.

'Will I have my own wardrobe?' was his sudden concern, followed by, 'will Miss Eagle have an indoor toilet?' and other such worries.

We were so deep underground, I think the humans could barely hear the raids that night, although I could make out the distant sounds of anti-aircraft fire and the occasional explosion. Then I fell into sleep myself, pressed up against George and Wilhelmina's basket, and dreamt of nothing but sausages.

CHAPTER NINETEEN

I had seen them in George's books, and I had seen them the day the war broke out, and the day Philip went away. Giant creatures puffing out steam and soot, and so loud. But I was quite nervous about actually riding on a train.

The next day, we climbed on board with George's suitcase, which was almost as big as he was, and Rose's bag for the two days we would be away. We walked along the train and found an empty little room with seats facing each other and a rack above them, where Rose put the luggage. George immediately jumped up on to the seat.

'Hooray. A whole carriage to ourselves!'

'Compartment, not carriage,' said Rose.

'What's the difference? Anyway, look, we can see out the window the whole way.'

He went to lean his head out of the window, but Rose immediately pulled him back in by his collar.

'No you don't, not unless you want to get your head knocked off. I'm not taking you out of London to avoid the bombing, only to get your head knocked off on the train.'

George sat glumly back down on the seat.

'You can look through the glass, though. Count the sheep. We played that on the way to Margate, remember?'

So far, all I could see were buildings. Houses and streets whizzed past so fast I could barely focus on any one thing. Every now and again, we stopped somewhere for a moment, and I saw flashes of London – a stretch of the river through a gap between two buildings, a man waiting at a bus stop, checking his watch, a woman cleaning her little daughter's face with her handkerchief. Londoners, going about their business in spite of everything that had happened.

Gradually, the landscape began to change. First the houses got smarter, then bigger, then smaller again. Then there were large patches of green, and before long, there were huge fields of green grass, and trees everywhere with their leafless branches poking up out of the earth.

'There's some sheep,' said George. 'One, two, three, four, five. I can't count them all!'

'Look at that one,' laughed Rose. 'He's gone down on his knees, as if he's praying!'

As well as sheep, we saw animals I had only seen in George's books and never before in real life. There was a bird called a kite which swooped down into a field, then rose up and landed on a fence post and surveyed the land, looking for food on the hard ground.

In a clearing, a group of deer stood in an opening. They looked up, and then scattered as the train passed by and sounded its whistle.

Then, all of a sudden, it all went completely black. I stood still, terrified, and began to growl.

'It's all right, Bertie. It's just a tunnel,' said Rose, stroking my head to reassure me.

Before long, the light came back again and the winter sun streamed through the window. Every now and again, the train stopped. We watched as people got on and off, and greeted loved ones or walked with their heavy suit-cases along the platform.

After what seemed like an age, the train shuddered to a stop once more and Rose stood up.

'This is us.'

'Benley-on-Clough,' said George, reading the sign on the platform. 'Like cough?'

'I think it's Clough, like clow,' said Rose, leaning through the window to open the door. 'Quick chop, get your suit-case. We don't want to miss the stop.'

As I jumped down on to the platform, I realized we were the only ones getting off. Almost immediately, the whistle went and the train started up again in a haze of smoke, and then snaked its way off into the distance.

Only when the train had gone did I realize how loud it had been. As we stood on the platform together, it was so quiet it suddenly seemed like I could hear my heart beating in my head. This place was a world away from our street and London. All the smog and noise, the sandbags and broken glass and ruined buildings and jostling for position in the underground; there was none of that here.

'Where are all the buildings?' asked George, looking confused. 'It's so quiet.'

'I know, it's wonderful, isn't it?' said Rose. 'The village proper is a few miles that way.' She looked down at the map. 'This way. Come on. It'll be dark in an hour.'

As we began to walk, a cold wind blew around our faces.

'Put your new gloves on, Georgie,' said Rose, pulling her coat around her ears.

The last of the autumn leaves were being whipped up by the wind along the narrow road ahead of us. A robin sat on the branch of a nearby bush and chirped out what seemed to me to be a very lonely song.

On either side of the road were high hedges which I couldn't see over, but every now and again, there was a gap with a gate revealing large sloping fields which stretched away into the distance. There were more sheep in their fluffy coats, and a herd of large brown-and-white animals called cows, which Rose explained to me was where milk comes from, the real stuff, and beef mince and steak, which then made me hungry just to think of it.

Through one gap in the hedge, I got a very strong smell of something, which Rose explained was the farmyard. A black-and-white dog came out of a large stone house and started barking at us. The ground in front of the house and its surrounding buildings was all churned up with mud.

'That must be the farm,' said Rose. 'Applegate Farm. It's on the map here.'

'Is that where the cows live?' asked George.

'Probably. I expect at night the farmer tucks them up in there.'

I moved quickly past the dog, who didn't sound like he wanted us to hang around. Perhaps he's protecting the sheep, I thought.

We had still not seen a single person or car the whole way. I was beginning to wonder how long the walk was going to take, when the road bent suddenly around a sharp corner beside a small pond with two large white birds floating about on it, next to a stream which flowed down the hill, away from the road. Ahead of us, on either side of the road, were houses of varying sizes, and on the corner was a grey stone church with a simple spire. On the opposite corner, there was what looked like a pub with no signs of life, its sign gently swinging in the wind.

The pub was a lot smaller than the ones I was used to seeing in London, which generally had people spilling out of them at all hours. Next to the church was a sloping hill with a large stone cross standing on it and rows of small gravestones.

'Oh, it's so pretty,' said Rose. 'Look at the little church. I'd stay here with you, Georgie, if I didn't have to go back for work.'

'Where is everyone?' asked George. 'It's scary. I don't like it.'

At the far end of the village, tucked back slightly from the road, was a small cottage with a grey tiled roof covered in moss. There was a small chimney with a thin stream of smoke drifting from it.

'Willow Cottage. This is it,' said Rose.

A tall, thin woman came out of the house and waved at us. She was wearing a grey shirt, buttoned up high, and had her hair tied back in a long pony tail.

'Brenda Eagle,' she said with a small smile. 'You made it. Good journey, I trust. And this must be little George.' She held out her hand for him to shake. George stiffened and went quiet. He shifted awkwardly from foot to foot and didn't say a word.

'Well,' said Miss Eagle. 'Shall we get in, out of the cold?'

'I'm sorry, he's normally fine,' said Rose. 'He's just nervous. Leaving London and everything. It was very sudden. But we're very grateful, of course.'

'And this must be . . .' said Miss Eagle, looking at me.

'Oh, this is Bertie,' said Rose.

I wasn't sure what to make of Miss Brenda Eagle and kept well back, hiding behind Rose's legs.

The cottage was quite dark inside, with wooden beams all up and down the walls and across the ceiling. Miss Eagle herself had to duck as we went through each doorway and into the kitchen. There was a strong smell, which I couldn't quite pinpoint but which reminded me of Rose's cooking and strong-smelling plants, like herbs, although it was much more pungent.

'You can put your things in here for now,' she said, pointing to a small room lined with books and with a small open fire at one end. 'But we'll take some tea first, shall we, and then you can meet the girls, and I'll show George his room.'

I didn't know who the girls were, but I couldn't see or hear anyone else in the house.

'Lapsang or Assam?' Miss Eagle asked Rose as she boiled the kettle on a large cream-coloured range.

'Lapwhat?'

'Lapsang Souchong or ordinary breakfast tea?' she said. 'I had a stockpile already, practically, when the rationing started so I've been all right. I don't know what I'd do without my daily dose.'

Rose settled for ordinary tea, and they sat down around a small wooden table. Miss Eagle poured the tea carefully from a large blue teapot into two fine blue cups. George had a glass of lemonade, which he drank quietly in the corner. I couldn't quite tell whether he was sulking or just feeling shy. Probably both.

Rose tried to make some small talk but was not met with much response from Miss Eagle, who seemed to be a woman of few words and remarkably comfortable with silence. I decided it would be best to keep my head down, so I sat quietly on the cold tiled floor at Rose's feet and eventually dozed off. I woke when Miss Eagle stood up and announced it was time to see the 'girls'.

'They're tough old beasts,' she said, and she showed us through the back door and into a large garden neighbouring a field. 'They don't mind the cold on account of their thick coats. From South America, of course. The Andes.'

In the field were half a dozen animals the like of which I had never seen before. They were rather like sheep but with long necks, longer hair, and taller, with long ears. One was baring its teeth, but they weren't sharp like mine; they were quite blunt, and they were munching away on hay. When the animals saw me, they moved away nervously, but when they saw Miss Eagle, they came over to the fence and leant their heads over. They made a kind of grunting noise, and she stroked their noses.

'What are they?' asked George, suddenly quite interested, but also a little frightened.

'Never seen a llama before?'

'What on earth . . . How peculiar they are,' said Rose. 'Where did you get them?'

'The zoo. When the war broke out. My cousin Joyce is animal mad. She started rescuing all these things, up at the manor. Asked would I take them. She's been distributing animals all over the place. Finding homes for the ones she couldn't find a place for at the big house. And I thought, well, I've got this field at the back and . . . anyway, I've grown rather fond of them.'

'See, Georgie. You find all sorts here,' said Rose.

'Do you want to feed them?' Miss Eagle asked him.

'Yes, please,' he said, rapidly cheering up. She handed him a big bucket of dry food, which he threw into the field, and they began munching on it. Seeing them eating made me realize how hungry I was. I was very relieved when Miss Eagle suggested we go back inside and have tea. They all had tinned salmon and peas, which meant I got a bit of George's salmon slipped to me under the table, as well as some dry dog food.

'Oh, it's getting late,' said Miss Eagle. 'You must all be exhausted. Let's show George his new bedroom.'

We all went upstairs. The room was plain and small but looked comfortable enough. As that was the only spare room, Rose had a bed made up on the downstairs sofa and I slept next to her on the floor.

'My cousin, Joyce's brother, will drive you to the station in the morning. I'm sorry he couldn't pick you up today. I don't have a car, I'm afraid. Up at six, if that's all right?'

Miss Eagle made her way up to bed and the house fell quiet.

'Night night, Bertie,' muttered Rose, half asleep on the sofa. 'He will be all right here, won't he? I have done the right thing, haven't I, bringing him all this way?'

As I lay in the dark, trying to sleep, I heard the sounds of the llamas in the distance as they grunted and settled down to sleep. An owl, somewhere far off, hooted, and there was a strange scratching noise, which might have been a mouse or a large spider, somewhere under the floorboards nearby. I couldn't reply to Rose, but I had the feeling that whatever happened, George's new life was going to be very different from the one he was used to.

The next morning was the hardest part. It was hardly light when a car pulled up outside and honked its horn.

'That'll be Kenneth,' said Miss Eagle.

'Darlings,' said the driver, leaning out of his window. 'Throw your bags in the back there.'

'Have I forgotten anything?' asked Rose, then she put out her arms. 'Come here, Georgie. I'll write to you as soon as I get home.'

'I'll be all right, Mum,' he said, and already he sounded just a little bit more grown up. But maybe he was just trying to make her feel better; I couldn't tell. The car outside honked its horn again. Rose gave George the biggest squeeze she could without suffocating him, and kissed him on the head.

'Be a good boy for Miss Eagle, won't you?'

'Bye, Mum,' he said.

Then he sat down on the floor and grasped my neck and pressed his head into my fur.

'Look after Mum, won't you, Bertie,' he whispered.

I barked back and wagged my tail. I'll do my best, I thought.

We put Rose's small bag in the boot of the car, and I jumped into the back seat. Miss Eagle said a few words to the driver, and I looked out of the window.

George stood there, waving, as we drove away, and he got smaller and smaller. Miss Eagle stood at his side until we turned the corner and they disappeared from view.

'What time's the train?' asked the driver. I recognized the voice, but I couldn't quite place it.

'Six forty-three, I think,' said Rose.

'Plenty of time, then. Up from London, are you? Cousin Brenda mentioned something about taking in an evacuee?'

'Yes, my son, George. We didn't want to, but . . . with the bombing. We lost our house and we really had no choice in the end.'

'I know what it's like. I've got a place in London myself. Been spared so far, but for the grace of God. I still go back when I can. Back and forth for my sister, mostly. And for business.'

'Oh, what business are you in?'

'Antiquities, mainly. Middle East, Greco-Roman, that sort of thing.'

I remembered where I had heard his voice before. At the house in Kensington with Clive. It was the man we had taken the Chinese vases to. His house had been full of cats and dogs, so it wasn't a place I was likely to forget in a hurry.

Rose had no idea about any of this, and Kenneth didn't seem to remember me. Before long, we arrived back at the station. Rose thanked him and said goodbye.

The train pulled in almost straight away. We climbed on board as before, and sat back in a quiet compartment, almost as though we had never been away. Without George, it was very quiet, and Rose wasn't her usual chatty self. She just stared out of the window as the fields and villages whizzed past us. I sat there and stared out of the window with her.

When we arrived back in London, it was as though we had never left. There were the same busy platforms, the same bustling streets with streams of people making their way to work. The same piles of sandbags, and shopkeepers sweeping up broken glass beside bombed-out buildings. None of it had changed, except one thing. George was no longer here.

Rose dropped me off at Victor and Mary's house and ran upstairs to get herself ready for work. She needed to earn money more than ever.

I was relieved to sit down in front of the fire after all the excitement of the train journey. Even though it had all but died out from the night before, there were a few grey coals in the grate giving off just a tiny amount of heat. I watched them burning away to nothing and found myself wishing for anyone, even Princess Wilhelmina, to come in and skulk about nearby, just for some company. But even she was nowhere to be seen. I felt empty inside, as though part of me was missing.

'Nancy will pop in and let you out. I won't be too late,' said Rose, poking her head around the door. 'Life's got to carry on, hasn't it, 'ey, Bertie. Otherwise we'd all go mad.'

CHAPTER TWENTY

'I'm starting a new job,' said Rose, coming in and putting her coat and gloves on the kitchen table. 'With a couple of the girls, up at the munitions works.'

I had no idea what the munitions works was. Rose was unpacking a bag of groceries.

'Had to queue for half an hour to get you these, Bertie, so I hope you like them,' she said, pulling out a piece of newspaper in which there was a large slab of unidentifiable meat. I assumed, from the smell, it was offal. It was a change from biscuits, so I gobbled it up eagerly.

'I'll be working there most evenings now. First shift's tonight. Nights mainly, so it won't interfere with the factory.'

'Isn't that a bit dangerous?' asked Mary. She was laying out a row of knitted blue socks on the edge of her armchair. She had been making them for a collection organized by the local women's volunteer place. They were to be sent to the men in the Navy who needed socks.

'Everyone's got to do war work now. And it's all very well making uniforms and parachutes and that with Dad, but I want to do something more . . . concrete. Something really actually useful. And now that George is away, I've got that bit more time.'

'Glad to hear it. We need all hands on deck,' said Victor. He was putting on a large pair of black boots and a heavy overcoat. He had also now joined the air-raid precautions unit with Frank.

'I'm getting too old for this lark,' he said as he put on his tin hat.

'I'll be leaving shortly, too,' said Mary, 'once I've finished this line.'

Mary also had a new job. Since the explosion at the shelter, she realized she had a particular skill, not only for bandaging up wounds, but also for being a calm presence for people, and organizing them, so she had taken on the role of running a local emergency hospital, which was in ever-greater demand.

I started to think I needed a job now, since everyone else had one. And I wasn't going to spend the night on my own in the house, so I jumped up and barked at Victor to see if he would take me with him.

'You want to come, too, do you, Bertie?'

I wagged my tail, and he put the lead on me. The first stop was Frank's house to pick him up, as the pair of them were on duty together that night.

Although Mary wasn't that keen on Frank and Maude, because she thought they were 'not quite of the right sort', Frank and Victor were becoming quite good friends and often went on their ARP duties together.

As we walked down our old street, it was a shock to see the space where our house had been. In the dark, it looked a sorry sight with just the few bits of brick wall remaining, and a few remnants of our old life – a bucket in the garden, and a scrap of carpet where the hallway had been.

A steady rain had been falling that evening. It had soon become heavy rain, and large puddles had started to form around the piles of rubble still scattered next to the large crater made by the bomb blast. The last bits of wall had been pulled down by the demolition men for safety, and the houses on either side had been shored up with great steel strips to stop them falling down. As we walked away, I was quite relieved to leave the old street behind.

'Gets me every time,' said Victor as we walked into the rainy night. 'And to think Philip hasn't even seen it yet. It'll break his heart.'

'Every day, we think how lucky it was Rose and George, and you, Bertie, weren't in there. Brings it all that much closer,' said Frank.

Victor looked up. 'The rain should hold the bombers off tonight at least.'

When it was rainy and cloudy, the German planes would often just turn back. For the first time in months, there was no air raid that night. After an hour of walking around the area, Frank decided we might as well all go home and have the night off.

When we got back, Princess Wilhelmina was in the lounge, sprawled out in front of the fire. I hadn't spoken to her properly since she had been found by the docks by Nancy. She had become so nervous and skittish since then, always hiding in things and hiding from me. One day, Nancy couldn't find her for hours. She eventually found her sitting on top of the wardrobe, right in the corner, just shaking, a big ball of white fur.

To see her out again in the open was a relief, even if we never had much to say to one another. I sat down next to her, and she flinched a bit, but she didn't move away. On such a damp and chilly night, I think it was just too tempting for her to stay by the warmth of the fire. We watched the flames flickering for a while.

'You know what happened to me, don't you?' she said plainly and quietly out of the blue.

'What? No,' I said.

'When I was away.'

'Tell me,' I said.

I genuinely wanted to know what had caused such a transformation in the poor cat.

'I can't remember it all,' she said. 'I heard that horrible noise and ran out through the window. I got lost. It got dark. I walked for ages. Then all I remember is being chased by this man with green boots. He pulled my legs. It was painful. Caught me and put me in a van. Then more darkness for ages. Then I was sick. Shut up in a cold, damp place. There were other animals there. Crying. There were bars and I got hungry. There were other cats there. I don't know how, but eventually I escaped. Slipped past the other man. The one with the moustache. I found myself on the street, was nearly hit by something. A stick made of fire. I ran away and hid in the darkness. Then . . . well, that's when Nancy found me.'

Blimey, I thought, she had gone from one extreme to the other. First she wouldn't speak to me, now I can't shut her up.

'What's up with Princess?' said Victor. 'She's making a right racket tonight.'

He was about to go up to bed and make the most of the brief respite from air raids.

'She hasn't been the same since her little escapade,' said Mary, padding through the room in her dressing gown with a mug of hot cocoa. 'What bliss. A night in our own bed.'

Princess went quiet again for a while. I was desperate to know more about what had happened to her out there. I had experienced my own fair share of adventures now, some of them quite scary. I'd even seen the dog catchers that day in the cemetery. I wondered if it was the same ones.

'You know the worst thing?' said Princess Wilhelmina after a while. 'I was so . . . excited to be outside at first. Yes, I was terrified. But when I first made it out there, everything was so big and new. It was . . . exciting. There was more to life than just this house.'

I thought about telling her about my own time on the streets, right back to when I was found by Annie in a bag in a bin. About how I kind of knew what she was going through, but I stopped myself. She looked so absorbed in her own memories.

'Then all I found was . . . nastiness,' she said sadly.

Wilhelmina stood up and stretched and went off to sleep in the kitchen without saying another word.

Nobody minded me being in the house any more, so I just stayed right in front of the fire, thinking about what else must have happened to Wilhelmina to make her so down in the dumps with life. I found it hard to sleep that night, although the bombing had stopped. I listened instead to the sounds of the rain hammering on the windows and spilling down into the gutter.

Just before dawn, the front door opened and someone crept into the house. It was Rose. I could smell her perfume.

'You still awake, Bertie?' she whispered. I let out a single quiet bark and wagged my tail on the rug.

'That was exhausting,' she sighed and kicked her shoes off. I still didn't know what her new job was. She went up to the spare room and I nodded back off to sleep until morning.

Rose couldn't have had much more than about three hours' sleep before she and Victor were up again and leaving for the clothes factory.

Mary didn't want to leave me and Princess on our own all day, so since she now had jurisdiction over the local hospital centre, she decided she would take us with her.

'You might be useful,' she said.

She put Princess in her basket and I trotted along beside them. My mind boggled as to how I would be useful. I certainly wasn't much good at tying bandages.

It turned out that the centre had taken over part of a school hall and converted it into a kind of rehabilitation centre, or makeshift hospital, since most of the children from the school had left for the country. Food was being served in the canteen, and inside the wards, there was a mixture of those who were made homeless by the Blitz and those with non-life-threatening injuries or traumas who just wanted a place to be with other people.

There was a row of beds full of people, some bandaged up, some just lying there, and others walking around the ward, or hobbling around with injuries. There was also a group of children listening to stories being read by a young woman in the corner.

'Orphans. Poor little mites,' said Mary.

When they saw me, they all got very excited, and one little boy, with a large gap where he had lost three of his front teeth, ran over and started pulling at my ears.

I let the children play with me for a bit, until the woman reading to them called them back over. Then I caught sight of a man sitting on a chair by the window. I recognized him. He had a flat cap on and was wearing a loose jacket and trousers with his shirt untucked.

'That's Tom,' said Mary. 'Lost his whole family, bless him. I've kind of taken him under my wing. But he helps out here now, too.'

I remembered who it was. The man from the church crypt that was hit directly by a bomb. He had been sitting outside, waiting for his wife and children, but they hadn't come out alive. It was a sobering reminder of why, although I missed him a lot, perhaps it was best that George was no longer in London, for the time being at least.

Before long, everyone was talking about Christmas again. But it was very different from the previous year. Many families were now separated. People had lost their homes, and loved ones were away or had died. There wasn't as much food about now either, and luxuries it had been possible to get the year before were now out of reach for most people.

Although Clive's services were in great demand because he seemed to be able to get anything, even oranges, Rose was reluctant to get too much from him any more. But for Christmas it didn't matter in any case, as we were making plans to travel up to Wiltshire again to see George. Rose had been on the telephone to him as often as possible, and I got to listen in. He seemed to be all right, a little quieter than usual, but he told us how he had been getting involved with the animal sanctuary at the nearby manor house, and how he had thoroughly taken to Miss Eagle's llamas and was now in charge of feeding time.

He said Miss Eagle herself was a little odd but perfectly friendly, and he had got to know the local farmer and even helped out with the milking of the cows. His other news was that he wanted to be a vet now when he grew up instead of a pilot. I couldn't wait to see him again. Hearing his little voice through the telephone was not only miraculous, but also very comforting.

Ever since she had been working extra shifts at the munitions factory, Rose had been saving up for a special present for George. She hadn't known what to get him, but after their conversation, Mary had a brainwave. She had some contacts with doctors from the rehabilitation centre and there was something she thought he might like.

Rose knitted him a stocking for Father Christmas's presents, which, somehow, Nancy had already got. And before long, it was time to head back to the train station, this time loaded up with parcels and suitcases.

The train was a lot busier than it had been last time. I had to squeeze in on the floor, and the compartment we were in was packed with people going to the country to visit relatives and escape London for a few days.

There were soldiers on leave, still in their uniforms. Some were clutching what looked like packages for their sweethearts. And there were other families who looked like they might be visiting evacuee children.

When we left behind the buildings again, and the countryside came back into view, I had to settle for counting sheep on my own, although Nancy had a game where she counted thatched roofs. It didn't really catch on with the others.

'I just love thatched roofs,' she said. 'Don't ask me why. It's my dream. To one day live in a cottage with about a hundred children and a thatched roof. Well, maybe not a hundred but, you know, maybe about six.'

'Heavens,' said Mary.

'Well, you better get busy then,' laughed Rose.

'Aren't you and that Baxter boy engaged?' said Victor. 'Or is that off the cards now?'

'Don't encourage her,' said Mary, who still had her doubts that Eric was good enough for her daughter.

'We're waiting until he can get some leave and I've saved enough money at least for a cake or something,' she said.

'I can make the dress, you know. I've always said that,' said Rose.

'I know. Thank you. But, I don't know. I've hardly seen him in months, anyway.'

'We're here already,' said Rose, looking out of the window.

We gathered up our belongings, and when the train stopped, we all piled out on to the platform. It was even colder than it had been before, and the sun was beginning to go down. A thin layer of frost was forming on everything. It was cold under foot.

'Go carefully. It's icy,' said Victor, taking hold of Mary's arm.

'Someone from the lodgings should be meeting us here,' said Rose.

Parked outside the station on the road there was not a motor car, but instead a large grey van with writing on the side.

'We're not riding in that thing, are we?' asked Mary, looking horrified. 'What is it anyway, the delivery van?'

'Looks like it's from the brewery,' said Victor. 'They might have a decent brew, then. I could do with a pint.'

'You the family staying up at the pub?' called out the small wiry man in blue overalls.

'That's us,' said Victor, heading over to shake the man's hand. 'Will we all fit?'

'If you squeeze up,' he said. 'The dog can go in the back.'

Rose lifted me into the van and the others all jumped up and piled in next to the driver. He didn't say much as he drove, but he whistled very loudly the whole way, and he went extremely fast along the winding road.

Mary gripped on to the edge of the door, which she was pressed up against. She was partly on Victor's lap, and his long legs were squashed up against the front of the van. Nancy and Rose were squashed together next to the driver.

We rounded a corner at quite a speed and the driver screeched to a halt, sending us all flying forwards. Mary gasped and Nancy let out a small scream.

Standing in the middle of the road there was a gathering of tiny horses with swishing tails.

'They're so . . . small,' said Rose. 'What are they for?'

'S'all right, missus,' said the driver. 'Just the forest ponies. They got the run of this place. We'll wait until they move on. Got to respect them, see. It's their land.'

So we sat there in the van for what seemed like ages, waiting for the ponies to finish whatever it was they were doing, which was just standing there, mainly. Eventually, the driver got out of the van.

'Shoo, come along,' he said, gently coaxing them. 'I got people today.' One by one, they trotted slowly off the road and on to a patch of grass. He jumped back in and we were on our way at just the same racing speed as before.

By the time we arrived at the village, Mary had gone quite white from the journey. We parked up outside the little pub. George and Miss Eagle were already there, waiting for us. As soon as I saw George, I ran over, wagging my tail with happiness, and he ran over to me and gave me the biggest hug ever. Rose bent down and hugged us both.

George looked different somehow. He was wearing a huge woollen jumper I didn't recognize and he had a kind of healthy glow in his face. Immediately, when he saw us, he started chatting away.

'Jack says he's going to teach me fishing and rabbiting and all sorts. And I get to feed the llamas and help put the cows to bed.'

The pub was run by a jolly-looking woman with white curly hair, who grew up on a local farm, and her husband, who was from a place called Cornwall and had a thick accent I could hardly understand.

It was Christmas Eve, and a crowd of people were sitting at the bar, laughing and drinking ale. There was a roaring fire in the corner of the room and two tiny white fluffy dogs sitting in an armchair curled up next to one another.

I ran over to greet them, and they jumped off the chair, and we circled each other for a bit, and they barked quite a lot, but playfully. I had to take care because they were so small, but they had fierce little eyes and were very playful and even nipped me once or twice.

'Those are my babies,' said the landlady. 'Had them since pups.'

Eventually, they wore themselves out and jumped back on to the chair. I ran back over to George.

'Let me take you up to your rooms,' the landlady said, and we all trooped up a tiny wooden staircase.

'It's supposed to be haunted, they say, up here,' she said. 'They told us when we took over, but I haven't seen any ghosts yet.'

I did feel something of a strange shiver as we got to the top of the stairs. There were three large paintings of people staring out at us, which made me uneasy. Their eyes seemed to follow me as I walked past.

'Oh, a four-poster bed!' said Mary as the landlady showed them into a room. 'I've always wanted to sleep in a four-poster. Like Queen Elizabeth or something.'

'It's a bed. That's all I care about,' said Victor.

I got the feeling he was keen to get back downstairs and start mingling with the locals.

Rose, Nancy and I were shown into a smaller room at the end of the corridor with two single beds and a tiny window overlooking a small courtyard at the back. It smelt of damp wood and lavender.

'This will suit us just fine,' said Rose, and she began to unpack her things, laying them all out, including a small bar of soap, which she placed on the sink. She even put her slippers out, all ready by the bed. Nancy ran over and sat on the bed by the window.

'It's lovely,' she said. 'Proper old pub, this. Think of all the exciting things that must have happened in here over the years, like back in Victorian times, and even Henry the Eighth and all that. Murder, probably, and all sorts.' She shuddered.

After everyone had unpacked, we had a small tea downstairs, and I was allowed a bit of the little dogs' food, which was some tinned meat.

Victor was soon talking to the locals as though he had lived there all his life. There were two jolly men at the bar, who turned out to be the farmer and his son Jack. The man who had driven us there was busy putting logs on the fire, which he obviously considered to be his personal job. It all felt very homely and cosy, and I hardly wanted to leave when it came time for bed.

Eventually, Mary pulled Victor up, and Rose and Nancy said they were tired, too. George had fallen asleep on a chair already, so Rose carried him back to Miss Eagle's so she could tuck him up in bed.

'I'll take Bertie out,' said Nancy, and before bed, we went through the village for a quick walk.

The small church spire stood out against a bright starry sky. The air was so clean and fresh, I breathed in deeply. I stopped and my ears pricked up. Something rustled in a bush. I jumped but then realized, from the smell, it was probably just a fox. We had them in London, too, but I usually avoided them. The ground was already twinkling with frost, and when I breathed out, a cloud of steam came out of my mouth and nostrils. It was strangely quiet, and for the first time in months I felt my bones and my whole body begin to relax. I felt an enormous weight of relief when I realized there would be no air raid that night.

CHAPTER TWENTY-ONE

It was strange waking up in a new place, and at first I didn't know where I was when I opened my eyes. I looked around and saw Rose's slippers, a spider under the bed, and a skirting board I didn't recognize.

I jumped up and looked out of the window, and then I remembered where I was. It was very early, but Nancy was already up. She always got excited about Christmas, even though she was a grown-up.

Instead of having Christmas in the pub, which was closed so that the owners could have a day off, we walked straight up the road to Miss Eagle's house.

'Give George his thing,' said Nancy, clapping her hands, barely able to contain her excitement.

Miss Eagle showed us all into her living room first, and poured everyone a glass of champagne and orange juice, even George.

'Ooh, posh!' said Rose.

'Give him his stocking,' said Nancy. Rose pulled a long blue stocking, which was bulging with presents, out of her bag and handed it to George.

'Look what Father Christmas brought us for you last night.'

George grinned and began pulling out the things one by one, first the bars of chocolate, and the orange from Clive, and two new toy aeroplanes to replace the ones he had lost in the air raid. Finally, it was time for his main present.

'It's from all of us,' said Rose.

He took hold of the package, which was wrapped in brown paper with silver stars stuck on it.

'I stuck the stars on,' said Nancy, then she whispered to Rose, 'oh gosh, I hope he likes it.'

George spent quite a while unwrapping the paper, which had been tied up with string quite tightly. Inside was a grey box.

'What is it?' he asked cautiously. 'Looks serious.'

'Open it,' said Nancy, clapping her hands.

He lifted the lid, and inside was a strange object. It was a round disc with two long cables sticking out.

'What *is* it?' asked George, still none the wiser.

'You do it like this,' said Mary, and she lifted it carefully out of the box while George was transfixed.

'Let's try it out on Bertie, shall we? Lie down, Bertie. Roll over,' called Mary, and I rolled over on to my back, thinking she was going to play with me. But instead, she put the two long things into her ears and lay the flat disc on my chest. I wriggled a bit and then decided it wasn't doing any harm so lay still, wondering what on earth she was doing.

'Well, he's definitely alive,' she laughed. 'Here, George, you have a listen.'

George took the object and put the things in his own ears and listened intently.

'I can hear something,' he exclaimed. 'What, though?'

'It's Bertie's heart beating,' said Mary.

'We thought you might like it. It's a proper stethoscope, like the ones real vets use to check animals' hearts,' said Victor.

'Oh,' said George, a little unsure what to make of it at first.

Then Miss Eagle had an idea.

'Let's take it outside and see if the girls are fit and healthy.'

So we all went outside, and Miss Eagle helped George to check the llamas' hearts were working.

'They're alive,' he said. 'It's so loud! It's amazing.'

The llamas soon got bored of the game and found better things to do, like eating. Miss Eagle told us all it was time for a Christmas treat.

Everyone put their warmest winter clothes on, and we walked up the road and out the other side of the village, where we'd never been. Instead of farmland, this way there was rougher ground with tall trees with spines on them, which were still green even though it was winter.

'Not far,' said Miss Eagle as we walked up the hill and out of the village. A large house came into view. It was probably the biggest house I had ever seen in my whole life. It had several chimneys on the roof, all with smoke coming out of them, and lots of land all around it, with hedges and trees, and even a pond with water spurting out of it and a naked lady standing in the middle of it, although I realized pretty quickly she must be made of stone, otherwise she would have got very cold, standing there.

'This is wonderful,' said Mary. 'Who lives here?'

'My cousin,' said Miss Eagle, smiling, 'and she's invited us all for Christmas dinner.'

'Oh, good lord. Are you sure? All of us? Can she manage?' asked Rose.

'It's all decided,' said Miss Eagle.

'Well, that's wonderful. Thank you!' said Mary with a half skip.

As we approached the house, I had another shock. There was a huge creature right in front of me. I growled. I couldn't tell what it was. It didn't move.

'Silly Bertie. He thinks it's a real bear,' laughed George, and he growled at me just like a bear. As I approached, I realized it wasn't a creature at all; it was made of leaves.

'These hedges are shaped like animals!' said Nancy, running over to look at them. 'How do you do it?'

'My cousin, Kenneth. He's a dab hand with the hedge cutters,' said Miss Eagle. 'Doesn't let the gardener near them. Insists on doing them all himself.'

Once I skirted around the hedge animals, which I still didn't quite trust, I ran about, this way and that way. I had never seen so much open space in all my life. There was hardly a building in sight, just the village down at the bottom of the hill with its church spire poking above the green, spiny trees, and fields as far as I could see into the distance.

'Hello, hello,' said a woman in a long purple smock dress. 'Come in, all of you.'

Inside the house, it was even more grand than I could have imagined from the front.

In the entrance hall, there was a huge staircase, and the floor was decorated with black-and-white tiles, intricately formed into patterns which sent me dizzy from looking at them.

'We're so sorry you couldn't stay here,' said the woman who showed us in. Her hair was tied up in a pink scarf and she was carrying a tiny kitten in her arms.

'The house is simply full to the gills,' she said. 'But we love it. We're so pleased you could come. When Brenda told us about George and that you were coming all this way from London, I thought, how wonderful! The more the merrier!'

She was holding the kitten rather casually, as though she was used to having an animal of some kind in her arms at all times. It didn't look more than a few weeks old, so I decided to keep my distance in case it was frightened.

'Oh, gorgeous,' said Nancy. 'A kitten. I love anything baby. It's the eyes.'

'Plenty more where this little one came from,' said the woman, who introduced herself as Joyce.

'My brother's in the kitchen. He'll be through later. He always insists on cooking at Christmas. Well, standing behind Cook and orchestrating proceedings, anyway. Very particular about his stuffing. Do come through for the guided tour.'

'You live here, do you?' asked Victor, hovering about as if he wasn't sure whether he should remove his shoes.

'Oh, leave them on,' said Joyce. 'We gave up trying to keep this place clean years ago. Yes. The old manor. Since dear Pa shuffled off this mortal coil, what is it, ten years ago now, Kenneth and I have been running the old place. But it does get harder. People think we're stinking rich, and we are in a way, I suppose, but really it's all tied up in this. Bricks and mortar. We haven't got a bean between us. Had to lay off half the staff a few years ago. That was awful. Letting them go. Grow most of our own food here on the estate now. But can't complain. Just look at the place. Could never sell it, of course. Not for all the tea in Yorkshire.'

Joyce showed us through to a room she called the library. Inside, there was a crowd of cats and dogs.

'Hope you don't mind. Well, of course you don't. You've got your own little chap,' she said, looking at me. There was a young woman in the library, dressed in black and white, trying to maintain order among the animals.

'This is dear old Lucy. She's been with us since she was a girl. Her mother was my maid. Known her since she was knee-high to a cricket.'

The young woman curtsied, then ran over and separated a nervous-looking greyhound from a very excitable spaniel.

'How did you all get here?' I asked, running over to the spaniel, who seemed the friendliest.

'My owner just disappeared,' answered the spaniel. 'One day I went downstairs and the whole family was gone. The house was all quiet. I barked and I barked and it was days before someone broke into the house and found me. I was taken to a kennel and then here.'

'How many of you are there?' I asked. I was tempted to stay; it looked a lot of fun. But I also had fun with the humans.

'I've no idea. Some come and go. Find new owners. Joyce looks after us all,' said the spaniel, before he ran off and skidded along the floor to catch a ball that Lucy had thrown him.

'Lucy's been an absolute angel with the animals,' said Joyce. 'This lot are about to be sent out to the kennels. The really little ones get bedrooms to keep them warm.' She was still holding on to the kitten, who was now wriggling to try and get inside her shirt sleeve.

Once Joyce had given us a grand tour of the downstairs, it was time for everyone to sit down for dinner.

George insisted that I be allowed to sit with the humans, rather than get put with the other cats and dogs. Although I would have liked to have a play with them, I did get the benefit of treats from the table. And, boy, were there treats.

Joyce's brother, Kenneth, came in, looking very red-faced and sweaty. He was carrying various jugs and plates, and was followed by two young men in suits, along with a woman I assumed must be the cook, who was equally sweaty and was carrying a large plate with a big bird on it.

'The goose,' Kenneth announced with a flourish of his hand. 'Darlings. Welcome, welcome to our humble abode. Or the madhouse, as we call it these days. Do tuck in.'

At that moment, I could see from Nancy's expression that she had recognized Kenneth as the man from the house in Kensington. She sank down in her seat. But it didn't seem like he remembered her.

On the table were potatoes, all kinds of vegetables, even ones I had never seen before, and a large plate of sausages wrapped in bacon.

'One of the benefits of rearing one's own,' said Joyce. 'Although this is nothing compared to how it used to be in the good old bad old days, as Pa would say. He'd cook up half the farm if he got the chance at Christmas. Not so now. We don't want to be . . . ostentatious. With the war and everything.'

All around the room, there were paintings which I assumed were family portraits of men and women, in various poses, who all had the same pointy nose and chin as Joyce and her brother. It must be the family face, I thought.

Far from having the austerity Christmas we were all expecting, we ended up having the most lavish feast we had ever seen. Joyce, Kenneth and Miss Eagle, or Brenda, as everyone was now calling her, also had a little routine which seemed to be their Christmas thing, during which they sang a song, and all three of them acted out little scenes and the others had to guess what they were doing.

This had everyone in fits of laughter. After a few glasses of wine, Victor started singing, and before the end of the day he and Mary, Rose and Nancy were giving their own renditions of all the songs they knew. There was 'Roll Out the Barrel', followed by 'The Lambeth Walk', and in the end everyone was singing, and I was howling away as best I could, although not necessarily in tune.

When I looked over at Rose, though, she seemed a little sad. She was singing all right enough, but she had this faraway look in her eye, as though she wasn't quite all there.

Finally, Mary, who had a very nice voice, sang a song she had learnt as a little girl. 'Ave Maria', the words went, and everyone was quiet while she sang. I started thinking about the war again, and Philip, and wondered where he was.

'Your father would have loved this,' said Rose softly to George when Mary had finished and everyone clapped.

Rose picked George up and put him on her lap, even though he was almost too big for that now, and she rocked him gently in her arms.

It was time to leave. Joyce and Lucy went to feed the animals, and the young men in suits came scurrying back in and removed all the plates.

As everyone was saying their goodbyes, I heard Kenneth telling Victor something in a serious voice, and I couldn't help overhearing.

'Darned awful shame,' he said. 'Ransacked the place. Broke a window at the back. Took the small pieces. The ones they could shift quickly, anyway. Not the big ones. But they did get away with two of my best Chinese vases. I was hoping to sell those to prop up this place. But what can you do? It's empty half the time these days. And the thing is, the looters know it.'

I looked at Nancy and she looked at me, and I wondered if we were thinking the same thing.

'Damn bloody shame,' said Kenneth, clapping his hands. 'I'd give my right eye to catch the buggers.'

CHAPTER TWENTY-TWO

Soon it was time to leave, say goodbye to George and head back to London.

It was an emotional send-off, as we had all just got used to being with him again. But Miss Eagle had kindly arranged a distraction by offering to take him up to the manor house again the next day so he could try out his stethoscope on the animals there like a real vet, which he was very excited about, and which made it easier to leave him.

The train on the way back was bustling with people returning from trips to the countryside. Nancy was strangely quiet, though, and as soon as we got back, she said she had to go and meet Clive.

Rose had to do a shift at the munitions factory, and, since the Blitz had started up again, Victor and Mary set about straight back to their war work, so I ended up staying with Nancy.

We walked briskly to a pub, where Clive often met a lot of his 'clients'. As we entered, he was sitting in a corner with two men. I stopped and growled and hung back. There at the table was Mad Carpet Tony.

'What's wrong, Bertie?' said Nancy, pulling me in.

One of the men, the one who I had seen before, who looked like a little rat, was twitching nervously and raising his hands defensively. Tony was sitting very upright in his chair with his hands on the table. He wasn't saying a word but was just staring at the man with an intimidating look in his eyes.

One of the other men appeared to have a weapon or something in his pocket, and he was getting ready to bring it out. The third man was smiling a sickly kind of smile. And next to them, Clive was sitting silently with his head down.

Nancy hung around by the door, and when Clive looked up, she managed to catch his eye. He made his excuses and left the group.

'What are you doing here?' he whispered angrily.

'Happy Christmas to you too.'

'Sorry, I mean, it's just, there's a big deal going down. Sensitive. Tony's on edge today. It could kick off at any moment.'

'Look, I need to talk to you,' said Nancy, sounding more serious than I had ever heard her. 'I need to know something. What I'm involved in . . .'

'All right. Meet me here in about an hour. Tony'll be gone. We can talk then.'

Nancy took me around the block for a stroll, but the wind was bitingly cold, so we stopped off for a cup of tea at a small cafe. When we went back, Clive was sitting on his own.

'What's all this, then?' he asked.

'I could be wrong. I hope I am, but I need to know. In Wiltshire. With George. We met this man. That man. The one from the big house up in Kensington.'

Clive had a blank look.

'I've no idea what you're talking about, woman.'

'The sculptures. The man with those dogs and cats. Remember?'

'Oh, right. Yes, what about him?'

'We saw him. He's got this big house. We had Christmas dinner there. It was incredible. Goose. They've got their own pigs.'

'You dragged me out of a meeting to tell me about your Christmas dinner?'

'No, sorry. It was something he said, as we were leaving, about his house being looted. Those Chinese vases. Nicked. Clive, it wasn't . . . look, I'm not accusing anyone, but . . . do you know anything?'

He paused and ran his fingers through his hair.

'That's not my end of things. I keep well clear of all that stuff.'

'But do you know? Because I couldn't bear it if I thought we . . . I had something to do with it.'

'You knew what this was when you got involved. Don't play innocent now,' he said, slamming his pint down on the table.

'I knew there was the odd bit of stuff Tony's lads had sneaked past customs. I didn't know we were dealing in burglary now,' said Nancy, looking Clive directly in the eyes.

'All right,' he said, backing down a bit. 'All I know is since we delivered those vases, Tony's been watching that house. Had some of the lads keeping an eye out. Said there was a lot of valuable stuff in there.'

'But he only knows that because we went in there!' said Nancy, getting exasperated.

'I had nothing to do with no looting. And you ought not be worrying yourself about it either,' he said, standing up. 'Come on, get your coat. I'll walk you home.'

As we were leaving, I caught sight of one of Tony's men. It was the man with the small moustache, standing around the corner by the bar. I couldn't help thinking he may just have heard every word.

Rose hadn't heard from Philip for months and was starting to get concerned. But she finally received a letter from him just after Christmas.

He said he was alive and well in France, and she was very relieved, because he also assured her she had absolutely done the right thing, sending George to Wiltshire, and that he was so sorry to hear about the house but that she shouldn't worry. They would sort something out when he was back. And he was just relieved they were all alive.

'It's like it's not real any more, Bertie,' said Rose as she put the letter down. 'I'm starting to forget things. Silly things like his smell. I can't remember what he smells like. I can't explain it. I just want him back.'

I tried to comfort her as best I could, but nothing I could do would bring Philip home.

Over Christmas, there had been a brief let up in the air raids, but it wasn't long before it all started up again. It was nearly the end of the year, but people were not in a celebratory mood. Instead, all around London, people began to do more and more to help with the effort on what they were now calling the 'home front'.

One morning over breakfast, Nancy came in and announced she was no longer working with Clive. She wanted to do something more useful.

'I'm going to join the auxiliary fire service,' she said, out of the blue.

'You're what?' asked Victor, almost choking on his coffee.

'I should be doing something. I can't just sit here and watch this city being obliterated, brick by brick.'

'I understand women have got to muck in,' said Victor, 'but there is a limit. There are some things the fairer sex ought to just steer well clear of. And I'm afraid firefighting is one of them. It's just too dangerous.'

'One of the girls from school. Mavis. She's doing it,' said Nancy. 'I bumped into her down the market yesterday. She says they're desperate for more volunteers. And that women are doing all sorts now. Even anti-aircraft guns.'

'Well, that really is the dog's biscuit,' said Victor, giving up. 'I don't know what it's all coming to any more.'

'If you want to do this thing, dear, just make sure you're careful, won't you?' said Mary, who was herself taking on more responsibility as the war went on.

I was sitting by the fire with Wilhelmina, who I don't think had forgiven me for going to Wiltshire with everyone and leaving her with the next-door neighbour, an elderly lady who wanted the company. Mary didn't think she would handle the train ride, but it sounded like she'd had a rather boring Christmas compared to ours.

I tried to get some more information about her adventures, but she was having none of it and was thoroughly sulking and ignoring me, so I wandered off to see if there were any scraps left over from anyone's breakfast.

In the afternoon, Nancy went for her fire service training at a local centre, and that very night she was called out to be on hand, and keep watch, while they were diffusing an unexploded bomb near a factory that made aero-plane parts down by the docks. She came home utterly exhausted. But it seemed she was good at the job and was praised by the team for her hard work.

Now that George was gone, and almost everyone was involved in war work, we didn't bother going to the shelter together any more. Rose had a separate shelter near the munitions factory, and there was a shelter right next to where Mary was running the makeshift hospital.

Victor and Frank and the air-raid precautions team all ducked into a public shelter if and when it got really bad, but generally they stayed out doing what they could to help the injured, put out firebombs when they saw them, or diffuse unexploded bombs with the help of the disposal unit.

When I got tired, Rose said I could stay with her rather than go on air-raid duties, as she insisted she didn't want to leave me at home alone. But she had to sneak me in under her coat in case I was spotted by her boss. As she worked, I sat at her feet.

The factory was based in a large open warehouse. In peacetime it had made motor car parts. Now it produced and then filled metal objects with a thing called cordite. Rose explained that the objects were for the men at the front and in the planes, so that they were able to fight the enemy. It was a very important job; without it, we might lose the war.

Rose sat next to a woman called Caroline, who hardly ever stopped talking. Despite the din and smell of the factory, she told Rose everything about her life. Her terrible boyfriend, Malcolm, who had proposed to her just before the war and then left her just days later and gone off with the woman who sells the ice cream at the pictures. About how she once nearly died on a holiday to Margate when there had been a storm on the beach and the water had swept her clean off her feet.

'Enough about me,' she said after her speech had ended. 'Tell me about you.'

'Not much to tell, really,' said Rose. 'I met my Philip at the bus stop, if you can believe it! The buses were all cancelled for some reason. I can't remember why. And you know how people start talking when things go wrong. We just got chatting. I wasn't that keen on him to begin with, actually,' she laughed.

The foreman of the factory came past and started pointing out things they should be doing differently. I tried to keep as still as possible so he wouldn't see me. I didn't want to get Rose in trouble.

'And no chatting, girls,' he said as he walked up and down the aisles with his hands behind his back. 'Mistakes cost lives.'

Rose and Caroline looked at each other and suppressed their smiles. As soon as he was out of sight, they started talking again but in more hushed tones.

'I thought he was a bit rude at first. Philip,' continued Rose. 'But then I realized he's just shy. After that, we would see each other often at the bus stop. And eventually he plucked up the courage to take me out to a dance. Although he wasn't much of a dancer. Kept treading on my feet, actually. But I had told him how much I liked it, so he obliged me. Then . . .' She paused and realized she may be saying too much to this complete stranger.

But Caroline seemed to be one of those who tell you so much, it makes you feel like saying a lot, too, so she carried on in a low voice, 'I got pregnant with little Georgie and . . . of course, then we had to get married. I mean, we wanted to anyway. Maybe not quite that soon. And I was lucky because Mum and Dad loved Philip as soon as they met him. Dad approved of his line of work, making furniture. And then when little Georgie was born, we never looked back.' She began to look sad as she thought about Philip.

The air-raid siren went and I got the prickly feeling in my back that I always got when I heard that ghostly wailing. It was a kind of mixture of sickness and tension and fear. But I was amazed that all the women in the factory just carried on as though nothing had happened.

'Only if the planes come directly over do we go to the shelter,' said Caroline to a new girl who had got up to start leaving her station. 'Work must go on.'

Someone from outside came in and said they thought they heard planes overhead, so the foreman came back out and told everyone they could put their things down. They all started making their way out. There wasn't much panic, although a couple of the new girls were getting a bit worried that it had been left so late before they were allowed to leave.

Rose picked me up and put me under her coat so nobody would make a fuss about having a dog down there. And I made sure to keep quiet. The shelter was a few hundred yards away under a grand building called the Town Hall. By the time we got there, it was full of people and completely airless. But we weren't down there long, anyway, because almost straight away the all-clear sounded and we all went straight back to the factory.

'Every minute you're not in here, girls,' said the foreman, 'is one less shell for our boys at the front.'

The siren had been a false alarm. Someone said it had been one of our own planes, not the Germans, and there was no bombing that night after all. As he walked past us, the foreman noticed something sticking out of Rose's coat. It was my tail. And he wasn't happy.

'You brought that creature in?' he said, horrified. 'Are you trying to get us all killed?' His face was right up close against Rose's nose as he spoke, and I could see her wincing.

'But it's just for a night,' she said meekly. 'I didn't want to leave him on his own, and the poor thing is exhausted.'

'No animals of any kind allowed on the factory floor,' he said. 'Under any circumstances. You'll have to take him outside right away. What the hell was she thinking?' he muttered as he walked away, but he quickly forgot about me, as he was very soon telling someone else off about something.

Rose carried me outside.

'Sorry, Bertie,' she said. 'I didn't mean for you to end up out here on your own.'

I lay down and put my head on my paws. Rose went back in and I spent the rest of the night on the floor outside the factory. It was freezing cold and a clear, frosty night. Across town, I could see searchlights flashing across the sky.

Just as it was getting light, Rose came out at the end of her shift. We walked home as the sun was coming up over the buildings.

'I'm sorry, Bertie,' she said. 'I tried to give you a night off. I think tonight you'll have to stay at home or go with the others.'

Over breakfast, everyone compared notes about their night shifts. Nancy had been busy training at the fire station, as there had been no bombing.

'Perhaps you can take Bertie with you tomorrow?' Rose suggested. 'He might be useful.'

CHAPTER TWENTY-THREE

Nancy got dressed up in her new fire service clothing, and seemed almost excited to be doing something that was usually only done by men. She was a little nervous, having heard how many firefighters had already been injured or killed doing their dangerous job. But she seemed more determined than ever to do something useful.

'Come on, Bertie,' she said as we left the house. 'You can be the head of the newly established canine fire department.'

We walked through the streets to a large shed containing a row of trucks equipped for fighting fires. They had ladders on them and long pipes snaking this way and that. We didn't get in one of those, though. Instead, we were told to jump in a nearby plain grey van.

'Back for more?' said a woman who was already sitting in the back of the van as we jumped in. 'Maybe we'll see some action tonight. This break in the bombing can't go on for ever.'

'I brought some moral support this time,' said Nancy, and I hopped in beside them.

Another woman jumped in the front seat, and we headed off towards central London.

Just after dark, the air-raid warning went, and not long after that, a swarm of planes flew over. I still wasn't used to the buzzing noise they made and the insistent way it grated on the nerves.

'That doesn't look good,' said Nancy as we watched them fly over. A woman on a motorcycle stopped to talk to the driver and then wheeled around and sped off.

'She says it's getting bad up by the city,' said the driver, calling back to us. 'They're asking everyone they can to head up that way.'

As we drove, we saw incendiary bombs start to fall, and every now and again, the van would stop so we could run out and extinguish them. There was one at a library and another right by a church, which had erupted into a small fire. I wasn't needed much to help with this, as it was all quite quick; Nancy and her team got hold of their stirrup pumps and tackled the fires with ease. A young man on a motorbike pulled alongside us and spoke to the driver.

'You're needed up by St Paul's,' he said urgently. 'They're calling everyone that way now.'

He hopped back on his bike and drove off. The driver turned the van around and we went somewhere I didn't recognize, down a small cobbled road, and spoke to some men, who filled the back of the van, all around us, with containers.

'Fuel,' said the young woman to Nancy. 'To keep the pumps going. It's going to be a bad one tonight.'

We headed back towards a more built-up area, and people were still making their way to the shelters. As firebombs were falling all around, people were starting to panic. Others were getting in their cars to get away from the centre of town.

'Lucky it's a Sunday,' said Nancy. 'And Christmas holidays. Can you imagine what it would be like trying to get all the people out of here on a normal weekday?'

I could smell and eventually see that fires were starting up all over the city. First there was the pungent smell of burning plastic and metal and wood. Then I could see the smoke and flames, glowing above the buildings. Then, eventually, I could feel the heat as we approached the actual fires.

'This is worse than we thought,' said the driver, wiping her forehead, which was already starting to sweat even though it was mid-winter. We drove to the next water pump, where the firemen were spraying as much as they could on the fires and struggling to handle the vast pumps. Instead of going out, though, some of the fires just seemed to be getting hotter.

'We're running out of water,' yelled one man over by a large pump. There was a lot of activity as people rushed to try and get more water from the river.

I was able to make myself useful by running between the firefighters attacking the blaze and Nancy and her crew, who had the fuel containers. I would let them know where they were needed and one of the women would run up with the containers. Then we would move on to the next area.

As the night went on, the fires began to join up into one large inferno. It was beginning to look like we would never bring it under control. Then everyone started talking about one thing. The cathedral. I knew it from my walks with Annie. I knew it was important to people in London. And saving it was fast becoming the main priority that night.

We jumped in the van again and sped through the narrow streets. As we turned a corner, I saw the huge dome silhouetted in the darkness. All around it were flames and smoke and glowing orange. In the middle of it all was St Paul's.

The van parked up around the corner and we jumped out. I moved between the groups of firefighters, checking who needed more of the fuel. I was even able to carry the odd empty bucket or pump. Pretty soon, we had also run out of water, and Nancy and I did what we could to help the firefighters with their pumps.

A little way down the road, one building was so wild and hot and orange with fire that it began to collapse. There was a group of firefighters right beside it, and they couldn't get away in time before the whole wall fell down on to them. There was nothing we could do to stop it. It was far too hot to get anywhere near.

'One's landed on the dome,' someone shouted.

A firebomb had hit the cathedral. There was a rush to bring the hoses as close as possible. Luckily, the incendiary dislodged itself and someone smothered it with a sandbag.

After several hours, the bombers eventually moved away. The fires were far from out, but St Paul's was still standing. The men who had been under that collapsed building were nowhere to be seen.

When Nancy and I got home, Nancy's face was black with soot and smoke from the fires, and my eyes were streaming and sore from the heat. My throat felt dry, and my body was aching. From our street, we could still see the smoke rising up into the sky in thick clouds above

London. Rose wasn't back from work yet. And when she wasn't back by lunchtime, I started to worry.

'Do you think we should nip down to Woolwich and just check she's OK?' asked Mary, pouring out some tea.

'I'm sure the girl's fine. Probably stopped off for a cuppa on the way back,' said Victor.

But Mary couldn't stop worrying.

'Why don't Bertie and I go down there? Just for peace of mind,' said Nancy, slurping down the last of her drink.

Mary agreed, and we took the bus to the riverside where the factory was. But when we arrived, I knew things weren't right. On the street, right by the factory, there was a huge crater, and the buildings either side had collapsed in on themselves.

'We didn't get an air raid,' said one woman, who was helping to shovel the rubble out of the way. 'It was an unexploded bomb. Must have been sitting there for a week or so, undetected, and chose last night to go off, of all nights.'

'There was no one in the shop, I don't think, but a few girls from the factory were passing,' said another woman nearby.

Rose was nowhere to be seen. Then I caught sight of her friend from the factory, Caroline. She was concentrating on lifting bricks one by one and putting them in a pile. I ran over and barked at her.

'Oh, it's Bertie. Rose's little dog. Hello, boy,' she said and patted me on the head.

'Are you a friend of my sister's? I'm Nancy.'

They shook hands.

'What's happened?' Nancy asked.

'Rose went on ahead,' Caroline said. 'I had a few things to do. Then, by the time I got here, there had been this explosion . . . the road was already completely blocked. Passers-by said there were a few people near here when it happened. It was in the early hours. I'm not sure if anyone was hurt. Did Rose not come home last night, then?'

'No,' said Nancy, sounding worried. 'She might have gone to the market, I suppose.'

But she didn't seem convinced. I began to dig down into the rubble with my paws. It felt almost pointless, but I had to do something. I whined and kept digging. After a while, I felt more certain someone was under there. There was dust flying all around me, and then I smelt it. A familiar scent. It was Rose's perfume. I was sure of it. She was somewhere down there. But I couldn't let anyone know, so I just kept digging and barking.

After a while, people came around and joined me to see what I was up to. The woman with the shovel helped shift the loose plaster, and Caroline and Nancy began to move the larger bricks. I saw something blue. It was the colour of Rose's uniform. Then I saw some human hair. I barked loudly. Everyone crowded around.

'Oh my God,' said Nancy. 'It's my sister.'

CHAPTER TWENTY-FOUR

Rose's body was completely covered in rubble. She wasn't moving. Nancy ran over.

'Rose,' she cried and knelt down.

People began to move the rubble away from the area. We could see her face. Her eyes were closed. She had a small bruise on the top of her head.

'Is she all right?' asked a woman in the crowd.

'Don't move her,' said someone else. 'Might have broken her neck.'

Once the worst of the bricks were cleared away, they lifted two large planks from on top of Rose.

'Rose, can you hear me?' said Nancy. Rose didn't move.

Eventually, people were able to lift her up and out, but because of the awful night in the city, there was no ambulance available. Instead, Caroline fetched the door of the shop which had fallen in. They lay Rose on the door and carried it to a nearby van, whose driver had offered it up as transport.

'Let's get her to my mother's hospital,' said Nancy as they lifted the door in and placed Rose down on the floor between the narrow seats. I jumped in the van beside Rose and licked her hand. I looked at her face and saw she wasn't moving. I couldn't bear the thought that she might be gone, like Annie.

Then her eyes twitched just a little. I waited, and then they opened.

'Oh, what a lovely dog,' she mumbled, and she tried to sit up.

'Did she say something?' asked Nancy, jumping up.

'Such a lovely little dog . . .' said Rose very quietly.

'Rose. It's me. Nancy. Don't you know who that is?' she said. 'It's Bertie.' Nancy took hold of Rose's hand. 'We're taking you to Mum's. To the emergency centre. It's going to be all right.'

'That sounds wonderful,' mumbled Rose. She had a vacant look in her eyes. 'Did you pack the chocolate?'

By the time we got to the hospital, Rose was drifting in and out of sleep. They carried her to where Mary was standing on one of the wards with a clipboard in her hand.

'Oh my goodness,' she said when she saw us. 'What's happened?'

'She got trapped after a blast down by the docks,' said Nancy. 'Might be a head injury. She was trapped right under the wall. Bertie found her.'

'Come on, dear. Let's get you down here,' said Mary, remaining calm and efficient.

They lay Rose on an empty bed in the main hall. There were a few people in beds nearby who looked in a lot of pain. There was a man whose eye was covered up; he had marks all across his face. Next to him was a woman, sitting up in bed, whose hands were all bandaged up and who had a large red mark on her face.

'Burns,' said Mary. 'From last night. We had so many in. It was horrendous.'

'You're all being so kind,' Rose slurred. Mary caught Nancy's eye and whispered. 'Does she not know who we are?'

'I think she's just in shock.'

'If there's anything I can do to help, you just have to ask,' said Rose, trying to sit up and looking around the room at the other patients. 'That poor lady over there has had such a terrible time. Look at her poor hands.'

'I think I should call the doctor,' said Mary, and she went away for a while, then came back with an older man with white hair and glasses. He had a stethoscope like the one George got for Christmas around his neck. He checked Rose's heart, and felt her pulse. Then he asked her a few questions.

'Do you know where you are, Rose?'

'Hospital, of course. These kind ladies brought me here. Though I can't for the life of me remember why.'

After he had finished talking to her, he took Mary aside.

'She does appear to have had a knock to the head of some kind. Even when there's no injury on the outside, you can't always tell what's going on inside with a knock like that.'

'Is it serious?' asked Mary.

'Hard to tell at this stage. We should keep her in. Keep an eye on her. Just in case.'

I lay down by the bed with my head on my paws. I was sad that Rose didn't know who I was. I hoped she would remember us all again soon.

After a few hours, I left the hospital with Nancy and we went to buy some groceries. Across the road from the shop, a large brown dog was sitting next to a pile of rubbish. It was looking very ill and thin, and sniffing around along the roadside, eating anything it could find, even bits of paper. I had been hungry, I thought, but never that hungry. I could see her ribs sticking through her fur. I wanted to go over and do something, but Nancy was in a hurry to get back to Rose.

As we were about to leave, a green van pulled up alongside and two men got out. One of them had on a pair of overalls and a pair of green boots. The other had a moustache. I had seen him before. He looked over at Nancy. His eyes narrowed. She didn't see him.

'Get this one, Reg,' said the man with the boots. 'Come around the side so we can catch her.'

'What? Oh, right. Yes,' he replied.

They managed to chase the dog into a corner and pick her up. But she still had a bit of energy left, and she wriggled free and jumped down. She started to howl. Then she lay flat on the ground and started shaking with nerves.

'That poor animal,' said Nancy. 'So many strays around now.'

They finally got the dog and threw her in the back of their van. I could see her face through the window as they drove away. I could also see the man with the moustache. He had his eyes on Nancy as we walked away.

The next day, the doctor said Rose was well enough to come home. But she still had no idea who we were or where she was, so we had to keep an eye on her.

Nancy kept explaining everything – who we were, who she was – but it was no use. Rose couldn't remember any of it; it was very frustrating for her. Nancy showed her some family photographs and Rose got quite upset because she had no recollection of them. Even of her wedding day.

Rose also found the air raid that night extremely scary, as she had no recollection of any of the previous ones. When the warning went, she said she could remember that it meant something bad but not what, and she started to breathe very heavily, and then she got into quite a panic. I sat next to her when that happened, and she stroked my fur; it seemed to help her.

On New Year's Eve, there was none of the celebrating that normally takes place among people at that time of year. We did hear some music drifting out of some nearby basements as people put on a brave face, determined to keep up their spirits. But for us, the night pretty much came and went without much ceremony.

'What shall we do? About George?' Nancy said to Mary. 'It's New Year and Rose doesn't even know what day it is. We'll have to telephone and tell him, but he'll be so upset if she doesn't remember him. He won't understand what it all means, will he?'

'Well, we can't bring him back. If anything happened to him, Rose would never forgive us,' said Mary.

'I agree. We can't do it while she's like this. She's not capable of making a decision on her own about something like that. Not yet.'

The next day, Clive came over to say hello and give Rose some chocolates.

'Oh, what a lovely young man,' Rose said. 'How kind.' But she didn't seem to know who he was or why he was bringing her chocolates.

'I heard you're not well,' said Clive.

'I'm fine. I don't know these kind people who have been looking after me. They say my house was destroyed! Can you imagine? I don't know. I just don't know any more.' She started to get upset and confused again, which was very distressing to watch, as we couldn't do anything to help her except be there. Nancy explained again to Rose that they were her own family, but she didn't seem to be able to retain any new information for long.

Everybody said it was a mad idea to bring George back to London, that Philip would never forgive them if anything happened, but the more I saw Rose like that, the more I had the feeling that if Rose saw her son's face again, she might just start to remember.

I quickly put the idea out of my head. There was no way I could bring George back to London.

Princess Wilhelmina came wandering in and sat on Rose's lap. She began stroking her head. Ever since Princess had gone missing, I had tried to get more information about her frightful time with the animal catcher, but she didn't like remembering it and had completely clammed up. But that evening, I told Princess about the van I had seen pick up that brown dog earlier, and she opened up again.

'Sounds like it could be the same people who picked me up,' she said. Her voice shook as she remembered.

'But what happened next? Can you remember anything else? It's really important,' I said.

She thought about it for a while then her eyes opened widely.

'Well, I do remember one thing,' she said. 'The day after I got taken in, this man came in. With glasses. He picked out some animals and took them away in another van. "Darlings," he said. He was with his sister, a woman with a pink scarf on her head. They seemed nice. She looked at me for quite a while. I thought she might take me with her. Then the man said they couldn't take everyone. So I was stuck. The next day, those two others came back, the one with the green boots and the one with the moustache. They took a load of cats and dogs away. They were screaming. I don't know where the men took them but I never saw them again. Some had already gone mad from losing their homes or their humans. Others were fit and healthy, though, and they just took them away.' She bowed her head. 'That's when I knew I had to get out. When the men came and tried to get more of us into the van, I managed to slip out.'

As I listened to Wilhelmina's story, I began to think that perhaps there might be a way I could get George to London after all. It would be a big risk, though.

CHAPTER TWENTY-FIVE

Nancy and I looked after Rose as best we could. I could remember the way to the market and the local shops, and when it came to getting the household rations, I could show her the way and make sure she didn't get lost. We had a list of everything we needed, and soon enough, all the local shopkeepers knew what had happened and what to do to make sure we got the right rations.

It was far too dangerous for Rose to continue working at the factory, but she was able to go with Mary some evenings and help out at the makeshift hospital. I went with her. She would sit for hours, listening to people talking about their experiences of the war, and how they had lost their houses and loved ones.

She couldn't remember her own loss, but she was still able to sympathize remarkably well with other people. I was also taken around to comfort people; they seemed to like having an animal around to stroke and pet.

There was an air-raid shelter right near the hospital that we often ended up going to. Although it was in a basement, it wasn't that deep, and it was still possible to hear the sounds of the bombing outside. Rose's eyes would often glaze over with tears during an air raid. She would start to panic, and her breathing would get heavy, although she never quite knew why. When this happened, I would press myself against her, and she would hug me. It seemed to calm her down.

They had still not told George about Rose, and everyone was getting more and more anxious about it. Mary had told him on the telephone that she was away with work and would be able to talk to him soon. But she already felt bad about telling him that lie.

'The sooner we can get that boy here, the better, as far as I'm concerned,' said Nancy one evening after Rose had gone to bed. It was a night off from the air raids, as the rain had come in.

'But if we bring him back and anything happens, Rose will never forgive us. And Philip. If he knew we'd taken a risk . . . I just couldn't,' said Mary.

She had written a letter to Philip, telling him about Rose's memory loss, but we weren't sure whether or not it had reached him or even where he was. That evening, I met up with Princess Wilhelmina by the fire.

'We need to bring the plan into action,' I said to her. And she agreed.

'I need your help, though,' I said. 'Are you up to it?' She told me she was.

The next day, when Victor let me out into the garden, Wilhelmina slipped past his legs behind me like a ghost. He was so absorbed in his first cigarette of the day, he didn't notice. There was a small gap in the fence he had been meaning to fix, but he hadn't got around to it. In a moment, Wilhelmina and I were both through it and out in the street. When we got to the other side, Wilhelmina started shaking. It was the first time she'd been out since she had gone missing, apart from the visit to next door's house at Christmas. I reassured her that I was by her side, and we began to walk away from the house. We didn't want to get noticed so slunk behind lampposts and post boxes and took care not to draw too much attention to ourselves. Wilhelmina said she knew a place where she had seen the men make their pick-ups while she was hiding.

'They come here every day,' she said. 'Guaranteed.'

It started to snow. First a few flakes, then a thick, heavy drift. Gradually, London was transformed from a bombed-out city of bricks and mortar into a timeless city, all covered in a blanket of snow. Snow settled wherever it could. On piles of rubble and sandbags. It settled on the tops of Anderson shelters and the roofs of cars and houses and in the gaps where houses once were. By the time we arrived at the docks, everything was covered in a thick layer of white.

'I don't recognize anything,' said Wilhelmina, getting worried. 'It all looks different now. I'm sure it was near here I saw them.'

We could see the river snaking away into the distance.

'I think it's the right place,' she said.

'Let's wait and see,' I said. We set up position in a corner of an old bombed-out warehouse.

'It was close to here, I think, that they picked me up last time,' she said and began to shiver at the thought of it. We waited. The snow had stopped falling, but it had settled all across the road, so the cars were going very slowly and carefully, and some were sliding about.

'Perhaps they won't be out today after all,' said Wilhelmina. 'Perhaps we should go home. I'm cold and hungry and I miss Mary and I miss my bed.'

I was feeling the same, and it was very tempting. But I thought of the mission we had agreed to take on.

'We've come this far,' I said. 'It's for George, remember. And Rose.'

Just as I was losing the will to carry on, as dusk began to fall, a pair of headlights flashed into our eyes. I could just make out that it was a green van crawling slowly through the snow. The engine stopped and the headlights went out. A man got out.

'There's something over there,' he hissed.

'What?' said a voice from in the car. It was Reg.

'Cat, oh, and a dog, I think. Double whammy!' said the other man, who was flashing a torch in our direction.

Instead of fleeing as my instincts told me to, I stiffened and moved closer to Wilhelmina. The man approached us. He was the one in the green boots. It felt so wrong, but we made his job easy and went willingly into the van. Inside was one other animal. A black-and-white Staffordshire bull terrier. I recognized her immediately. It was Jane.

'Let's make that the last catch, shall we?' said the driver. 'Snow's getting too thick. We'll take this lot back and call it a day.'

Jane looked relieved to see me, but she was frightened and confused. She said that she had been out with Tony and some of the lads, preparing for some big job, and she had become separated from them. The police had come by, and everyone had scattered, and she got left behind in the confusion. When the snow started falling, she had lost her way and was then picked up just as dusk was falling.

'Where are they taking us?' she asked nervously.

Wilhelmina was scared of Jane, and when she first saw her she had crouched in the corner of the van. I reassured her that Jane was a friend, and Wilhelmina finally, reluctantly, emerged and told her about how she had been caught before and to try not to worry too much. It was a strange sight to see this fluffy white cat reassuring a stocky Staffordshire bull terrier.

'What on earth are you doing here?' asked Jane, when she finally calmed down.

'It's a secret plan,' I said, getting excited again.

'I've had it up to here with secret plans,' said Jane glumly. 'Tony's been planning a secret plan for ages. It's all about what he's calling "finishing off" some big house in Kensington where he knows about an object that's worth a lot of money. That's all he seems to care about, money. Planning on cleaning up there in a few days, if the snow lasts, as they think it will cover their tracks.'

The van stopped. It was dark outside. I could just make out the shapes of buildings.

'Is this it?' I whispered to Wilhelmina.

'I think so. Yes, I recognize that,' she said and pointed her nose towards a bit of railway track and a large warehouse next to it. I could hear the sounds of other dogs barking and cats meowing inside the building. They did not sound very happy.

'Come on, you lot,' said the driver. 'Reg, get the boxes.'

They put Wilhelmina into a small box. I could see she was having a moment of panic, but she was brave and didn't resist. Then they put me and Jane on leads, as we weren't putting up any resistance either, and they took us towards a row of dark outbuildings with thick, locked gates on the front of them.

'Placid lot, these are,' said Reg. 'It's weird. Almost like they want to be here.' He laughed a cackling, hoarse kind of laugh. 'But I doubt it, somehow. Unless they're mad!'

I hoped they would put us near one another. Luckily, they put me and Jane in the same area. It was a large cell-like outhouse with a stone floor and a small bucket of cold water in the corner.

Inside I saw a dog: the brown female we had seen outside the grocer's. She looked thinner than ever and was curled up in the corner, hardly moving. Alongside her there was a little terrier. They seemed content with one another, so we found a space on the other side of the outhouse, out of sight.

Instead of bringing Wilhelmina in with us, the men took her off to another area, but we didn't know where. I whined and barked, but it was no use. I began to have doubts about the plan. Perhaps I should have left Wilhelmina out of it.

'She came of her own accord, though,' said Jane.

'I know you're right,' I said. 'But . . . I just hope she's OK.'

But it was done now and there was nothing we could do.

Despite the snowfall, the aeroplanes and the bombs still came over the city that night. Because we were virtually outside, with only a thin roof over half of the kennel, and no walls at the front at all, just the metal gates, we saw and heard it all – the lights, the flashes and crashes. We could smell the burning and heard several large explosions and a steady crack crack crack of anti-aircraft fire all through the night.

At one point, there was an explosion not far away, and the ground rumbled around us, and the bars of our cage rattled until my ears hurt. I snuggled up against Jane, and we tried to comfort each other. I was pleased that she was with me. Even though I hardly knew her, I felt like we had a connection. It was a long night, but we comforted each other as best we could. Eventually, at some point in the middle of the night, we drifted off to sleep, and the bombing finally stopped.

I woke up suddenly, cold and shivering. I opened my eyes. Jane was still there. I was relieved. We huddled up together. More snow had fallen in the night and settled all around the front part of the cage where there was no roof.

There was a small robin, a sprightly little bird, hopping about in the snow right in front of our cage. It flew off when a man I hadn't seen before came out to check on us. Although there wasn't much food, they didn't starve us. The man even said a few kindly words as he threw in a couple of biscuits and filled up the old bucket in the corner with fresh water. I gulped it down; I hadn't realized how thirsty I was. Then we waited. A few kennels along, I could hear a commotion, some barking and howling, and it sounded as though several dogs were being taken away. I don't know where they went, but they never came back.

'What about this lot?' growled Reg, walking past our cage.

'They look half starved,' said another man I couldn't see.

'Might as well get rid of them, then,' said Reg with a menacing grin below his moustache.

'I'll do it,' said the man. The key turned in the gate and a pair of green boots appeared in front of my face. I saw the green boot fly through the air, and it kicked Jane sharply.

'Out of the way, you mutt.'

Jane was flung backwards and let out a terrified shriek. She ran into the corner.

I don't know what came over me, but I suddenly felt fiercely protective of Jane. I wasn't taking that from anyone. I barked at him and went for his leg, and he momentarily backed off, but then, out of the blue, I felt a large whack on my back and crumpled down in pain. The man in the green boots now had a big stick in his hand and he was hitting out at me and shouting.

'You bloody dogs. You make my life hell. I never asked to work here. I bleedin' hate animals.'

I carried on barking and trying to get between him and Jane, who was also barking. I dodged back and forth as the stick came down either side of me.

'Get them in the van,' shouted the green-booted man to Reg, who was inching his way along the wall to avoid us. He was still waving the stick wildly, and after a while I couldn't dodge out of the way quickly enough any more, and the stick came down sharply on my back and I fell to the floor.

'Stop barking,' shouted Jane. 'He'll kill you.'

'I think he already has,' I said. We both stopped barking, and eventually he laid off and I managed to limp over to Jane. She licked my back and we lay down together again, both shivering.

In the end, we realized it wasn't us they were after. Instead, Reg went over to the two very thin dogs, the brown one and the terrier, who had settled down for the night together in the other corner. I couldn't tell whether they had even made it through the night alive; they were so quiet and hadn't even moved during all the commotion. He picked them both up, and as he walked past, I could see they were both alive and were whining very quietly.

'I can't spend another night in here,' I said to Jane when they had gone. But there was no way out.

There was nothing we could do except sleep and stay close to keep warm. The only time I woke up after that was when we heard barking or howling from another cage. If I strained my ears, I could also hear meowing from the cats, which were further away. At one point, I was sure I could hear Wilhelmina, but when I listened again, the sound had gone.

By the end of the day, we were absolutely starving. The nice man never came back with any biscuits, and I could tell Jane was getting weaker. I didn't think I would make it through another night in there without going mad, but I didn't have any choice for the moment.

I thought about George and hoped our plan would work.

That night, the air raid was worse. The sky had cleared, and although the ground was still covered with snow, planes were flying over in full force. There were several loud explosions, which set my teeth on edge every time.

I thought of Rose and felt guilty for leaving her. She would be frightened. I felt guilty about Nancy, who would be worrying about where we were, and I thought about

Mary and Victor, who would be especially worried about Wilhelmina. Then I felt bad again about Wilhelmina. I had no idea if she was all right. Had I done the right thing? Was I mad? I just didn't know any more. The only thing I was grateful for was being with Jane, who, I reminded myself, would have been all alone in this cage if I wasn't there.

By the time I had finished worrying about everything, it was morning. The robin was back and hopping about in the courtyard again as though everything was right with the world. I could smell the fires from the night's air raid and see smoke rising up over the nearby buildings. A train puffed its way past on the nearby railway track, and a large car pulled up outside the kennels. It wasn't the green van, but I was sure I recognized the sound of the engine.

I could hear the mumbled sounds of voices. A man was talking to Reg. The dogs in the other cages started barking, and as one barked, another barked more loudly until the whole place had erupted. They all wanted to be saved. Jane and I kept quiet.

The human voices got louder, and I could hear footsteps on the stone floor. The next moment, a smiling face pressed up against the cage and peered in at us.

'Oh, darlings! I love a staffie,' said the face. '"Nanny dogs", they're called. So good with children. And that little terrier cross,' he said, pointing at me. 'A lovely little thing. Sure I've seen one just like that before.'

'Is that him?' asked Jane.

'Yes,' I said under my breath.

We sat and stared up at the man, and tried to look our most cute and lovable. The next thing I knew, I was being led to his car. But he must have seen so many dogs recently, because he still didn't recognize me. When I looked back for Jane, I realized she had been left in the kennel.

'I can only take one,' he said to Reg. 'I think I've just got the space if I re-home that whippet. I'd love the Staffie, but we don't have the room. Maybe next week, if she's still here?'

I was torn. My mission was to find George. But now I realized that Jane was about to be left in that hellhole on her own. In a moment of blind panic, I tried to run back. The lead strained. I couldn't leave her there. I barked and ran wildly towards the kennel.

'He's not a tricky one, is he?' asked Kenneth, pulling me back. 'Here, boy.'

'He's been pretty quiet today, that one. Although there was that little . . . incident yesterday. Perhaps he's a bit skittish. I don't know.'

George had to be my priority, I told myself. I let Kenneth put me into the back of his car and didn't make another sound. The back door slammed. I looked around the car and saw a small basket. Inside it, there was a bundle of white fur, looking just like a ball of snow, with a white face and blue eyes.

I breathed a brief sigh of relief.

'Thank goodness you're here,' I said to Wilhelmina, and I crawled over to her. She licked my nose through the railings of her basket. I sat down beside her, and she started to purr.

The plan had worked so far. But there had been one major setback I could never have foreseen. As we drove away, I could hear Jane barking and then howling, and it broke my heart to leave her.

CHAPTER TWENTY-SIX

It was a long journey through the snow by car. The wheels were skidding from side to side, and we had to go very slowly in order not to slip off the road. This was the first time Wilhelmina had ever been in a car, other than her journeys in the van, and she started to feel very sick. Kenneth was kind and stopped a few times once we were out of the city to give us some air and something to eat and drink.

'What happened to you in there?' I asked Wilhelmina when we got out of the car for a break.

'Nothing much,' she said quietly. But I saw that she was shaking just at the thought of it. I think she was very relieved to be out of there for the second, and hopefully the last, time.

'Where are all the buildings?' she asked as we got deeper into the countryside.

Just like me and George, she was a city animal, and this was the first time she had ever been outside London.

'They don't have many buildings here,' I said.

I pointed out the things that Rose had shown me, the fields and animals, although they looked quite different now in the snow. Wilhelmina was wide-eyed and a little nervous of all the new sights.

Kenneth was so kind, and he even had some treats for us, some biscuits and some tinned meat. It felt like luxury after our time in the kennels. After several hours, I started to see things I recognized. The railway station, with its sign swinging in the wind, was now covered in a layer of snow.

It was strange to think George was just around the corner somewhere, knowing nothing about the fact we were in the village.

As we drove up to the grand house again, I had a feeling of relief and fear at the same time. I hadn't been anywhere outside London without Rose before. I also began to worry, because now that I was there, I wasn't sure how to get to George, let alone get him back to Rose.

The gardens were all white with snow. It looked beautiful but so different from the last time. I was suddenly worried about what might happen. What if I never found George and we got stuck here for ever?

'So this is where you all came for Christmas, is it?' asked Wilhelmina enviously. 'While I was stuck in that old lady's house on my own.'

'Yes, we did,' I said, getting excited. 'It wasn't that good, though,' I added quickly.

'Yeah, right,' she said sulkily.

Joyce came out of the house to greet us, as she did all her new arrivals. When I saw her, I cheered up.

'Oh, what a darling puss cat,' she said to her brother when she saw Wilhelmina.

Wilhelmina immediately softened when she saw Joyce, and she started purring and nuzzling her. I think Joyce would have recognized me if she hadn't been so preoccupied with Wilhelmina, but Kenneth took me straight to the kennel, so I didn't get a chance to see her properly.

'Keep an eye out tonight and try to distract them all as much as possible. I'll try and think of a way out to find George,' I called to Wilhelmina as I was led away. I think she heard me, but I couldn't be sure, as she was purring so loudly at Joyce.

When I was put in the kennel, I kept myself to myself. These were a lot nicer than the London kennels. They had comfy beds in them, with blankets and water bowls always full of fresh water.

I didn't want to draw attention to myself, so I slunk into the corner. There were a couple of other dogs in there, a very timid bull dog and a particularly chatty Yorkshire terrier. I kept my head down and pretended I was in shock. I didn't trust anyone yet. Only when they all went to sleep did I creep out to have some water.

I remembered from Christmas that Kenneth liked a drink in the evening, and he left the feeding to the maid, Lucy. Sure enough, just after dark I heard the clatter of keys, and Lucy came down the hall with an oil lamp lighting up her face. She had a large sack of dry animal food. I hid in the corner of the kennel so she wouldn't see me.

'Come on, you lot, dinner's up,' she said and shook the bag.

The others were so hungry, they woke up immediately and ran straight over to the bowl. The terrier nudged its way in ahead of the bull dog who tried to nudge his way back in again, but failed. While they were engaged in this battle over the food, and just before Lucy shut the gate behind her, I slipped out very quietly and softly past her. No one, not even the other dogs, who were all eating noisily away, noticed as I made my way out and along the dark corridor.

Once I was out, I ran as fast as I could without looking back. My heart was beating so loudly, I could hear it pounding in my head and I didn't realize that I had been holding my breath the whole time until I stopped for a moment and started panting heavily and gasping for air.

I breathed in again and carried on. I didn't know where I was, but I suddenly found myself outside. I stopped and listened. There was a small shaft of light ahead of me. Perhaps they weren't as strict about the blackout here. I realized I was behind the big house. The silhouette of its tall chimneys towered up against the starry sky. Through a chink in the curtain, I could see Joyce on the floor, playing with Wilhelmina with a ball of wool. I was relieved. They were distracted. Well done, Wilhelmina. I inched my way along the back of the house. Suddenly, I heard a very loud dog barking. I froze. The barking carried on for about five minutes. It was warning whoever was there to get away quick or he would be on them. Then I saw him, a large Alsatian-type dog on the other side of the house. He hadn't seen me, so it was just a general warning, so far.

Joyce looked up from playing with Wilhelmina. I saw her say something to Kenneth and point outside. He was pouring a drink from the cabinet. He swished it around in the glass and sniffed it, then he said something back to Joyce before swilling it back. She laughed and went back to playing with Wilhelmina.

The Alsatian stopped barking and disappeared from view around the other side of the house. I breathed out again and continued my way past the end of the house and down the hill towards the village.

I had felt sure I would be able to remember my way back there, but in the dark and with the snow covering everything, the landscape seemed different and alien-looking. Trees took on scary shapes and seemed to be talking in the wind. Their huge trunks loomed up and their branches, all empty of leaves, waved about as if they were warning me of some awful thing that was about to happen.

A huge white face appeared in a tree, making me jump. Then it swooped down without making a sound. Must be a type of bird, probably looking for food, I thought. Unsuccessful at the hunt, it landed on the branch of a nearby tree and let out a screech.

Eventually, I found myself on a small road. I thought it looked familiar, but it was so dark I could hardly see the ground ahead of me. Only the white snow left along the edge of the road, reflecting the moonlight, guided my way. The road was icy where the snow had melted during the day and refrozen. I slipped across the ice a few times but kept going, determined to find the village and George.

I saw the spire of the church poking up through the trees. Then the houses with their thatched roofs came into view, and soon I was standing outside Miss Eagle's house. The windows were all dark and the curtains were drawn. There was a thin trail of smoke coming from the chimney. I was suddenly overcome with tiredness. I didn't think I could last the night out there. It was so cold, my nose had started to freeze, with small icicles forming on the end. I crept to the back of the house and looked for somewhere to get some rest until morning.

The llamas must be safely tucked away in the barn at the end of the garden, out of the snow, I thought. There was a small gap in the wooden door to the barn; it was not big enough for a llama to fit through, but it was just big enough for me. I squeezed my way in. When I got inside, I could smell the llamas, and then I could just make out their muddy beige coats in the darkness. They were lying down in the corner, all together. When they heard me, they woke up and started grunting. They stood up and moved into the corner together, shifting nervously. I was too tired to do anything else. I found a patch of hay far away from them, dug my way deep into it with my paws, and then fell fast asleep.

When I woke up, a llama had come over and was sniffing at me under the hay, out of curiosity. I jumped up and barked. I had no idea where I was or what this funny animal was doing. It was getting light outside but was still grey.

The llama let out a strange loud bark, which I didn't understand but I knew meant it was more scared than I was. I remembered where I was. I heard the back door slam. I froze. The barn door opened. Miss Eagle was standing in the doorway, holding a long stick, and the long stick was pointing right at me. At least, I thought it was a stick, until I realized it was a gun. I had seen soldiers carrying guns in London before but had never had one pointed directly at me.

CHAPTER TWENTY-SEVEN

I tried not to move as I looked down the barrel of the gun.

'Who's there?' said Miss Eagle. 'Is there someone here?' She was trying to sound brave. I didn't want her to do anything rash. Unfortunately, I breathed in a bit of hay and couldn't help but let out a huge sneeze. The gun went click.

'Who's there? Declare yourself or I'll shoot,' she said, walking slowly towards where I was hiding under the hay. The llamas were shifting and snorting in the corner. The back door slammed shut again and a small voice called out.

'Miss Eagle. Where are you? I heard a noise. Shouting.'

'I'm in here, George. Don't move. There's an intruder. I've got him cornered. Don't you worry.'

George couldn't resist a bit of action, and he peeped his head around the door. I took my chance. I darted out of the hay and across the barn. The gun followed me and Miss Eagle was just about to shoot when George yelled out.

'No! It's Bertie. It's Bertie,' he screamed, running right across the path of the weapon.

Miss Eagle dropped the point of the gun just in time, and I jumped up at George with a feeling of joy, mixed simultaneously with sheer terror at what had just happened.

George started to cry, and Miss Eagle looked very confused by the whole thing. The llamas were still snorting and making strange noises, so she went over to comfort them.

'How on earth . . .' she said as she stroked their faces. 'Well, you'd better bring the dog in.'

I was shaking as I sat down in the kitchen. George smothered me with hugs and kisses, and I wished I could tell him about my adventures and how I had got there. I sat in front of the stove, which Miss Eagle stoked up with wood. My nose and cold paws were soon thawing out nicely.

Although I couldn't talk to George, there was one thing I could try and use to get his attention. I ran upstairs.

'What is it, Bertie?' he asked and followed me. I barked and looked back, and he followed me into the little bedroom. He had on his bedside table a small photograph of Rose, which had been salvaged in the special box she had saved from the bombing.

I barked and looked at the photo, then jumped on the bed and nudged it with my nose.

'What is it? Is it Mum?' he asked. 'Has something happened? What's wrong with Mum, Bertie?'

I barked over and over again, and then ran back downstairs. George followed.

'I know it sounds weird,' he said to Miss Eagle, 'but I think Bertie is trying to tell me something. About my mum. I think something's happened. I don't know how he got here. It's so strange, but . . . I've just got this feeling I have to go to her.'

Thank goodness. He understood. I ran up and scratched the front door. George opened it. I ran into the road and started walking in the direction of the manor house. Now that I had started to get through to George, I hoped he would follow me all the way.

Miss Eagle was so confused by events, she just put on her coat and started following us, too, but it was all she could do to stop from slipping on the slushy, icy ground.

It seemed a lot easier to get back with the sun now coming up, and before long we were standing at the main door of the house. We must have looked a right trio, me half mad with all my travels and frights, George in his pyjama bottoms, with just a jumper on top, and his boots on. And Miss Eagle in a huge woollen hat and great coat, still with her gun in her hand.

'What's all this?' said Joyce, opening the door. George had been ringing the bell frantically.

Miss Eagle answered her. 'This dog appeared, and it's the boy's dog, and . . . well, he seems to have some kind of "message" from London about the mother. I don't know. It's completely extraordinary, but . . .'

Princess Wilhelmina appeared in the doorway and began rubbing against Joyce's legs and looking as though she'd lived there all her life.

'That's my granny's cat!' said George in disbelief. 'Wilhelmina, with the blue collar.'

I ran over and greeted her. 'You did it, then,' she said quietly.

'You're having a nice time, I see.'

'Making up for my missed Christmas,' she said with a smile that only a cat that literally just got the cream could produce.

Kenneth appeared at the top of the stairs, looking a little grey in the face. He clearly wasn't used to being up that early.

'What's all this commotion?' he said. 'Lucy, can you be a darling and fix me up with one of your raw egg specials?'

Lucy, the maid, was looking very sheepish.

'I'm so sorry, sir, but you know that dog you brought in last night? Well . . . I just went to give him his breakfast, and . . .' Before she could finish, she caught sight of me in the doorway. 'God alive, he's out here now. But how in the world? I'm sure I locked the gate.'

I couldn't work out who was the more bewildered out of everyone standing there.

Eventually, Joyce suggested the only sensible thing in such a situation. 'How about we all have a cup of tea?'

Everyone agreed that was a damned good idea.

'How did you end up picking up young George's pets?' asked Joyce as she poured the drinks. I was lying in front of the fire in the drawing room, next to Wilhelmina, who was asleep and purring so contentedly I wondered whether we'd ever be able to get her back to London.

'I'm damned if I know,' said Kenneth, dipping a hot crumpet in his tea and eating it down in one. 'But I do know we'd better get them back before the boy's family get worried about their dog. And their cat!'

'Can I come, then?' asked George, getting excited at the idea of a trip back to London. 'I'm really sure Bertie had something important to tell me about Mum.'

'Why don't you telephone?' Joyce asked her brother.

'The line's out,' he said. 'I was trying all yesterday afternoon to get hold of my man at the British Museum about that marble. I'll have to go down there again myself and arrange things now. All right, George, you can come. We'll be back tonight. You can visit your mother and return your wayward pets at the same time. And we'll have you back in time for supper.'

'Hooray!' said George, and he jumped up and punched the air.

We walked back down the hill to Miss Eagle's, and George put on some warmer clothes.

Before long, Kenneth's car was back outside, hooting its horn. Wilhelmina was a little disgruntled about being back in the travelling box, but despite all that, she did look quite splendid. She had been washed all clean by Joyce, and her fur was shimmering in the morning light.

Kenneth had a tweed cap on, and he produced another one for George, who was over the moon. Together they looked like a couple of country gentlemen, out for a drive.

'You promise you'll be back tonight?' said Miss Eagle, leaning in at the window. 'If anything should happen to that boy, I'll be . . .'

'Don't worry, cous'. They're in safe hands,' he said before she could finish. Then he started up the engine, honked the horn, and off we went.

Kenneth liked to sing while he drove, and between the village and London, we must have learnt about six different songs. There was one about a rabbit running in case it gets shot by the farmer. That made me shiver a bit, that one, after my experience with the gun that morning. There was another one about packing up your troubles, and one about how far away Tipperary was, and saying goodbye to Leicester Square. George found it all great fun, and I joined in with some howling on the final line, 'but my heart's still there!' I think I was becoming quite good at this singing lark.

When we reached London, George tried to remember how to get to Mary and Victor's house, but we got lost. Eventually, he remembered the pub on the corner, the Dog and Whistle, and then the number, seventeen, because it was his birthday. By lunchtime, we pulled up outside the house. I felt a sudden moment of trepidation. What if they were cross that George was back in London? Maybe I'd done the wrong thing.

'I'll leave you here, boy, and pick you up in a couple of hours once my business in town is finished with,' said Kenneth, then he hopped in the car again and drove away.

George rang the doorbell. There was a pause. Perhaps they're not in, I thought. Maybe it was all for nothing. Then I heard a quiet shuffling of footsteps on the carpet. The door opened. Rose was standing there in her housecoat. She still had that glazed look in her eyes.

'Sorry it took me so long,' she said. 'I was in the kitchen.' She did not seem to recognize any of us. She squinted. 'What can I do for you, young man?' she asked George.

He ran over and hugged her, not realizing she didn't know who he was.

'Mummy,' he said, 'Bertie came all the way out to get me, and I think he was trying to tell me . . . Now I feel silly. I was so worried, but you're OK.'

She stood back, alarmed.

'I'm sorry . . . I don't know . . .'

'What's the matter, Mum?' asked George, sounding older suddenly. He started to panic. He couldn't understand why she was being so strange.

'You'd better come in,' she said quietly.

We both went into the house, and George started looking around, now a little apprehensive.

'Where is everyone?' he asked, putting Wilhelmina's basket down and opening it so she could run out. Rose didn't seem to notice that the cat was back.

'She wrote me a note so I'd remember,' said Rose, feeling around in her housecoat pocket. 'Here it is. "Just popped out to shops. To make tea, heat kettle on hob. Tea leaves in pot. Pour into cup. Use powdered milk. Won't be long. Your loving sis, Nancy." Oh, yes. My sister has just popped out. My sister Nancy,' explained Rose, as though she was reminding herself. 'What a lovely dog,' she said suddenly, and knelt down and patted me on the head.

'It's Bertie,' said George. 'Don't you remember?' Now his voice was really becoming anxious.

'Wait,' she said, feeling around in her other pocket. 'I've got another note here. "My name is Rose. I had a nasty knock to the head. I live at 17 Fairbridge Road with Victor, Mary and Nancy. My husband is Philip. He is away in the war. I have one son, George, who is nine years old. He is evacuated in Wiltshire."' Tears began falling spontaneously from her eyes as she read.

'Did you get hurt, Mum? Don't you remember?' He looked at me but I couldn't say anything to reassure him.

'I remember something,' said Rose. Her eyes lit up. 'I remember . . . a window. Light. A man's face. He was holding a little . . . a baby . . . it was a little boy. I noticed straight away. He had the same eyes. His father's eyes.'

She looked at George. It looked as if she might remember, but then her eyes went blank again.

'What did you say your name was?' she asked him, as though she had just forgotten the whole episode. George looked like he was about to cry. I nuzzled up against him.

'Bertie,' he whispered. 'What's happened?'

Rose looked up at George again. Then she suddenly grabbed his shoulders and held him tightly, as though she never wanted to let him go again.

'My boy.' She had remembered.

The three of us stood there for what seemed like an age until Rose finally let go of George. When she looked at him, he had tears streaming down his face in confusion and relief.

When they finally both began smiling again, Rose pulled out the note reminding her how to make a cup of tea and went to the kettle and put it on the hob.

George ran upstairs and came back down with Mary and Victor's leather-bound photograph album. Together, the three of us looked through it, and as George spoke, Rose began to remember her old life again.

Bit by bit, the memories came back. It was slow, but once George got used to Rose's struggle to remember, he was able to reassure her and remind her of things she had forgotten. She looked through the photos and saw her wedding to Philip. The dress she made herself with her father's help. George's first birthday party. That little sailor's suit. Philip in his army uniform, just before he had left. Eventually, she even remembered me arriving. With a little prompting from George, she started to recall how I had turned up in their garden and how they had taken me in and given me a home.

'Bertie,' she said. 'You old thing. Did you go all the way to Wiltshire just to get George for me?'

There was another photograph. It was taken in the garden at their old house. Our old house. Rose put her finger on it. She remembered the bombing all over again, as though for the first time, and we all felt sad, sitting there, thinking of our old house and how we would never see it again.

'Do I have to let you go again?' said Rose sadly to George, touching his arm gently.

'You've got Bertie,' he said. I whined as if to say I would always be there.

'Where's Auntie Nancy, anyway?' he asked, jumping up and looking out of the window. 'I've got things I need to tell her.'

In the excitement of Rose's memory starting to come back, they had completely forgotten that Nancy had only popped out to the shops and should have been back ages ago. The doorbell rang.

'That'll be Kenneth,' said George. 'I promised Miss Eagle I'd be back tonight so I didn't get blitzed and Daddy wouldn't be angry at her.'

'Who's Kenneth?' asked Rose. Then she remembered George was supposed to be away in Wiltshire. 'Oh, how silly. Yes. Of course,' she said when she went to open the door. 'You must get back there, mustn't you?'

But it wasn't Kenneth. It was Clive. He was out of breath from running and was red in the face.

'Where's Nancy?' he asked. He was holding on to the door frame to get his breath back.

'She's . . . out at the shops . . . why? Well, actually, she should be back by now. Shouldn't she . . . ?' said Rose, looking at George for reassurance. 'It's . . . Simon . . . no . . . Clive, isn't it?' she said, looking relieved to have recognized someone at last.

'Yes. But. She's not here, then? Oh God,' he said, his face getting very serious.

'What is it?' asked Rose.

'I don't know for sure, but I think . . . Tony's men might have . . . taken her.'

CHAPTER TWENTY-EIGHT

The panic in Clive's voice was rising. It took a while for Rose, who was still a little confused, to realize the enormity of the situation.

'Taken her where?' said Rose, getting upset.

'I don't know. Look, there's a job going down tonight. I can't say much. I've kept out of it up until now. My brother, Tony. He's behind it all and Nancy . . . well, she clocked on to it. And I heard them talking and now she's gone and . . . oh God. I should never have got her involved in all this.'

'Going down? Clocked on? What do you mean? What on earth is going on?'

'Up at the big house. In Kensington. Some ancient statues or something, a load of them, worth a bunch of cash. Tony's got his eye on pinching the lot before they go to some big museum. Priceless, he says. Got a buyer already. I mean, we're talking thousands here. Millions, maybe . . .'

'Where the hell is my sister?' said Rose, changing from being upset to being angry. 'Have you put her in danger, you . . .'

The doorbell rang again. George opened it. This time it was Kenneth.

'My Auntie Nancy's gone missing,' said George, bold as brass.

Clive had no choice but to bring him in on the secret. Pretty soon, it transpired that it was Kenneth's house they were going to rob, anyway, that very night under cover of darkness.

I could have told them all that ages ago, if only I spoke human.

'Mum, you can't send me back tonight,' pleaded George. 'We've got to find Nancy and help Kenneth keep his ancient statues. Just tonight. Please . . .'

'Oh, I don't know,' said Rose. 'We've got to find my sister. Of course. I don't know anything about any statues. But I'll do whatever needs to be done to find Nancy.'

'Well, shouldn't we just call the police?' asked Kenneth. 'Be done with it.'

'I don't think so,' said Clive. 'I think it's best we keep this . . . between friends.'

'I better write a note for Mum and Dad,' said Rose. 'They'll be wondering what on earth is going on.'

She found a piece of paper and scribbled down to say that she was feeling much better, and she and Nancy had popped out for the evening and not to worry. I could imagine the look on Mary's face when she saw the note and then saw that Wilhelmina was back safe and sound, as though she'd never been away, and looking clean as newly fallen snow.

We all piled into Kenneth's car, and Clive directed us to the warehouse.

'If they haven't left yet we might just be able to head them off.'

But when we arrived, there was no one there. Not Mad Carpet Tony. And none of his lads, nor Jane, nor anyone. I had no idea what had happened to her since we were separated at the kennels. I feared the worst. There was no sign of Nancy, either.

'What do we do now?' Rose asked, anxiously looking around at the bleak landscape of the docks. They seemed to be even more desolate-looking with the patchy brown snow dotted all around.

'Both vans have gone,' said Clive, running back to the car.

'Should we head straight to my place, then? I can call the police and be done with this whole thing,' said Kenneth, getting quite exasperated.

'If the police get involved now they'll dig about, and we'll all really be up the proverbial creek without a paddle,' replied Clive. 'Including Nancy, and you, Rose. You've had your fair share of stuff off me. And Kenneth, where do you think those Chinese vases came from? How do you think we got them into the country in the first place, 'ey?'

'I thought you said that was all through . . . official channels.'

'In your dreams, mate,' said Clive. 'Look, we haven't got time to stand here chatting. We've got to get there before Tony and the lads do.'

So that was that. It was impossible to get the police involved without everyone, I suppose even me, being implicated in some way.

'Come on,' said Clive. 'Let's go. I know who we should talk to first.'

We jumped in the car again and he directed the way down some dark back streets, over a small river and down a row of scruffy terraced houses where the road reached a dead end. Many of the streets in the area had been destroyed and some looked like they had been abandoned altogether. There were children on the road, playing games with skipping ropes and footballs. As we drove up, they all stopped and stared at the smart car. We stopped outside a house right at the end. It was painted white, while all the others were brick and falling apart, and it had a smartly painted blue front door. Remarkably, all the windows were intact. On the windowsill were brightly coloured flowers in window boxes.

We all got out of the car and Clive knocked on the door.

'I still knock, so as not to scare the old lady. Even though she never locks it,' he said.

A sprightly-looking elderly woman answered. She was small and slight, with a thin nose and small eyes with large, expressive eyebrows. Her hair was in tight grey curls. When she saw Clive, her face broke into a large smile.

'My littlest lad,' she said. 'What's kept you so long?'

'Ma,' he said. He held out his arms, picked her up and swung her around.

'Been busy, you know what it's like. This is Rose, Kenneth, little George and Bertie. Ma Finch.'

Ma Finch's house was full of books. Every inch of wall space was taken up with shelves and books, some of which looked very old. Once we were inside, she told us the story of how she had taken Clive in as a boy when his parents, her best friends, had died from TB, both in the same year.

'I came from nothing. Father was a poor street sweeper. Mother died while I was just a baby. I got by on my wits,' she said. 'Taught myself to read and pestered the local bookshop owner for work until he gave in. It was unpaid at first, of course, then after a few years I started helping him restore the old books. Before long, I got to knowing what they were worth, and eventually I was able to deal them myself. And that's how we started the family business.'

When the bookshop owner died, she told us, his errant son came and took over and sold the shop, and Ma Finch was turned out. But she had saved enough money to rent the house and do it up nicely and bring up her young son, Tony, with her husband Arthur.

'Arthur ran off after a few years with a local barmaid,' she said. 'But I was quite happy with my boys and my books, thank you very much. Tony, the eldest, wasn't too happy, of course, when this one turned up.' She laughed, nodding her head towards Clive. 'Picked on the poor sod mercilessly. But what can you do?'

'All right, Ma. Enough of the family history. We're in a hurry today.'

'Why? What's going on?'

He told her what Tony had planned and how Nancy had disappeared and how, possibly, it was one of Tony's men who'd kidnapped her.

'He's gone too far now,' said Ma Finch. Her eyes developed a steely look which made me nervous, and she wasn't even looking at me.

'It's about time I gave him that clip around the ear I should have done years ago,' she said and slammed her small fists on the table so that all the bookshelves shook.

'What about my sister?' asked Rose meekly. 'Is there anything you can do about her?'

'I'm thinking about that one,' Ma answered seriously. 'Where might they take the poor girl?'

I could think of one place that the man with the mous-tache might take Nancy. It came with ready-made cells.

With Ma Finch now in the car as well, it was getting quite packed. But the more the merrier, as far as I was con-cerned, especially when it came to 'staking out', as Clive put it, Kenneth's house in Kensington. On the way, we passed the old railway line. The large, grey outhouses looked familiar. I started barking, and I jumped up and looked out of the window.

'What's Bertie up to?' asked Clive, leaning back.

'He's seen something,' said George.

'Stop the car,' said Ma. 'I know this place. Gives me the creeps.'

'What is it?' asked Rose.

'It's the old abattoir. Been shut for years now, but old Reg uses it for his animal things. He lives here, I think. When he's not doing Tony's dirty work.'

Then I remembered where I'd seen the man with the moustache. It was in the pub with Clive that day. The day Nancy said she knew it was Tony who'd burgled Kenneth's house.

I didn't know what an abattoir was, but it gave me a nasty feeling in the pit of my stomach. If I strained my ears, I could hear dogs barking and, further away, hungry cats crying out. It gave me a shiver to remember being in that place, even for a night.

'What time's this thing going down?' asked Ma.

'About nine o'clock,' said Clive. 'Give or take.'

It was just starting to get dark. Kenneth stopped the car and pulled it into a corner, out of sight. There were no lights on in the outhouses, just the sound of distressed barking. But next door there was a small wooden hut with light coming out from around the edge of the door frame; enough light to think there was most likely someone in there. There was also a small chimney in the roof from which a thin stream of smoke was wafting out.

As we approached the hut, I could hear a man with a gruff voice, laughing at the radio. George and Rose stayed in the car and kept watch. Kenneth kept an eye on the hut, while Ma and Clive went along the rows of kennels. I followed them. I wasn't only looking for Nancy.

In the first kennel there was a single Alsatian dog, which looked very thin. As we approached, he came up and started barking at me weakly. I told him there was nothing we could do yet but to hold on. We'd be back. The next two kennels were empty and smelt very bad. In the third there was a small bundle in the corner. And next to that, a larger bundle of clothes. The bundle of clothes moved and a face appeared.

'Clive!' said a weak voice.

'You don't half get yourself in a fix, do you?' he said.

'Oh, you beast!' said Nancy. 'They pulled me into their wretched car and I've been in here for hours now. How did you know?'

'Bertie's canine instinct,' said Clive.

I whined quietly, as if to say hello, without drawing too much attention to myself.

'Well, thank goodness for Bertie,' she whispered. 'Now, can you get me out of here? It stinks! And I'm freezing.'

The air-raid siren went.

'Quickly,' she said. 'I am not spending the air raid in a dog kennel.'

The other bundle had woken up and wandered over. I couldn't help barking with joy when I saw it was Jane. She was looking thinner than ever.

'Thank goodness for this little one,' said Nancy, stroking her head. 'We kept each other warm, didn't we? She doesn't look well, though.'

Footsteps were approaching on the stone floor. We all stopped moving.

'I got the key,' a voice hissed in the dark. Thank goodness it was Kenneth. While Reg had gone to the loo, he had managed to slip in and grab a bunch of keys from the hook.

'I hope it's the right ones,' he said. 'I only had a minute before he came back in. Nearly caught me. But he's gone off somewhere now. In his car.'

I had a feeling I knew where he'd gone.

Clive tried all the keys; as usual, it was the last one on the ring. His hands were shaking as he opened the gate. He bundled Nancy out, and Ma Finch came over and picked up Jane, who was so weak she could hardly walk. When Nancy saw Rose and George in the car, she squealed.

'What are you doing here?' she whispered.

'We'll explain everything on the way. Get in. We've got to get to Ken's place before Tony gets away with the burglary of the century.'

Kenneth agreed with that sentiment and put his foot down. We sped across London, cutting corners. The blackout was now in force, so we could barely see the road in front of us. Rose held her breath and hung on to George, who was wriggling to get a better look as we raced along.

'Are you OK, Georgie?' she asked.

'I should say so,' said George, who was having the time of his life.

'Rose. You remember!' said Nancy, putting her hand on the roof as we went around a sharp corner. 'Wait, hang on a minute. How did George get here, anyway?'

'Good question,' said Rose.

'Bertie,' everyone else said, and they all laughed.

I was in the back part of the car with Jane, and I barked back at them as if to say, 'Well, yes, what did you expect?'

Ma Finch stayed quiet throughout all this. She was squashed up in the corner of the back seat with a look of deep concentration on her face.

Nancy and Rose chatted all the way, and although we had heard the air-raid siren, there was no sign of any bombers in the sky above. Nancy had a very sick-looking Jane on her lap and was stroking her head. All in all, we were quite the car full.

'Perhaps we should drop George and me off at home,' said Rose.

'No way,' said George. 'There is no way I'm missing this one.'

After everything that had happened, she was too tired to argue with him this time.

'This is it,' said Kenneth, and he pulled up under some trees and switched the engine off. We all kept quiet and watched the big house. Nothing happened.

'I think I should go in,' said Ma Finch after a while.

'Take Bertie,' said Rose.

'I'll come, Ma. Kenneth, you show us the way in,' said Clive. 'You lot, just stay put and keep an eye out.'

For once, Nancy was quite happy to sit this one out and look after Jane and keep Rose and George company. But what we hadn't anticipated was the bombers coming over at just that moment. A woman came running down the street in high heels and a long coat.

'Follow me,' she said. 'There's a public shelter this way.'

So Rose and George and Jane and Nancy followed the woman to the shelter. And Clive, Kenneth, Ma Finch and I made our way towards the house. There was a huge explosion in the next street. I flattened myself to the ground. Clive grabbed hold of Ma Finch.

'It's all right, lad,' she said. 'I'm here.'

She carried on fearlessly towards the house.

'There's a back gate here. We can get through. I keep a back door key under the minotaur,' said Kenneth.

'Are they here yet?' asked Clive.

'Don't think so. No lights on. Let's hope not, anyway.'

Kenneth lifted up a large statue of a half-bull, half-man creature, and sure enough, underneath it was a key. He opened the back door, which creaked loudly. The house was silent.

'Come in,' he whispered and beckoned for us to follow.

'You can bet they're looting whoever's place just got it on the next road,' said Clive, looking angry.

'Well, he doesn't get it from me,' said Ma Finch. 'Must be his father's influence.'

There was the sound of breaking glass from the other side of the house.

'Shhh,' said Kenneth. 'What was that?'

'What?'

'That!'

There was another smash and then a thud, followed by another thud, and a third.

'They're in,' said Clive.

We all breathed in.

'Where's the best stuff?' asked Ma Finch.

'Well, the Mesopotamian items . . . they're in the library.'

'Where else would they be?' muttered Clive.

'Which way?' asked Ma. Kenneth signalled for her to follow.

'Bertie, you stay here by the stairs, and if you see them coming, let out a single bark,' she said.

When they had crept away, I was left alone in the dark corridor. I could hear the sounds of movement and a few crashes and bangs from the other side of the house, followed by footsteps and quiet whispers. Then the footsteps got closer. And some more whispers. I let out a single bark.

'What the hell was that?' said a voice.

'Flippin' animal. Where'd that come from?'

'I don't know, but get a move on. We're late as it is.' That was Mad Carpet Tony.

I slunk into the darkness behind a statue of a man with goat hooves. Tony turned the door knob to the ballroom with a gloved hand and opened the door. The house shook. It was another explosion, somewhere not far away. Tony didn't flinch. I held my breath.

CHAPTER TWENTY-NINE

It was completely dark in the ballroom. He flashed his light around, and I slipped in behind him silently and hid in the corner.

'Have you got it? The box,' Tony asked one of the men.

'I thought he was bringing it.'

'Yes. I've got it,' said the other one. It was Reg. He came running in behind them.

'Keep it down, will you?' hissed Tony.

Then his light flashed on to something. It looked like a statue, but it moved.

'What the . . .'

'Clive. What the hell are you doing here?'

'Just checking the coast was clear,' he said, improvising.

'You scared the bejeezus out of me,' said Reg.

'Well, make yourself useful,' said Tony, and he handed him a big iron bar. 'Use this to break into those cabinets over there, would you? We missed them last time.'

'Righto,' Clive said, playing along. He began to fumble about with the cabinet.

Kenneth was nowhere to be seen. But just as Tony was about to remove a large piece from a pedestal next to the mantelpiece, a small electric light flipped on in the corner. Ma Finch was sitting in an armchair with her hands clasped in front of her, and her eyes of steel were staring right at Tony.

'Ma!' he jumped.

'Nothing dodgy,' said Ma Finch. 'That's what you told me. A few knocked-off stockings here and there, you said. But this. Have you gone stark staring mad? Is that how I brought you up? Creeping about in the dark like Jack the Ripper's ghost.'

Tony dropped the iron bar he was holding, and it clattered to the floor.

'You.' Tony looked at Clive and ran over and grabbed his head and got it between his arms as if he might snap it off. Ma Finch rose to her feet quietly and walked over to them.

'You picked on him then and you pick on him now,' she said, pulling at Tony's ear. 'It's got nothing to do with him.'

Clive's face had gone quite blue, but Tony released his grip when Ma grabbed his ear. The other two men just stood awkwardly in the corner, not knowing what to do. At that moment, the bookcase began to move. It sort of rumbled and then began to turn around. Standing on the other side was Kenneth. He was clutching his prize sculpture, the marble Adonis. One of Tony's men started to make a run for him.

'Leave it,' growled Tony. 'It's over.'

'Good boy,' said Ma Finch, and she rubbed her hands together.

The all-clear sounded.

'We might get some rich pickings down the road,' said Tony's man, heading for the door, and Reg ran out after him.

When we finally got outside the house, Rose and Nancy were coming back down the road in the darkness, with little George in tow and Jane now walking alongside them.

When she saw Tony, she hopped along on her thin legs and barked at him.

'Janey,' he said. It was the first sound of affection I had ever heard come out of his mouth. Jane began to jump up at him and bite his hands affectionately.

'I thought I'd lost ya, you little scamp.' His face soon darkened when he looked at Clive.

'I won't forget this,' he whispered, right up against his brother's face. Then he bent down and scooped Jane up and walked away down the road.

I didn't want to be there if and when Tony realized that one of his own men had locked her up.

For the first time in what felt like weeks, I relaxed. Rose was back to her old self. Kenneth's precious objects were safe. With this relief came an overriding realization that I was absolutely starving. Kenneth said he knew an Italian restaurant where they were sure to let me in, so we drove in the middle of the night back towards the West End and stopped outside a building with light coming from its basement. Once we got down the stairs, we discovered a brightly lit place, with people drinking and eating and generally trying to forget the Blitz.

'Luigi,' said Kenneth. He seemed to know the waiter well.

He ordered a plate of delicious liver cooked with the finest gravy I'd tasted since Annie's Sunday roasts. Rose and Nancy celebrated with a glass of wine, and George even got an ice cream. He was so tired that he fell asleep under the table next to me as soon as he'd finished it.

Since the air raid was over now, anyway, Rose took George back to Mary and Victor's, and we got to spend the next day with him before Kenneth offered to drive him back to Miss Eagle's, out of harm's way. He put up a bit of a fight, but Rose was insistent; she'd promised Philip he would not stay in London while the Blitz was on.

At least we now knew he was in good hands. He may not have admitted it, but I think he was also rather keen to get back to the animals at the sanctuary and see the llamas again.

We all hugged him goodbye, but as they drove off into the distance, it didn't feel like he would be quite so far away any more.

The next day, Rose went for a check-up, and it seemed she was well on her way back to health.

'It must have been temporary shock,' said the doctor, smiling, 'and seeing your little boy shook you back out of your shock.'

That evening, Rose made an announcement.

'I want to find our own place again. Another place. For Philip. If . . . when he comes home.'

'But you're welcome to stay here, love,' said Mary. 'Both of you, if it comes to it.'

'I couldn't bear it, Mum,' she said, 'if he came back and we didn't have a home. A home that's ours. Even a small place. I can do extra shifts and . . . We'll make it work.'

'We've got some savings,' said Victor. 'It was meant to be your inheritance anyway. We can help put some money towards a place for you and Bertie, and George and Philip when they're back.'

'I know it's not logical,' said Rose. 'It might even get bombed as well. I know that. But it's something I have to do.'

The next day, Rose started going through the local newspapers to find somewhere for us to move to. With all the bombing, there was a great demand for homes, but she managed to get three places lined up to look at.

The first was a tiny flat at the top of a building over-looking a large industrial area.

'It's a bit . . . fishy,' said Nancy as we walked up the four flights of stairs to the top room.

'That'll be the fish-processing plant,' said the woman who was showing us around. 'It's stronger at this time of the day.'

'It's making me feel sick. You can't live here,' Nancy whispered to Rose.

'I don't know. We can't be too picky.'

We finally reached the top floor, and the woman unlocked the door. Inside, the walls were peeling and there was something growing on the ceiling. It was all dark inside with just a tiny window and only two rooms. There was an even stronger smell of fish which did not seem like it was going away any time soon.

Nancy looked at Rose and they both exploded into laughter. It was so awful.

'I don't think it will work,' Rose said politely to the woman, who tutted. It looked like it might have been the hundredth time she had walked up those stairs only to be told no.

The second place was a little better but, again, far too small and dark inside.

Finally, we went to a small house on a quiet street. It had two bedrooms and a very small courtyard at the back. It was a bit further away from Mary and Victor's, towards north London. But as soon as we walked in, I could tell Rose liked it.

'Ooh, there's a lot of light in here,' she said and walked over to the window.

An elderly man in a dark suit was showing us around. 'It was my son's place,' he said. 'He was a teacher at the university, before the war. This was his first proper house. Then he got called up and . . . Dunkirk . . . stepped on a landmine, never made it back.'

'I'm so sorry,' said Rose.

'We don't ask for much because we just want someone who loves the place. Who'll love it like he did.'

In the kitchen was a small stove, which I could see myself sitting in front of on many an evening to come. It was a bit more expensive than the flats they had seen, but it came with all the furniture included. Rose looked set on moving in right there and then.

'We'll take it,' she said.

The man smiled. 'Robert would be so pleased.'

Over the next few days, Nancy helped Rose move what remaining possessions we had, and they went out and bought some new things like kitchen equipment to replace what they had lost.

Although there wasn't much room at the back of the house, just a tiny courtyard, the house did back on to a waterway, which Rose told me was a canal. It was still quite cold outside, but I liked to sit by the canal and watch the boats being led by horses, making their way along. The boaters often waved at me. Every now and then, I would see another dog, standing on top of a boat which was carrying coal or other items for delivery.

A few houses on our new road had been boarded up, their occupants having left during the Blitz. One or two others had some bomb damage, but the street was generally quite intact. The next-door neighbours were two Italian women whose husbands were away, locked up for being Italian, since the Italian leader Mussolini had joined the war on Hitler's side. Rose had a lot to talk to them about, as they were both dressmakers who worked in the West End. They said they could get her some extra shifts at their place on Oxford Street. In the evening, I could smell all kinds of lovely smells coming from their house, and every now and then they would throw over some off-cuts they could spare for me, which Rose was grateful for, and I was, too.

I began to spend more time outside, enjoying the first real signs of spring. A few flowers were sprouting between the cracks in the ground out the back. The leaves on the trees were beginning to uncurl, revealing a fresh green colour. It began to look like the Blitz may be coming to an end. London was no longer being hit every night, and sometimes we would have whole weeks without any bombing at all.

The threat of invasion was also passing, and people were less worried that German spies would come parachuting down, or that Hitler would come and try to take over the country.

By April, the weather was warming up. Rose had received a long letter from Philip, who was really pleased about the new house and relieved to hear she was better after her accident. Rose got regular letters from George, too. He was doing fine in Wiltshire and was becoming a regular assistant to the local vet. He told us how he had helped deliver a baby lamb and a little calf, and how the cat and dog shelter was managing to find local homes for all the animals rescued from the bombed-out cities.

Nancy came over when she could to check Rose was still OK after her injury. She had stopped working with Clive since the unfortunate incident over the burglary, and she was helping out at the fire department more often.

Eric had barely been in contact with Nancy since she had seen him at the pub with Clive, but one day she received a letter from him, telling her all about his work on the anti-aircraft guns. She then got the news that he would soon be back in London.

'I'm scared,' she said to Rose one Sunday when they were both working on making some new clothes for George. It was his birthday soon.

'Scared of what?' asked Rose, squinting as she threaded a very small needle.

'I don't know exactly,' said Nancy. 'What if he's changed? What if we don't have anything to say to each other any more? And so much has happened, and I wouldn't begin to know where to start explaining everything.'

'We all feel like that. We're all different now. The world's a very different place.'

'But . . .' said her sister, looking down at the engagement ring Eric had given her nearly a year ago, 'will we have to start all over again, do you think?'

'God only knows. But if we do, then that's what we'll do.'

A few weeks later, Nancy came over. She had a big grin on her face.

'He's back,' she said to Rose. 'Mother's not too happy about it.'

Mary had never been very keen on Eric. She thought he was surly, and unambitious, and that her daughter could do better.

'He's still on the ack-ack guns,' said Nancy. 'But I can see him after his shifts now sometimes.'

'That's wonderful,' said Rose, giving her a big hug. 'Does that mean we're making wedding plans again?'

'Don't tell Mother just yet, but we've booked the church already. End of next month.'

Rose and Nancy began secretly making preparations for the big day. They managed to get hold of some white satin from Victor's workshop and swore him to secrecy. Then, every evening, Rose worked on the dress, while I dozed in our new living room and listened to the wireless, which sometimes played music and sometimes gave news of the war that rambled on in the background, and I hardly understood anyway.

'You'll have to tell Mother eventually,' said Rose. It was only a matter of weeks before the wedding. 'We'll have to start inviting guests. Arranging some food.'

'Eric says he's spoken to the Dog and Whistle, and they'll put on a spread there,' said Nancy.

We were around at Victor and Mary's for dinner one evening when it all came out.

'You seem positively giggly, girl,' Mary said to Nancy. 'What's happened? You look like the tiger that got the cream.'

Wilhelmina's ears pricked up at the mention of cream.

'Nothing,' said Nancy. She looked at Rose, who looked at Victor, which did not go unnoticed by Mary.

'What are you three conspiring at?' she asked.

'Nothing much. Except . . . now that Eric's back and based in London and . . . we don't want to miss the chance as he might get sent away. Out of the country this time. We're getting married,' Nancy blurted out, barely pausing for breath.

'Oh, you are, are you?' said Mary, putting her knife and fork down carefully on her plate and chewing her food slowly.

There was silence around the table. Rose looked down at her food, and Victor looked at the newspaper. Mary swallowed.

'And when was this all planned, exactly?'

'Not long ago,' said Nancy airily.

'Did you know about this, Vic?'

Victor mumbled something and turned the page of the newspaper. 'Looks like the action's heading towards Russia.'

'What about that Chipping lad? I thought you liked him. Not that surly boy.'

'Mother, please!' said Nancy. 'You hardly know him.'

'I've seen enough of that Eric boy to know he lacks ambition. Is he going to be able to provide for you? That's what I want to know.'

'I can provide for myself, thank you very much,' she said. Nancy had found a new confidence since her adventures with Clive, and was enjoying her job working with the fire department.

'You can't be a fireman for ever,' said Victor. 'As soon as this is all over the men will want their jobs back.'

'Firewoman. And yes. I know that . . . I've got other plans.'

*

The days were getting longer again, but one evening, just after dusk, for the first time in a few days, there was an air-raid warning. We ducked into our new local public shelter. No one seemed to care about pets down there. It was by far the biggest shelter I had ever seen, almost like a small village. It was a huge area with what seemed like hundreds of people crammed into a network of tunnels.

There were stalls with people selling things, and noise and smells and the sounds of children crying and laughing. We bumped into our new neighbour, Mrs Salieri. She made space for us to sit down.

'Some of this lot hardly ever leave here now,' she said. 'Some of their houses have been bombed and what have you, and they live here, practically, now.'

It smelt pretty bad down there, and I wondered how healthy it was to be stuck in such a confined space.

Although we were quite deep underground, we could still hear the sounds of the air raid. I pressed up close to Rose, who had become more nervous than she used to be about air raids since her accident.

'I can't remember it, exactly. What happened that day,' she said to Mrs Salieri, 'but when I hear the sounds of explosions it brings something back. A feeling. A blackness.'

A young-looking woman with a clean-cut look ducked her head down and entered the tunnel a little way up. She had a camera around her neck and a smart suit on.

'Not another one,' said Mrs Salieri.

'Another what?' asked Rose.

'Tourists from up West. They come here to see what it's like down here in the "worst shelter in London", as they're calling it over there.'

'Heavens,' said Rose. 'How strange. It seems all right to me.'

But it wasn't a tourist visiting this time.

'Hello,' said the woman, approaching us cautiously. 'Miss Peabody,' she said, holding out her hand.

Rose and Mrs Salieri looked at her for a while, not sure what to say, and she carried on regardless.

'I'm writing a piece for the paper about public shelters. What they're like. Who's down here. Real-life working people, that sort of thing.'

'Real-life working people,' whispered Mrs Salieri. 'I ask you. What planet are these people on?'

Miss Peabody saw me and came over and stroked my head.

'Oh, what an absolutely darling dog,' she said to Rose. 'Can I take a photograph?'

'Of course,' said Rose. The woman held up the camera and there was a flash and a click. I blinked.

'What's his name?' she asked.

'Bertie,' said Rose. 'He's been a bit of a hero, actually. Saved a few lives. Including my own.'

'Bertie the Blitz dog!' said Miss Peabody. She liked the sound of her own headline.

The next day, there was a picture of me in the newspaper, sitting in the shelter with a slightly startled look on my face. Me, in print, sitting next to Rose, alongside the story of how I had saved her from out of the rubble.

There were other photos of people in the shelter, along with complaints from people who said that it wasn't hygienic enough and that the government needed to do something to help people who were being forced to live down there because they had no homes.

A few days later, we were out shopping for food and didn't have time to get back to the public shelter before the bombs were dropping again. It was almost hard to believe it could get any worse, but this was really the worst I had ever seen.

There were hundreds of aeroplanes in the air; the whole sky seemed to be black with the shape of them in motion. Rose broke into a run. Before long, we were not far from Mary's makeshift hospital.

'Let's go in and look for Mother,' she said. I could see she was starting to panic.

By the time we arrived, part of the hospital had already been struck by incendiaries and there were fires breaking out all over the place. Nurses, doctors and volunteers were rounding up all the patients from the undamaged part of the hospital and moving them as quickly as they could to the underground shelter next door.

'Have you seen my mother?' asked Rose as we ran through the corridors, but no one had. Rose was breathing fast, and I thought she looked like she might have some kind of attack. I barked at her and got her to look at me.

'Bertie,' she said and stroked me. 'Thank goodness you're here.'

It seemed to calm her down as she continued her search for Mary. Nearby, I could hear the loud firing of anti-aircraft guns. The sounds began to lessen and the all-clear sounded. People began to move about the building, assessing the damage, piling sandbags into fires and spraying at the flames with the pumps and buckets. Part of the canteen roof had fallen in, and there was broken glass and debris all over the floor. Around the back, where they kept supplies, the whole roof had caved in. A little way along the corridor, I thought I could smell fire again. I barked. Just over the wall I could see the large anti-aircraft guns in position. They were still firing intermittently. Then they stopped. As soon as the all-clear had sounded, I recognized the voice of a man. I barked again.

'What is it, Bertie?' asked Rose.

A man's head popped over the wall.

'Eric!' she exclaimed. I ran over to the wall and started barking.

'What are you doing here?'

'Working the guns,' he said. He was covered in sweat and oil from manning the huge machine. 'What's up?'

'I can't find Mother,' said Rose. 'We took a hit, and . . . I don't know . . . I'm fearing the worst. I suppose I'm just so nervous now after the house and . . .'

Eric hopped over the wall. 'I probably shouldn't, but what the heck,' he said, brushing off his hands.

I barked. I thought I could sense someone in the room next door. I saw flames. Something had caught fire. Rose grabbed a stirrup pump and they ran towards it. I heard screaming. I ran into the room. It was so hot, it scorched my whiskers. I pressed myself low to the ground so as to avoid the smoke, which was filling the room. Over by the window there was a pair of legs. The flames were flickering all around me. I saw an arm, then a face. It was Mary, out cold on the floor, with the fire fast approaching.

Through the smoke, I heard a voice.

'Bertie? Are you in there?' It was Eric. He came running in. He shielded his face from the heat of the fire. As soon as he saw Mary on the floor, he picked her up and ran back out of the room. I followed, narrowly avoiding getting my tail completely burnt off.

We lay Mary on the floor of the ward. She was all covered in soot and her hands were a little burnt. But otherwise, she seemed to be unhurt. When she opened her eyes and looked up, the first thing she saw was Eric.

'Are you all right?' he said. 'There was a fire. You're out now.'

In a kind of shock, she screamed. She must have thought she was having a bad dream.

Eric lifted Mary to her feet and took her to the ward she was normally in charge of. It had only taken a slight hit, and a few windows had been smashed. Otherwise, it was back working, with patients back in their beds.

'Do you know what day it is?' the doctor asked Mary, shining a light in her eyes.

'Eleventh of May, 1941,' she said. He patched up her burns and said she was fine to go home. She, of course, then insisted on going around the rest of the hospital and checking everyone else was all right.

That was the night we all said the Blitz ended, although it had been one of the worst nights of the whole bombing campaign. Mary, having survived, was one of the luckier ones.

As we were leaving, Miss Peabody appeared with her camera in hand. She was striding towards us with a purposeful look.

'I heard the hospital took a hit,' she said excitedly. She put the camera to her eyes and snapped a couple of shots. 'There was a fire, I heard. You don't mind?' she said, snapping away. Then she saw me. 'And here's our Bertie. How wonderful,' she said and took another photograph of me, alongside Eric and Mary and Rose.

We took Mary home, and when we walked in, Nancy couldn't believe it; her mother was arm in arm with Eric. The rescue certainly made the wedding preparations an awful lot easier, as now Mary had decided that Eric was the perfect gentleman.

The day after the rescue, when the newspaper arrived, there was a photograph of all of us on the front page, with the headline:

BERTIE THE BLITZ DOG AND BRAVE GUNNER IN MIRACLE HOSPITAL RESCUE

CHAPTER THIRTY

The rest of May turned out to be a busy month. The Blitz had ended, and although the war was far from over, an invasion seemed less likely as Hitler made other plans. The weather was getting warmer and the days longer. Rose announced that she had decided it was time for George to come home, just in time for his birthday.

'Do you think he'll like the new place, Bertie?' she asked. She had decorated the little bedroom upstairs, and was dusting and polishing the whole house to get everything spick and span for his arrival. I couldn't answer, of course, but I barked cheerfully to try to reassure her.

It had been nearly five months since we had last seen George, and although he had been on the telephone and writing letters, I was almost nervous about seeing him again myself.

On the morning he was expected to arrive back home, Rose couldn't sit still for more than five minutes. She stood up and plumped up the cushions on the sofa. Then she rearranged the flowers she had picked and put in a vase on the kitchen table. Then she would sit down and try and read a book. Then she'd get up again and look out of the window and plump the cushions and sit back down again. This went on for some time until we heard a car pull up outside. She jumped up and ran to the front door. I followed.

Kenneth, who had driven George home, was in the car, waving. He got out and went to the boot and took out George's suitcase. Then a tall boy got out. I didn't recognize him at first. He looked older. His hair was fuller and he had a healthy glow about him. Rose ran out of the house and hugged George, who stood awkwardly on the pavement.

'Oh my goodness, my little boy. You're about twice as tall!'

'Mum,' he said. His voice cracked slightly.

'Oh, you're a little man now, nearly,' she said, ruffling his hair.

'Hello, Bertie, old fellow,' said George to me, and he bent down and gave me the biggest hug.

I thought his voice sounded a bit different. A bit more like Kenneth's and Joyce's, which weren't quite the same as the people we knew in London.

Kenneth brought in the suitcase and said goodbye. He had to go and pick up some more animals from the new shelter. The old one had closed down because of bad practices, he said, mainly thanks to Ma Finch's intervention.

'We're having a little party tomorrow. For your birthday,' said Rose as she showed George into the new house. 'A kind of house-warming, too. I hope that's OK. I couldn't resist.'

She stopped talking and looked at him. His face was thinner, but he looked healthy and happy. He was almost as tall as her now.

'Did I do the right thing?' she asked, pushing his hair out of his eyes. 'Sending you away?'

'It's all right, Mum,' he said. 'I'm back now.'

Up in his new bedroom, George unpacked his things, including his precious stethoscope, which he placed in its box on his bedroom desk. He also laid out his shrapnel in a line in order of size and showed me the new treasures he had found in the countryside, including what he informed me was a badger's skull, a large beetle with antlers, and a fossil he had found on a beach. It was from a creature he said had lived before humans, and most likely dogs, even existed.

'We'll go back there soon, you and me, Bertie. When this blasted war's over.'

'Goodness me, you did pick up some language,' said Rose, coming in with a plate of chocolate biscuits she had been saving. She sat on the bed next to him, but George went strangely quiet as he finished laying out his new finds.

'What have you got there?' she asked, trying to make conversation.

'Nothing much. Just a few things I found.'

'Ooh, lovely,' said Rose, looking around the room. 'Is it all right? The room.'

'Yes, it's fine,' he said.

There was an awkward silence. It was as if they didn't have much to say to each other, all of a sudden. I decided to break in by putting my head on George's knee and getting him to rub my ears. That was always a fun game. It worked.

'Old Bertie, demanding attention again,' he said.

Then he and Rose both laughed, and it felt like old times again.

The next day was George's birthday. Rose spent all morning pulling together all the rations she could get her hands on, including some real eggs from a friend at the factory who kept chickens, so she could make proper custard pies. She also did her best to improvise some other treats and made a flan using carrots in place of apricots and a cake with carrots and raisins, with mock cream on top made of margarine and a bit of sugar.

Although we didn't have much of a garden any more, as soon as George was up and about he went outside to look at insects. There was a small ants' nest in the corner of the courtyard, and he spent hours watching as the tiny ants made their way up and down in lines, carrying things much bigger than themselves. He got very excited about a large orange-and-black creature with wings which settled on Rose's window box. George identified it from a book as being a Silver-washed Fritillary butterfly.

At lunchtime, the doorbell rang. It was Nancy, Victor and Mary. They were so excited to see George again, they smothered him in kisses.

'You're nearly as tall as your father!' said Mary. 'How did that happen in just a few months?'

'I don't know, Granny,' he said. 'Feels like a lot longer than that.'

Before the food was served, everyone had presents for George. Rose and Nancy gave him the clothes they had made to replace what he had lost when they lost the house.

'I'll have to take them down, those trousers, though,' said Rose.

Victor and Mary had bought him a new book of natural history which showed pictures of all animals throughout time and a family tree of evolution.

George seemed a bit shy of all the attention, as though his family was somehow strange to him after all the time away.

When it came time for food, the doorbell rang again. A young girl with a bobbed haircut and a simple dress stood on the doorstep.

'Pamela!' said Rose. 'You're back. How lovely.'

'Is George back yet? I walked all the way,' she said proudly. 'Mum said you were living here now. I've been on a farm.'

'Well, you can tell us all about it over lunch,' said Rose, showing her in.

Both the children, who used to play together so easily, now looked slightly awkward together as they stood there in their party clothes in the new house. George even held out his hand for Pamela to shake it.

'My auntie was strange but not horrible. I think she was lonely. Her husband could get quite angry. But I spent most of my time doing the lambs when I could. Just to get out of the house. It smelt a bit, too. Of cabbage,' said Pamela. 'Where were you?'

'Wiltshire,' said George. 'We had three llamas.'

'Blimey, lucky. We only had sheep.'

'Shall we eat?' said Rose as everyone hovered politely around the table, not wanting to be the first to start the food. Before long, everyone was tucking in.

When they had finished eating, George and Pamela went back outside to look at insects together. They were soon chatting as though no time had passed.

Just as Mary, Victor and Nancy were getting ready to leave, the doorbell rang one more time.

'Who's that? We're all here,' said Rose, cramming in a last bit of carrot cake as she passed the table. I followed to see who it was. She had barely finished chewing and was brushing the crumbs from her dress when she opened the door. A tall man in a well-worn army uniform, with dark hair and a fresh suntan, was standing on the doorstep with a canvas bag.

'Hello, love.'

Rose swallowed the last of her cake with a gulp.

I felt awkward, standing in the doorway. It felt like a very private moment. For a while, neither of them spoke. It was as though the past year, which Rose and Philip had passed separately, had created a new gap between them.

'You look different . . . thinner,' said Rose.

'Army rations.'

'Was it . . . I mean. I can't imagine . . . the house . . . you know already, of course. We lost everything. I couldn't save . . . even your gramophone records. I'm sorry.'

'Don't be daft. It doesn't matter,' he said. 'They're just things.'

They looked shy together suddenly. It seemed like Philip was a stranger on his own new doorstep. I decided that was the moment to nestle my way in and say hello to him. I couldn't hold back any longer. I ran up to him and jumped up and barked and wagged my tail.

'Bertie,' he said. 'You've been running things just fine while I've been away, I hear.'

'Yes,' said Rose. 'He's certainly been a star. Even been in the papers!'

Eventually, I calmed down, and they looked at each other again.

'I feel like running away somewhere. Just for a while. Alone together,' said Rose. 'But I know we can't. It's George's birthday.' She said it as if she had suddenly remembered, as if she had just come out of a dream.

'I know,' said Philip. 'They gave me two weeks. I wanted to surprise him. And you.'

'Well, you certainly did that.'

She put out her arms and nestled into Philip's chest, and they held on to each other. For a while, neither seemed to want to let go.

'Any cake left?' asked Philip after a while.

Rose, who had tears in her eyes, breathed in deeply. Without a word, she took his arm and they walked back into the house.

'We thought you'd run away,' said Mary, without looking up. Then she saw who was with her. 'Oh Lord. What a surprise! What a marvellous surprise. George,' she called out. 'Your father's here.'

Everyone clapped Philip on the back and welcomed him home. George came in from the garden.

'Hello, lad,' said Philip and put his arm on the boy's shoulder. 'I hear you've been having some adventures while I've been gone.'

'Are you back for good, now it's all over?'

A year without his father must have felt like a long time.

'It's not quite over yet, son. But . . . happy birthday. I've got a bit of time, anyway. I brought you something,' he said and fished a package out of his bag. 'I hope it's all right.'

'Thank you, sir,' said George. He opened the package while everyone waited to see what it was.

'I made it,' said Philip.

Inside the box was a little wooden model aeroplane painted in the colours of a Spitfire.

'We had some spare time over there,' he said. 'I found bits of wood around the village we were near. Had a damned job getting that paint, mind.'

'It's super, Dad,' said George, smiling. 'Thank you.'

'Well, we ought to leave you to it. To settle in,' said Victor, getting up to go.

As they were leaving, Nancy whispered to Rose. 'Now that Philip's back, do you think . . . well, I might ask Mother if we can bring the wedding forward. So he can be there.'

Over the next week, Philip spent as much time as he could with Rose and George and me. We had a day trip along the river and a picnic outside the Tower of London, and we felt like we were on holiday in our own city. Nancy made all the arrangements with Eric, and a week later she was in our house having her dress fitted by Rose.

'I feel sick,' she said.

'Don't be silly,' said Rose, speaking through the pins in her mouth.

'Does it fit?' she asked.

'Of course. You look lovely. I'm just taking up the hem a bit.'

I was a bit scared of the dress as it had a long bit at the back that kept startling me every time I saw it. But I got used to it and realized I was not to play with it under any circumstances. And definitely was not to get any mud on it.

The vicar had said I was allowed in the church, so I became Eric's honorary best man, or best dog, as he called me. There was a sadness about it all, though, as Harry, who would have been his other best man, wasn't there.

Everyone gasped as Nancy walked into the church. She looked beautiful. Victor took her arm and they walked towards Eric, who was standing by the altar. They had taught me how to pick up the rings, which were in a box on the floor. When Eric made the command, I picked them up and everyone clapped.

I could tell Eric was nervous as he said his vows. He and Nancy sounded all small and young all of a sudden, despite what they had both been through.

Rose was in tears before it even started, and even Victor had a little glisten in his eye as he saw his youngest daughter married.

After the ceremony, we all piled into the Dog and Whistle pub, where they had laid on a nice spread of food for everyone, at least, as much as they could with the rations on.

Victor gave a moving speech about Nancy, and his regret that Harry wasn't there. Maude also made a speech, which had everyone in tears with laughter, in which she recalled some of Eric and Harry's pranks as children. Then everyone said a prayer for all those who had been lost and who had lost loved ones.

The landlady of the pub, who was about ninety, played the piano, and everyone sang their favourite songs well into the night.

Everyone danced, and I joined in with my new howling singing technique. Philip and Rose were dancing together by the window in a world of their own, as though the war was happening in another time and place. George danced along with me, and Mary and Victor, who used to win prizes for their dancing, got a round of applause.

As the evening wore on, Frank got a little too drunk and Rose got a little too loud, at least according to Mary. Eric and Philip were drinking together in the corner, quietly, perhaps in mutual recognition of what they had been through.

Nancy looked over at Eric. I thought she looked suddenly nervous, perhaps thinking about the reality of him going away again. It occurred to me then that we had also seen things over the past year that we would never forget. We had seen people losing their lives right in front of our eyes. Seen people lose their houses and loved ones. We had lost our own house and our own loved ones. I would never forget the damage a war could do.

'We'll stick together, you and me,' said Rose, putting her hand on Nancy's arm.

I barked and looked up at them both, and they broke into a smile.

'And Bertie.'

Epilogue

Although the war was far from over and the worst was still to come, that day was a moment of light and of celebration. Soon afterwards, Philip went back to the front line and Eric was called back to his regiment, while we all continued our work on the home front.

There was one more nice surprise that summer. Nancy, Rose and George were sitting together in the living room one sunny evening, playing cards while I watched and tried to work out what on earth the rules were, when a car pulled up outside. I looked out of the window. It was Clive, carrying a cardboard box.

'What's that?' asked Rose. 'What's he got? Hello, Clive,' she called and waved him in.

I don't know why, but I felt a prickling feeling on the back of my neck. A kind of excitement I had never felt before. A churning in the stomach like butterflies.

'I've got a surprise,' said Clive, and he laid down the box on the floor. When he opened it up, inside, looking up at us, were three little puppies with huge eyes. There was one that was ginger and white, one fluffy ginger-, brown-and-black one, and one that was black and white with short hair. They were wriggling about and biting each other playfully.

'They're three months now,' said Clive, picking up the little black-and-white one. It let out a little yelp.

'Oh, they're adorable,' said Nancy, and she scooped up the fluffy one.

'I'm keeping this little thing,' said Clive. 'I've named her Chloe.'

'Oh, lovely,' said Rose. 'They're feisty, aren't they?'

'This one's so small,' said Nancy. 'He looks shy.' She was holding the fluffy little ginger-, brown-and-black one. It had a white patch across its eye. I thought for a moment how familiar they looked. I could see a little of Jane in each of them, especially the black-and-white one. But I could also see a little of myself in the little one Nancy was holding.

Then I remembered that night in the kennel at the dog pound. We had both been so alone and in need of comfort. That was about five months earlier. I'm sure I blushed inside a little when I remembered that.

'Whose are they?' asked Rose, and Nancy and Clive put their puppies back down.

'They're Tony's dog Jane's. He's looking for homes for them. Can't keep them. We're not sure when she . . . you know.'

Once they were all back on the floor, I barked and ran over and sniffed them. They seemed so familiar to me and I instantly fell in love with them. They started calling out and looking up. Tony had appeared at the door with Jane. I stiffened when I saw him. I looked over at Rose, and her eyes narrowed. Nancy looked afraid.

'Sorry about bringing Tony,' whispered Clive. 'We don't want to separate Jane from the pups yet, but I really thought you might want to, well, have a chance to take one when they're ready. If you want?'

Tony approached the front door and nodded his head towards us without smiling. Jane and I sniffed one another and she licked my face. I felt so relieved that she looked so healthy and happy. We didn't need to say anything; we both knew these little pups were the most amazing things we had ever seen. All three of them bounded over to her. She looked like the proudest mum ever.

Rose and Nancy didn't look at Tony, and he was starting to look a bit awkward. But the puppies had softened them, and just for a moment, the past didn't seem important.

'This one looks a bit like Bertie,' said Nancy when they had finished snuggling with Jane.

The little fluffy ginger-and-white one jumped up at her legs.

'A little Bertie!' said Nancy, and she scooped her up.

'She's a girl, that one. I think she's chosen you,' said Clive.

They all looked at me.

'Did you see that?' laughed George. 'Bertie's smiling!'

The End

He just wanted a decent book to read ...

Not too much to ask, is it? It was in 1935 when Allen Lane, Managing Director of Bodley Head Publishers, stood on a platform at Exeter railway station looking for something good to read on his journey back to London. His choice was limited to popular magazines and poor-quality paperbacks – the same choice faced every day by the vast majority of readers, few of whom could afford hardbacks. Lane's disappointment and subsequent anger at the range of books generally available led him to found a company – and change the world.

'We believed in the existence in this country of a vast reading public for intelligent books at a low price, and staked everything on it'
Sir Allen Lane, 1902–1970, founder of Penguin Books

The quality paperback had arrived – and not just in bookshops. Lane was adamant that his Penguins should appear in chain stores and tobacconists, and should cost no more than a packet of cigarettes.

Reading habits (and cigarette prices) have changed since 1935, but Penguin still believes in publishing the best books for everybody to enjoy. We still believe that good design costs no more than bad design, and we still believe that quality books published passionately and responsibly make the world a better place.

So wherever you see the little bird – whether it's on a piece of prize-winning literary fiction or a celebrity autobiography, political tour de force or historical masterpiece, a serial-killer thriller, reference book, world classic or a piece of pure escapism – you can bet that it represents the very best that the genre has to offer.

Whatever you like to read – trust Penguin.

read more
www.penguin.co.uk